Queen of the Orcs

BOOK I

King's Property

To rule her fate,
a peasant girl will
challenge a kingdom.

MORGAN HOWELL

Ballantine / Del Rey /
Presidio Press /
One World

DAR WAS TRAPPED, AND SHE KNEW IT

Marked as she was by her brand, escape was suicide, while life in the regiment seemed only a slower path to death. Women were easy to replace and valued accordingly. In such an atmosphere, men's "generosity" and "protection" were hollow promises. Though Dar racked her brain, there seemed no refuge. Then she had an inspiration.

Dar lagged behind until the orcs overtook her. Soon she was walking in their midst. Spying Kovok-mah at the rear of the column, Dar slowed down until they were walking abreast. "Tava, Kovok-mah."

Kovok-mah didn't reply or even turn his head.

"Tava, Kovok-mah," said Dar, louder this time.

The orc regarded Dar. An iron helmet enclosed his head and his green eyes peered out from it like a beast's from a hole. With a sinking feeling, Dar realized the vastness of their differences, and her plan seemed as risky as it was desperate.

Advance praise for *Queen of the Orcs: King's Property*

"*King's Property* tests your presumptions of 'the other' and brings to mind the cultural prejudices and wars born from betrayal that are so sadly evident throughout our own history."

—Karin Lowachee, author of *Warchild*

THE QUEEN OF THE ORCS TRILOGY

By Morgan Howell

King's Property
Clan Daughter
Royal Destiny

QUEEN OF THE ORCS

BOOK I

King's Property

MORGAN HOWELL

DEL REY

BALLANTINE BOOKS • NEW YORK

A Del Rey Books Mass Market Original

Published in the United States by Del Rey Books, an imprint of The Random House Publishing Group, a division of Random House, Inc., New York.

This book contains an excerpt from the forthcoming mass market edition of *Queen of the Orcs: Clan Daughter* by Morgan Howell. This excerpt has been set for this edition only and may not reflect the final content of the forthcoming edition.

ISBN 978-0-345-49650-8

Printed in the United States of America

www.delreybooks.com

OPM 9 8 7 6 5 4 3 2 1

This book is dedicated to
Beryl Markham, Lúthien Tinúviel,
and Carol Hubbell

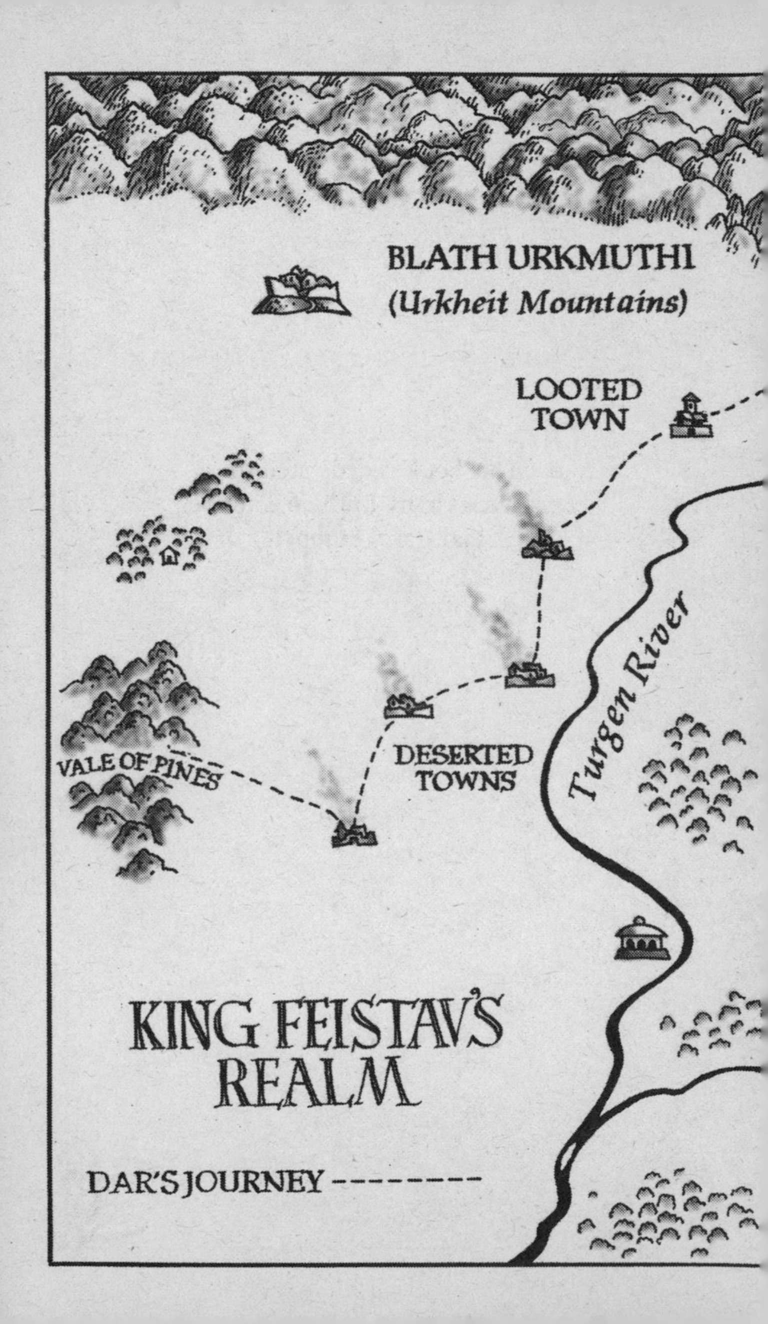
BLATH URKMUTHI
(Urkheit Mountains)
LOOTED TOWN
Turgen River
DESERTED TOWNS
VALE OF PINES
KING FEISTAV'S REALM
DAR'S JOURNEY

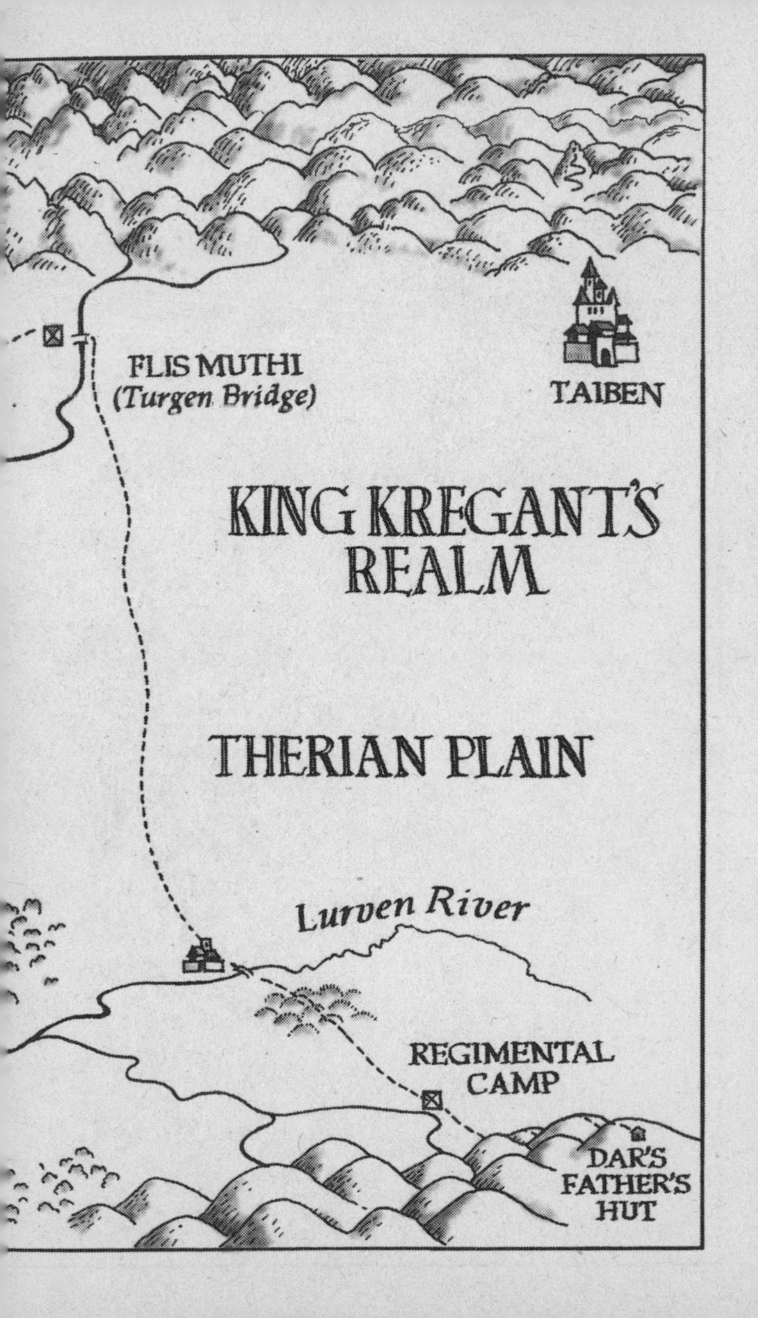
FLIS MUTHI
(Turgen Bridge)
TAIBEN
KING KREGANT'S
REALM
THERIAN PLAIN
Lurven River
REGIMENTAL
CAMP
DAR'S
FATHER'S
HUT

Glaciers have erased the past. The mountains are diminished. The plains are scraped bare. The First Children have departed, and their works have perished. Only tales remain, worn thin by retelling.

One

♛

Dar walked alone down a mountain path, bent beneath a load of firewood. The trail she followed hugged steep rocky walls that blocked the morning sun, so the air and ground still held the night's chill. Nevertheless, she walked barefoot and wore only a tattered, sleeveless shift with a rag to cushion her shoulders. Dar moved quickly to keep warm, but the sound of a distant horse stopped her short. None of her neighbors owned one, nor did anyone in the tiny village beyond the far ridge. Only strangers rode horses, and strangers often brought trouble.

Dar listened. When the hoofbeats died away, leaving only the sound of wind in bare branches, she continued homeward and arrived at a hollow devoid of trees. Its stony ground had been prepared for spring planting. At the far side of the hollow lay the only building—a rude hut, built of rocks and roofed with turf. The horse was tied nearby. Dar was considering leaving when her father's wife emerged from the low building with a rare smile on her face. The older woman called out. "You have visitors."

The smile heightened Dar's wariness. "What kind of visitors?"

Dar's stepmother didn't respond, except to smile more broadly. She moved aside, and six armed men stepped from the dark hut followed by the village headman, whose air of self-importance was subdued by the soldiers' presence. Dar's father came after him. Last emerged Dar's two little half sisters, looking frightened. All watched Dar carry her load over to the woodpile. She set it down, then asked her stepmother again, "Thess, who are these men?"

"King's soldiers," replied Thess.

"Why are they here?"

"There's a levy for the army," said the headman. "Our village must provide two."

"Then they've come to the wrong place," said Dar. "My brothers are dead, and Father's too old."

"It's not men they want," said Thess.

"I'm no fighter," said Dar.

Thess laughed humorlessly. "Then you've fooled me."

"Not all who serve the king need fight," said the headman. He turned to one of the soldiers. "She's the one."

"Father, what's going on?" asked Dar, already guessing the answer.

Her father looked away.

"This was his idea," said the headman.

"It's for the best," said Dar's father, his eyes still elsewhere.

"Best for *her*," said Dar, casting her stepmother a resentful look. "She'll be pleased enough to have me gone."

"I'll be glad for some peace," retorted Thess. "Always the proud one, you."

"Unlike *some*, who'd tup a man for a space by his fire."

"You'd be a wife, too, if you weren't so willful."

"She's best suited for the army," said the headman.

"*I'll* determine that," said the soldier in charge. Though he was the youngest, his helmet and arms were finely made, and his armor was metal, not leather. "Murdant, see if the girl's fit."

The murdant, a man half again the age of his officer, slowly circled Dar, taking in her sturdy grace. He thought her old to be unmarried, perhaps two dozen winters. Though unkempt, she had pleasant features—large dark eyes, a delicate nose, russet hair, and full lips—making him surmise it was her temperament that had kept her single. As if to confirm this, Dar stood with a defiant expression, fists clenched at her sides.

"Show me your teeth," said the murdant.

Though Dar realized the murdant was unlike some suitor who could be scared off by a show of temper, she pressed her lips tightly together. The murdant only grinned, then roughly pinched her cheeks with his thumb and forefinger to force open her jaws. He got a quick glimpse into Dar's mouth before she struck a blow that he easily warded off. "She's got her teeth and the rest of her looks sound enough."

"She'll do," said the officer.

The headman bowed. "Tolum, we always fulfill our duty to the king."

The officer regarded him disdainfully. "This spinster's no great sacrifice."

Thess entered the hut and returned with a small bundle wrapped in a threadbare cloak. "I've gathered your things," she said, handing them to Dar.

The tolum mounted his horse. "March her to our camp and be quick. I'll be waiting." Then he rode off.

The murdant addressed the other soldiers. "You heard the tolum. Move!" He turned to Dar, who clutched her bundle with a stunned look on her face. He had seen that expression before. *Her people have given her up*, he thought. *She has nowhere to turn.* Still, he doubted her defiance was extinguished. "You fixing to give us trouble?"

Dar shook her head.

"Then come along, we have to catch up with a horse."

Dar turned to bid farewell, but her family had disappeared into the hut.

At first, only the tread of the soldiers' booted feet broke the silence. Dar walked blank-faced among the men, considering what to do. To buy time, she trod as though her feet were tender, hoping to slow the pace. Dar knew the path would pass a steep slope that was covered with loose rock. *They won't expect me to scramble up it barefoot.* Dar was certain she could elude the soldiers, whose armor would encumber them, and escape into the heights above.

Dar tried to imagine what she would do afterward. *I can't go home.* The headman would declare her an outlaw, and Dar was certain no neighbor would risk sheltering her. She would have to go far away, and that was her dilemma. In the highlands, a woman without kin had no rights or protection. To dwell anywhere, she would have to beg some man's leave, and Dar had no illusions what price would be exacted. She recoiled at the thought.

When the soldiers marched past the rock-covered slope, Dar made no escape attempt. Having weighed her options, she chose what seemed the lesser evil—an uncertain fate with the army. The path turned away from the tumbled rocks and headed into a valley. As Dar trudged toward a new life, she thought of the one she was leaving.

She would miss her half sisters but little else. Her relations with her father had been strained ever since her mother's death. This day's betrayal was only his latest. Life in the stone hut had consisted of hardship, visits from unwanted suitors, and the barbs of a spiteful stepmother. Dar tried to cheer herself with the thought that she was abandoning these afflictions; yet she already suspected they would be replaced by different ones.

As the marching warmed the soldiers, their tongues loosened. "Do ye think the tolum will get himself lost?" asked one in an accent foreign to Dar's ears.

"Even he can follow hoofprints," said a companion.

"And his horse has sense," said another, "even if he lacks it."

"At least he listened to the murdant today," said the first soldier. "This one came easy enough."

"That's 'cause she's like you," said a soldier with a grin, "worthless."

His companion regarded Dar. "You worthless?"

Dar's face reddened. The soldier leered and answered his own question. "Well, you're good for one thing."

"Unlike you, Tham," said the murdant. The others laughed.

"At least my mum cried when I marched off," said Tham. "I saw only dry eyes today."

"Not like yesterday."

"Aye," said the murdant. "Get one that won't be missed—that's what I told the tolum. Hey birdie, will you miss them?"

Dar remained silent.

"Maybe she's happy to be gone from that dung heap," said one of the men.

"Sure," said another. "It's fun being a soldier."

A soldier laughed. "Especially if you're a woman."

"I've heard no talk of war," said Dar. "When did it begin?"

The murdant grinned. "For sooth, you've lived under a rock. Kregant's been at war since the day he was crowned. Soldiering's been steady work."

"What's the king fighting over?"

"Whatever he wishes. I just follow orders."

"And what will I be doing?" asked Dar.

"Cooking."

"You marched all this way to get a cook?"

"The tolum's commander wanted mountain girls. Said they're tough."

Dar regarded the murdant and the others. They bore the look of men who lived hard. *It would take a strong woman to serve with them*, she thought. Yet a glimpse at the murdant's eyes warned Dar he wasn't telling all the truth.

"How long will I serve?" she asked.

"Not long," said the murdant, his gaze fixed elsewhere.

For a while, the route was familiar to Dar. It crossed the valley, climbed the far ridge, and followed it. By noon, they left the ridgeline and descended into a winding valley Dar had never visited. At the lower altitude, the trees had already leafed out. The marchers halted by a stream for a brief meal before moving on. By early afternoon, they reached camp. The tolum paced about the clearing where his horse grazed. Several soldiers stood nearby. One was tending a small fire. A short distance away, a blond-haired woman sat with her back against a tree, facing away from Dar.

"You took your time," said the tolum.

"The girl's barefoot, sir," said the murdant. "She slowed us down."

"That's no excuse, Murdant!" The tolum shot Dar an irritated look. "By Karm's tits! How can you not own shoes?" Then he took the murdant aside, and they talked in low tones. Afterward, the tolum returned his attention to Dar. "Lie on your back."

"Why?"

"You don't question orders," said the murdant. "Soldiers who do are whipped. Now, lie down."

Dar obeyed. The murdant nodded, and a large soldier walked over, straddled Dar, and sat upon her chest, pinning her arms with his knees. Another soldier grabbed Dar's ankles. A third knelt down and gripped her head between his knees like a vise. From the corner of her eye, Dar spied another soldier approaching. He bore something in his hand that glowed. She fought to free her arms, but the man on her chest shifted more weight to his knees until the pressure was excruciating. "Don't struggle," he said.

Dar grew still, and the soldier on her chest eased up a bit. By then, the fourth soldier stood over her, and she could see that the glowing object was a brand. Its end resembled a five-pointed crown outlined in fire. As it came closer to her face, Dar closed her eyes and gritted her teeth. An instant later, she felt a searing pain on her forehead accompanied by the smell of burned flesh. Dar fought against crying out, but failed. The men released her, and she sat up. The pain was intense.

The murdant tossed her a water skin. "Pour water on it," he said. "It helps."

The water eased Dar's pain just enough so she could control her voice. "I came without resisting. There was no need to do that."

"All women in the orc regiments are branded, lest they run away."

"Orc regiments!" said Dar, her pain momentarily forgotten as she recalled the nightmare tales.

"Correct," said the tolum, "and a branded head bears a bounty. To keep it on your shoulders, you must stick with your regiment."

"What do orcs want with women?"

"I have no idea," said the tolum. "I fight alongside men, not monsters."

"They have women wait on them," said the murdant. "I've seen it often."

"You also told me I'd not serve long," retorted Dar. "This brand betrays that lie."

"Aye, I spoke false," said the murdant. "But now that you're marked, I have no need."

"We're done here," said the tolum. "Chain her to the other girl and move out. We must return by the morrow."

A soldier went over to the tree where the woman sat and pulled her to her feet. Then Dar could see that the woman's ankles and wrists were bound and an iron ring was locked around her neck. Attached to the ring was a long length of heavy chain from which dangled several bells. The soldier removed the woman's bonds, but not the iron ring. Using the chain, he led her closer to Dar. At the far end of the chain was a second ring, which he locked around Dar's neck. "You'll wear this till you reach your regiment."

The chain wasn't overly burdensome, but Dar saw how it would hinder an escape. The belled links were noisy, and, off the road, they would tangle easily. She approached the stranger at the other end, who appeared several years younger. Dar's fellow captive was well dressed by highland standards; her clothes were clean and almost new. She also wore shoes. She turned to gaze at Dar. Beneath the angry brand on her forehead, her eyes were red and puffy from weeping.

Despite her pain, Dar tried to smile. "I'm Dar."

"Leela," replied the woman in a nearly inaudible voice.

"Move out," commanded the tolum, who had mounted his horse. He urged his steed forward, setting a brisk pace for the soldiers and women that followed.

Dar gathered up the links of chain so it wouldn't snag on something and so she could walk next to Leela. When they were side by side, she saw tears flowing down Leela's face.

"It'll be all right," Dar said.

Leela stared ahead, oblivious. Dar gently touched her arm without getting a response. The girl's face was emptied of every emotion except sorrow. Its desolation made Dar wonder how Leela's parting differed from her own. The bundle that Thess had prepared was an indication. At lunchtime, Dar had inspected it. Within the worn cloak were a spare undergarment and a shift even more ragged than the one she wore. Dar's footwear and good shift were missing, as were the beads her mother had given her. Leela's garments bespoke a loving send-off, one that made Dar both envy and pity her.

Soon, the tolum's pace had Dar panting, and she gave up trying to start a conversation. She trudged along, concerned only with keeping up and her own misfortune.

Two

The sun was low when the tolum called a halt for the night. Leela and Dar were allowed to rest while the soldiers set up camp. A fire was built, and grain was boiled in a small pot to make porridge. This was dinner for everyone except the tolum, who also had wine and cheese. The soldiers ate first, then gave the pot to Dar and Leela, who dined on what was left using their fingers. When a soldier came to retrieve the pot, he said to Dar, "Use the bushes before I chain you for the night."

After Dar squatted in the undergrowth, the soldier placed a manacle around her ankle, looped a chain around a large tree trunk, and locked both ends of it to the manacle. Since Leela was already chained to Dar, the soldier didn't shackle her further. His work done, he headed back to the campfire and his companions.

Dar lay down on the ground. "Share my cloak. We'll both be warmer."

Leela moved close, but she didn't lie down. "The tolum will give us to the orcs tomorrow," she said in a terrified voice. "*Orcs!*"

"Maybe they're not as bad as the tales say," said Dar.

"They're demons. Not even human."

"An evil reputation gives an edge in a fight. Perhaps the king uses orcs because they frighten his foes."

"They've earned that reputation," whispered Leela, "from eating human flesh."

"Who told you that?"

"My cousin has a friend whose brother saw it. They don't even kill the people first. They just tear them apart and eat them raw!"

"That can't be true," said Dar. "The murdant said we're going to cook for them."

"He lied. Can't you see why we're branded like cattle? We're going to be devoured!"

"You're crazy, Leela."

"It's supposed to be a secret. That's why they take girls from the hills—so word won't get out."

"Then how did you learn about it?"

"I told you. He hid and saw it."

"Tomorrow, you'll see you're wrong," said Dar, trying to sound confident.

"Tomorrow, we'll be walking the Dark Path."

"Get some sleep, Leela. Things will seem different in daylight."

Leela lay down, and when Dar pressed against her for warmth, she could feel Leela trembling. Despite her fatigue, Dar had trouble falling asleep. Her forehead throbbed and her thoughts were uneasy. The savagery of orcs was legendary. *They say orcs pull out hearts with their bare hands. Might not they eat them also?* Dar had no answer. Lying branded and chained in the dark, she began to wonder if Leela was right.

The moon had risen, filling the clearing with pale light, when Leela shook Dar awake. Dar looked at her stupidly. "What's the matter?" she asked in a sleepy voice.

"Nothing," replied Leela. "I just need your help."

"Now?"

"Yes, now. Don't wake the soldiers."

Dar was puzzled, but the look on Leela's face reassured her. Dread had been replaced by calmness. "What do you want me to do?"

"Help me up to that branch," said Leela, pointing to a tree limb several feet above Dar's head.

"Why?"

"There's something I need to do. Come on. Hurry before someone sees us."

Still foggy from sleep, Dar rose and entwined her fingers to form a stirrup with her hands. Leela stepped into it and rose to grab the tree limb. Dar watched as Leela pulled herself up and threw a leg over the branch. After a brief struggle, Leela stood upon the limb, grasping the next higher one. The bells on the chain were silent; Leela must have stuffed them with grass.

"Leela!" whispered Dar. "What are you doing?"

Leela didn't answer, but climbed until the chain prevented her from ascending higher. She stood balanced on a stout branch, steadying herself with one hand on the tree trunk. "Dar," she called down, not bothering to lower her voice. "Grab the chain with both hands and hold on tight."

Dar was about to ask why when she guessed the reason. "Leela!"

Too late. Leela stepped off the branch and plummeted to earth. The chain and the iron ring about her neck jerked her to a stop before she hit the ground. The chain dug into the bark of the branch that Leela had stood upon an instant before; otherwise, Dar might have been pulled upward and strangled. "Help!" she cried. "Someone help Leela!"

As the soldiers stumbled toward her, Dar looked for

signs of life. Leela's feet kicked spasmodically, but her neck seemed unnaturally long and her eyes stared from a head held at a strange angle. The murdant arrived first and spun the dangling body so it faced him.

"Get her down!" said Dar.

"No hurry about that," said the murdant.

The tolum strode over. "What's going on?"

"One of the girls killed herself."

The tolum kicked the dirt. "Shit! Shit! Shit!" He stared angrily at the still twitching corpse, then drew his sword and swung it with both hands. Leela's body dropped at Dar's feet, while her head tumbled in another direction. He stood glaring at Dar, sword in hand. "You stupid bitch! You let her do it!"

For a moment, Dar thought he would decapitate her also. Instead, he released the sword hilt with one hand and slapped her so hard that she tasted blood. He seemed about to strike her again when the murdant asked, "Sir, what will we do?"

"Stop on the way and grab another girl."

"Our commander wanted highland girls."

"He also ordered me to report tomorrow. We don't have time to go back to the highlands."

As two soldiers dragged Leela's body away, the tolum found her head and picked it up by the hair. "He wanted two mountain girls? Well, we got two—both properly branded."

"What will they do with a head, sir?" asked the murdant.

"They can eat it, for all I care. I fulfilled my orders."

The tolum sauntered over to where Dar was chained and thrust out Leela's head. "Take it and see that nothing drags it off tonight. Tomorrow, you'll carry it."

Dar was too cowed to disobey. Despite her horror,

she grasped the long, blond locks. Leela's eyes glistened in the moonlight, staring at something beyond living vision. They seemed peaceful, and Dar imagined their owner's spirit walking the Dark Path, clad only in memories, and shedding even those as she traveled westward.

Three

The soldiers quickly returned to sleep. Dar, however, remained awake. Leela's suicide gave credibility to her dire predictions, making sleep impossible. Dar prayed to Karm for protection with little hope of receiving it. The Goddess seemed remote and abstract in contrast to the immediacy of branded flesh and Leela's severed head. Dar spent the remainder of the night leaning against the tree trunk, waiting for dawn, and fearing that the upcoming day would be her last.

When the sun rose, the soldiers woke eager to finish their business. Breakfast was hurried, and the march was also. On the journey, Dar's lack of sleep quickly took its toll. Leela's head was surprisingly heavy, and Dar's arms soon ached from carrying it. Her brand throbbed, as did the bruise from the tolum's blow. Dar stumbled frequently, causing the tolum to eventually take the head and tie it to his saddle by the hair. The murdant also unlocked the ring about Dar's neck, permitting her to walk without the chain. Dar's exhaustion made it unnecessary, for escape was beyond her.

Thus unburdened, Dar got enough of a second wind to take in the country about her. She had never seen any place like it. The land was fertile and in the full lushness of spring. The trees, unlike the stunted highland ones, were tall and full. The fields were neatly bordered and filled with sprouting crops. The homes reflected the bounty of the land; even the most humble ones exceeded all but the richest highland dwellings.

Yet the surrounding beauty and abundance didn't ease Dar's growing anxiety. She sensed that they were nearing the orc regiment, for the soldiers grew jittery and their talk turned to their destination. "I'd rather go to battle," said one, "than visit orcs."

"Me, too," said another. "It's like going near wild dogs. Ya never know if they'll bite."

"Aye, one false step can get yer neck snapped," said a third.

"They're dogs, all right," said the murdant. "Mad ones."

"And the men are curs," said the third soldier.

Dar perked up a little. "Are there men in the regiment?" she asked.

"Aye, the army's dregs," replied the murdant.

"Are they branded like the women?" asked Dar.

"There's no need," said the murdant. "The orcs do all the fighting. The men are barely soldiers—more like flies around shit. It's an easy life for them."

"If ya don't mind the stink," added a soldier.

"Or piss off an orc," said another, grinning and passing a finger across his throat.

"How do they serve the orcs?" asked Dar.

"They don't," said the murdant. "They serve the orcs' commander, and he's a man. Some general. They call him the Queen's Man. Don't ask me why."

"So a man commands the orcs?" asked Dar, who found this news encouraging.

"Aye," said the murdant. "And they say he's as bad as them."

When the road neared a small river, a lane diverged

from it and headed for the waterway. The soldiers followed the lane, which soon turned muddy. Wagon wheels and hoofs had churned the damp ground, and Dar noted footprints that were larger than any man's.

When the lane turned with a bend in the river, Dar saw a broad, open area. The regiment's encampment sprawled over most of it, a chaotic jumble of tents, wagons, and animals. The air smelled of manure, wood smoke, damp earth, and garbage. No orcs were visible, but a few men lounged about the wagons. The tolum directed his horse toward them. The soldiers and Dar followed.

Though the camp seemed peaceful, entering it filled Dar with dread. She felt as if she were an animal being led into a slaughter pen. With each step Dar fought rising panic. *I must seem calm and keep my wits about me.*

The tolum halted before three slovenly men who squatted on the ground and tossed bones in a game of knockem. They looked up at the mounted officer, but didn't rise. Ignoring their disrespect, the tolum addressed them. "I'm Tolum Krem," he said. "Where's the Queen's Man?"

"Out hawking with his officers," said a man in a greasy leather jerkin.

"Who's in charge?"

"Murdant Teeg," said the man as he scooped up the bones and tossed them.

The tolum's murdant stepped forward and scattered the bones with a kick. "Then, you'd best go get him."

The man in the jerkin scowled and rose, taking his hand from his dagger hilt as he did. A few minutes later, he returned with a large, coarsely featured man with a thick black beard. He wore an ancient-looking doublet, made of quilted cloth and sewn with metal plates. Murdant Teeg regarded the young officer indifferently. "What brings ye here, sir?"

"My commander sends the Queen's Man the two highland girls that he requested along with his regards."

Murdant Teeg looked at Dar. "Two? I see but one."

The tolum jerked Leela's head loose from his saddle and tossed it on the ground. "Two girls, both properly branded."

Teeg used his foot to roll the head so it faced upward. "It seems ye brought her least useful part." He turned to the man who had fetched him. "Stick it on a stake next to the other one."

As the soldier carried the head away, Tolum Krem said, "We're done here."

Murdant Teeg flashed a sardonic smile. "Do ye not wish to dine with the Queen's Man tonight? I'm sure he'd be interested in learnin' what happened to the rest of his girl."

"Give him my regrets, but we must report to our unit."

"I'll do that."

Tolum Krem turned his horse, and trotted off with his soldiers hurrying behind. Murdant Teeg spit. "I'll *bet* he's regretful, the little horse shit!" He turned to Dar. "Well, birdie, what's yer name?"

"Dar."

"What happened to the other one? She run off?"

"She killed herself last night."

"There's plenty who'd have saved her the trouble. Bear that in mind if yer thinkin' of boltin'."

"She was afraid of the orcs. She thought they'd eat us."

Teeg grinned, revealing broken, yellow teeth. "And so they might, little birdie, if ye do not as yer told." He turned to the two remaining men. "Get her to Neffa." Then the murdant walked away.

The men regarded Dar as cats might a mouse, and their interest put Dar on her guard. She watched warily as one slowly circled her, his eyes roving over her body. "You're a fresh one," he said. "Not yet scabbed over. Ever seen a piss eye?"

"What's that?" asked Dar.

"An orc. Fancy meeting one?"

Dar shook her head.

The soldier stopped behind her, so close she could smell his sour breath. "We could put it off," he whispered as he squeezed her bottom, "and go to my tent instead."

Dar quickly pivoted out of his reach.

The other man caught the look in Dar's eyes and laughed. "Better watch that one, Muut. She looks like she'd bite."

"She'll lose that look soon enough," replied Muut. "Why don't we take her to Garga?"

His companion grinned. "That would be a bit of fun."

Muut seized Dar's upper arm and held it tightly. "Come on, birdie, it's time you met a piss eye."

Clutching her shabby bundle, Dar was marched along in Muut's grasp. They entered an area filled with haphazardly erected tents of varying size. Many consisted of no more than a bit of weather-beaten cloth draped over a line stretched between poles. The ground between the crude shelters was muddied by traffic and littered with garbage and worse. As Dar passed among the tents, she spied men lolling inside some, while ragged women with brands on their foreheads scurried about with bundles of firewood and other burdens.

Muut didn't stop at the tents, but dragged Dar past them toward a slight rise. Its top was crowned with what looked like a collection of conical haystacks. These man-high grass-and-reed structures were enclosed by a wide circle of bare branches that were set upright in the ground. The purpose of the circle wasn't clear, for the branches were placed too far apart to form a barrier. Whatever its significance, the men's boisterous mood dampened as they approached the circle. They halted at its edge, and Muut pointed to the nearest cone. "Go over there," he said, releasing Dar's arm.

Dar nervously obeyed.

"Garga-tok," called Muut in a loud voice.

Huge hands, darkly tanned and tipped with claws, thrust from the straw and parted it like a curtain. A pair of yellow eyes peered from the shadows.

Muut yelled, "We brought you a new girl."

The grass parted further and Garga-tok emerged into the sunlight. His body was shaped like that of a very large man, though it was far more massive and muscular, particularly about the chest, neck, and shoulders. He wore a short-sleeved tunic that extended to his knees. It was covered with small, rounded iron plates that overlapped like fish scales. The armored garment was rusty and ponderous-looking, but the orc seemed oblivious of its weight. A broad-bladed dagger hung from a wide leather belt. His shoulders were covered by a short cape with a curious fringe sewn on its edges. In horror, Dar realized the fringe was made of human ears, some of which bore women's earrings.

Dar's gaze lifted from the gruesome cape to the orc's

large, grotesque head. A heavy brow shaded his inhuman eyes. Above the brow was a wide forehead, covered with a pattern of ridges and knobby growths. Behind these was a thick and tangled mane of long, reddish hair. The ridge of his nose was sharp, but turned broad close to the large nostrils. His thin-lipped mouth was wide, while his chin seemed disproportionately small and pointed for so massive a head. A design of black lines covered the lower part of his face, completing its savage look.

Yet it wasn't Garga-tok's bizarre appearance that terrified Dar—it was the way he regarded her. His yellow eyes, though as inscrutable as a wild beast's, possessed an alien intelligence. She was being examined, but she had no idea why. The orc's interest might be malign, casual, or even culinary. Unable to fathom it, Dar felt dangerously vulnerable.

"Youz name is what?" asked Garga-tok in a deep voice that had the rawness of a growl.

The orc appeared so bestial that Dar was stunned when he spoke, and she stood mute until Garga-tok said more loudly, "Youz name!"

"Dar," she answered in a tiny voice.

The orc curled back his lips and hissed, exposing teeth that were pearly black. A pair of sharp fangs jutted from both his upper and lower jaws, while the rest of his teeth were not unlike a human's. "Dargu?" he said, then hissed again.

A second orc emerged from a nearby grass cone and Garga-tok spoke to him. "Kala washavoki theefak Dargu."

The second orc curled back his lips and said something equally incomprehensible. Then he and Garga-tok hissed together.

Dar turned to ask the men what the orcs were saying and discovered they had fled. When she faced Garga-tok again, he had moved so close that she had to look upward to see his face. She remained frozen to the spot, uncertain what to do and fearful of provoking him.

Garga-tok's nostrils flared as he stared down at her. "You stink." He turned away and uttered something in his strange tongue before disappearing into his shelter.

The remaining orc grabbed Dar's upper arm, encircling it entirely with his fingers. "Sutat," he said, pulling her arm so forcefully that she was briefly wrenched off her feet. The orc strode toward the river, gripping Dar so she was forced to half run to keep up. He was shorter than Garga-tok and the markings on his face were different. He also wore no cape. Dar, however, scarcely noticed this. Her attention was fixed on the hatchet dangling from his belt. It looked very similar to one her father used to butcher game.

The orc took her to where the sandy riverbank was littered with boulders. One was the size and shape of a table. *That's where he'll slaughter me*, Dar thought, *and clean my carcass*. To her surprise, the orc didn't grab his hatchet. Instead, he marched her into the river. Once Dar stood in water up to her calves, he released her arm and said, "Splufukat."

Dar turned so she could face the orc. "I don't understand."

The orc bent down, scooped water with his huge hands, and splashed her, drenching the front of her shift. "Splufukat. Splufukat."

Dar stood motionless—terrified and uncomprehending. The orc's face gave no more clues to his mood or intentions than an animal's would. Dar shook her head. "What do . . ."

The orc seized Dar and tossed her into deeper water. She landed with a splash, fell backward, and submerged completely. Dar had never seen a body of water larger than a mountain stream, and being immersed panicked her. She struggled to her feet and dashed toward the shore. The orc blocked her way, one hand reaching for his hatchet. "Splufukat," he said again, this time in the low, harsh tone of a growling dog.

Dar's terror, frustration, and exhaustion combined to burst forth in a great sob. Her body shuddered with its force, which shattered her self-control. She began weeping, and the sound attracted a second orc, who descended the bank. As Dar fought to stifle her sobs, the two orcs spoke briefly in their strange language. The first orc left, but the second one remained. He was even taller than Garga-tok, though not as massively built, and his features were more finely formed. Like Garga-tok, he wore a short cape, though it lacked the fringe of ears. The orc watched Dar with green-gold eyes, blocking the shoreline and seeming to wait for her to cease crying.

When she did, he spoke. "Washavokis have unpleasing scent when they bathe not."

Dar guessed what "splufukat" meant. "You want me to bathe?"

"Is not that plain?"

"But it's unhealthy."

The orc curled back his lips. "Do I look unhealthy? Wash body and clothes." He pointed to Dar's partly submerged bundle, drifting in the current. "You losing some."

After Dar retrieved the bundle, she splashed water on her arms and legs, then headed for the shore. The orc seized her arm. "Wet washavokis stink worse. Scrub all skin with sand. Then wash clothes."

Dar blushed. "Must I take them off?"

"Garga-tok said you will be clean."

Dar assumed he meant yes. *Oh well, it's not like undressing in front of a man.* Then she recalled the two men who had taken her to Garga-tok. She glanced along the riverbank. Sure enough, they were spying on her from a distance and grinning broadly. "I can't bathe now."

The orc's body tensed, and he opened his mouth wide to expose his fangs. Puffing up his chest, he growled. The growl grew louder and became a roar that echoed along the riverbank. All the while, his greenish eyes bore into Dar. There was no mistaking his menace. Ignoring the men, Dar quickly shed her clothes and tossed them on the bank. While the orc watched, she scooped up river sand and rubbed it on her bare skin. After she rinsed it off, she headed for the shore. The orc blocked her way and sniffed. "Still stink," he said.

Dar waded back into the river to scrub some more. When she finished, the orc sniffed her and sent her back yet again. By then, Dar had realized that she wasn't about to die, and her fear gave way to irritation. Though she dared not defy the orc, she glared at him angrily. She had no idea if he understood her look; he simply curled back his lips and muttered, "Dargu nak theef turpa ala ga."

When Dar was finally permitted to leave the river, her skin glowed rosy pink and her arms and legs were several shades lighter. She hurriedly washed her shift by pounding it on a submerged stone and donned it wet before washing her other clothes. When the last garment was clean, the orc seemed satisfied. "Come," he said. "You go to Neffa."

The orc led Dar to a part of the camp outside the circle of branches, but close to it. He headed for a long, open-sided tent that was twice the height of the others. Its cloth was black with soot, for it spanned a pit where food was being cooked. "Neffa!" bellowed the orc.

A woman left the smoky tent and hurried over. Her clothes, hair, and skin were soot-stained and her eyes were bloodshot. "Here is new washavoki," said the orc. Then he walked away without waiting for a response.

Neffa seemed harried, and she had a worn-out look that made her age hard to determine. She gave Dar a cursory inspection. "We're supposed to get two girls," she said. "Where's the other? Tupping some soldier?"

"She's dead," replied Dar.

Neffa seemed unsurprised. "Already?"

Four

Dar thought Neffa would help her settle in, but all she said was "Feed the fires." There were over a dozen blazing within the long pit. Women were gathered about them, tending large kettles. As Dar waited for more complete instructions, Neffa turned and struck a woman who was listlessly stirring porridge. "Mind what you're doing," she yelled. "Don't let that scorch!"

"Neffa!" shouted Murdant Teeg. "The men are hungry."

"There'll be porridge soon," said Neffa.

"Porridge? I gave you bitches roots this morning."

"They're cooking."

"Well, cook them faster," yelled Murdant Teeg.

Neffa glared at Dar. "Why are you standing there?"

Dar set her wet bundle down and went over to the nearby woodpile. She grabbed a large branch and dragged it over to where a woman stirred a kettle filled with roots. The woman grabbed Dar's arm. "Hey, scabhead. What are you doing?"

"I'm supposed to feed the fires."

"Fool! That's way too big. Do you want to burn down the tent?"

"I'll chop it up," said Dar. "Where's an ax?"

The woman rolled her eyes. "How should I know?"

Dar dragged the branch outside and looked about for

something to chop it into smaller pieces. She was still searching when another woman called, "Wood, scabby! Bring wood!"

Dar dashed over to the tangled pile of branches for one that she could break with her hands and feet. She hurriedly snapped it into pieces and threw them on the woman's fire. Already, someone else was shouting for wood, and others quickly joined her call.

"Wood, you slug! Wood!"

"Move your ass, scabby!"

"Hurry, hillbitch, food doesn't cook itself!"

Used to an isolated life, Dar felt nearly overwhelmed by the clamoring voices. The suddenness of the shouting made Dar suspect she was being baited. Nevertheless, she scurried back and forth, trying to satisfy everyone. It was impossible, and her harassment ceased only when the food was ready.

Neffa appeared with a woman in tow whose brand looked only recently healed. The woman had a young face that was framed by long black hair and marked by a purple bruise beneath one eye. "You'll serve with Memni tonight," said Neffa to Dar. "Go with her."

"Come on," said Memni. "We have to wash first."

"I've already bathed today."

"It doesn't matter. You're sweaty, and orcs have noses like hounds."

Memni led Dar to a tent. Inside was a large copper basin containing hot water that had been mixed with herbs. The steam that rose from it smelled of them. "The herbs help mask our scent," said Memni. A naked woman stood in the basin and hurriedly scrubbed herself with a cloth that she dipped in the scented water. The rest of the women in the tent, about a dozen in all, appeared to have already washed, for they wore clean robes.

"Have you lain with a man today?" asked Memni. "If so, wash extra careful. Orcs hate that smell."

"I try to keep away from men," said Dar.

Memni seemed pleased to hear that. "What's your name?"

"Dar."

"This is Dar," said Memni to the others in the tent. The women cast Dar indifferent glances; otherwise, they didn't acknowledge her.

"You're from the hills, aren't you?" said Memni. "I can tell by your accent. Lots of the girls come from there. I was born in Luvein, but my uncle . . . oops, it's your turn. Be quick."

Dar undressed, stepped into the basin, and began washing. Recalling her experience at the river, she scrubbed thoroughly.

"Put on one of those robes when you're done," said Memni, pointing to some linen robes draped over a line. "After you finish serving, bring it back here and wash it in the basin."

Dar finished washing and donned a robe. "What will I be doing?" asked Dar.

"Giving orcs their food. They sit. We serve. It's like a ceremony. Just copy me. And you have to say 'mootha-yer-rat-thas-affa' when you do it."

"What does that mean?"

"Who knows? But it's important," said Memni. "The orcs get mad if you forget. Some will hit you. You don't want that. I've seen one kill a man that way. Just one blow. I'm not even sure he meant to do it. They're so . . ."

"Memni!" shouted a woman. "Stop blabbing with the scabhead and get ready."

Memni quickly shed her clothes, exposing several

more bruises. After she had washed and put on a clean robe, all the women left the tent. The food they were to serve stood ready. A large kettle of porridge had poles inserted in its handle so a pair of women could lift and carry it. There were also baskets that held steaming roots. The women lifted the food and walked toward the circular enclosure in a slow procession. Memni and Dar were assigned to bear the kettle. Memni grunted from the effort of lifting her end of the pole. "No one likes to serve," she said. "Especially porridge. By the time we're done, all we'll get is scraps. But I have my soldier, so . . ."

"Shush!" said another woman as they entered the circle of upright branches. The women proceeded past the conical structures into the open area they surrounded. There, row upon row of orcs sat cross-legged and motionless. The woman leading the procession called out in a loud voice, "Saf nak ur Muthz la."

Deep voices answered in unison, "Shashav Muth la." To Dar, the voices sounded like the roar of an avalanche. The fear and awe she experienced when she first saw Garga-tok returned as she gazed upon the monstrous faces. Each was different, yet all possessed a common inhumanity. Their animal-hued eyes glowed like those of cats in the fading light, and Dar dreaded walking among them.

"Hurry," whispered Memni. "Fill your ladle and start serving. Don't forget to say the words."

The kettle was too cumbersome to carry among the orcs, so serving them would take many trips back and forth. Each orc had a wide, shallow metal bowl set before him. Dar watched Memni ladle porridge over the roots that had been served already. *At least they're not fussy how their food looks*, thought Dar, as she imitated

Memni. When she turned to refill the ladle, the orc she had just served grabbed her ankle. His claws dug into her skin. *The words! I didn't say the words!* For a long moment, her mind went blank. The hand squeezed tighter.

"Moo . . . uh . . . Mooth . . . Mootha-yer . . . yer-rat . . . thas-affa," said Dar. "Mootha-yer-rat-thas-affa."

The orc released Dar, and she hurried back to the kettle, her ankle bloody. After that, Dar was careful to recite the phrase. All the orcs she served received their food without reacting, except the orc who had forced her to bathe. He curled back his lips and said, "Dargu."

Dar pretended not to notice as she poured the porridge over his bowl. "Mootha-yer-rat-thas-affa."

"No," said the orc. "Muth la urat tha saf la."

Dar repeated what he said. "Muth la urat tha saf la."

"Hai," responded the orc. "Yes."

By the time Dar and Memni had ladled out the last of the porridge, it was dusk. The other women had departed. Memni looked inside the kettle as she and Dar carried it back to the cook tent. "If you scrape the sides," she said, "there's enough for your dinner."

"What about you?" asked Dar.

"I have my soldier," said Memni. "He'll give me something."

The cooking tent was nearly deserted when Dar and Memni returned. A lone woman was cleaning up, and a paunchy soldier watched her. When he saw Memni approach, he held out a handful of cooked roots. "Hey, bird," he said. "Got some supper here."

"Aren't you sweet," said Memni.

"Ya might get some," he replied, "if yar sweet ta me."

"I'm always sweet to you, Faussy."

"Come 'n' prove it."

"Soon as I change," said Memni, heading for the bathing tent. "Dar, you should change, too."

Dar looked at the porridge kettle and hesitated. "I'm going to eat first."

The woman glanced up from her scrubbing. "You can only wear those robes while serving," she said. "Don't worry about the porridge. It'll be safe."

"Thanks," Dar said, and followed Memni.

After Dar changed into her shift and washed the robe, she returned to the kettle. To her dismay, the woman was washing it. "You must be Dar, the new scabhead," said the woman, who had a round, pleasant face with kind eyes. She appeared Dar's age, though her brand was old enough to have faded to a pale, raised scar. She was also very pregnant. The woman smiled and held out a cooked root in addition to a bowl of crusty porridge. "I saved these for you. I'm Loral."

Dar took the food. After an exhausting and terrifying day, Loral's kindness felt overwhelming. Dar started to thank her, but burst out crying instead. Loral watched sympathetically as Dar struggled to stifle her sobs. It took a while before she succeeded. "I never cry," said Dar, feeling embarrassed, "and now I've done it twice today."

"I cried for a whole moon after they took me," said Loral.

"Everything has been so . . ." Dar paused to suppress a sob. ". . . so horrible."

"You'll get used to it," said Loral. She gave Dar a hug. "Eat. You must be starving."

"I am."

Loral watched Dar devour the root, then hungrily

scoop the porridge from the bowl with her fingers. "You needn't eat like an orc," she said. "No one will take it from you."

Loral didn't speak again until Dar finished licking the bowl and her fingers. "I rescued your bundle of clothes. I'm afraid someone trod it into the mud."

"On purpose?"

"Of course. You're lucky she didn't toss it in the fire."

"Why would anyone do that?" asked Dar.

"The men fancy new girls, and that stirs up trouble. Everyone's afraid you might take their man."

"Except you."

Loral laughed ruefully. "No man wants a plugged womb-pipe."

"Well, I want no man," said Dar. "So no one should worry."

"You may not want one, but you need one. Where will you get shoes, if not from a man? Women have no share in the plunder. Only through a man's generosity . . ."

"Generosity?" said Dar. "Don't make me laugh! The only thing a man gives a woman is a big belly. Nothing else comes free." Dar recalled her suitors, who seemed to think a wife's sole purpose was to serve their needs.

"That's the way of the world," Loral said. "We're subject to men."

"My father's favorite lesson," said Dar.

"Why so bitter?" asked Loral. "It's natural for fathers to teach about life."

"There was nothing natural about his lessons. Even beasts show more restraint."

"But men aren't beasts," said Loral. "They're the masters here. You'd best look for a generous one."

"Have *you* found such a man?"

"Perhaps," said Loral, "if I bear him a son."

Dar looked dubious. "And that's how I should live my life?"

"That's how you *must* live it."

Five

After Loral banked the embers in the cooking pit, she led Dar to the women's tent. Its floor was covered with straw and bodies. Although it was only a little past dusk, all the women there were asleep. Loral and Dar carefully picked their way through the crowded gloom to a space large enough to lie down. Though Dar's cloak was still damp from washing and covered with muddy footprints, she was too exhausted to care. She wrapped it around her and sank down on the trampled straw.

Loral touched her shoulder. "Share my cloak," she whispered. "Yours is wet."

Dar cast her damp cloak aside to be enveloped by Loral's dry one. She felt Loral's bulging belly briefly press against her back and recalled lying next to her pregnant mother. It was the last of her happy memories. After Dar's older brothers died in an avalanche, her father had become obsessed with replacing his male heirs. Only when Dar's mother conceived again had peace returned. Yet what came afterward convinced Dar that her mother hadn't swelled with life, but with death instead. Dar shuddered, reliving the bloody night it had burst forth. She pressed her back against Loral, wishing her a better fortune.

* * *

It was still dark when Neffa entered the tent. "Up!" she shouted. "Up! Up! Where's Memni? Is Memni here?"

"She's with Faus," answered a sleepy voice.

"Taren, then," said Neffa. "I doubt *she's* tupping. Taren!"

"Here," answered a voice.

"Show the new girl how to make porridge," said Neffa. "Rise, girls. The Queen's Man is back. The men will be up early."

The women slept in their clothes, so dressing consisted of little more than slipping on shoes. Lacking these, Dar was one of the first out of the tent. A woman emerged soon afterward, spotted Dar, and stopped. "Scabhead, you know how to make porridge?"

"Of course," said Dar.

"Have you made it for a hundred?"

"Only for five."

"Well, there's a big difference," said the woman, who Dar assumed was Taren. Her appearance was the opposite of Loral's; she was bony, with a sharp, pockmarked face, and long dirty-blond hair, which was plaited into a single, greasy braid. She bore the same worn and hardened look as Neffa, which made it difficult for Dar to judge her age. "Come on, scabby," she said. "I'll show you how it's done."

"My name's Dar."

"So? You're still a scabhead."

Taren led Dar over to the fire pit. "First, you roast the grain over embers. You know how to do that?"

"Of course."

"Then light a fire. I'll get the grain."

By the time Dar had a fire going, Taren appeared, struggling with a heavy sack of grain. Dar went over to help her. "Do we always rise before dawn?"

"When you tup a soldier, you get to sleep in."

"Neffa allows that?"

"She has no choice. If she stuck her nose in a man's tent, he'd whack it off."

"Well, I'm used to rising early," said Dar.

"You'll get to sleep in," said Taren. "Men will choose you."

The bitterness in Taren's voice surprised Dar. Then she regarded the woman's ragged clothes and shoeless feet. They made her recall Loral's remark about needing men's generosity. *Taren's seen little of that.*

When Dar's fire burned down to embers, she and Taren placed a large kettle upon it. Roasting grain for a hundred turned out to be little different from doing it for five, except it was harder work. The mass of kernels had to be stirred constantly to keep from scorching. As she had in the dark highland hut, Dar judged when the roasting was done by smell rather than sight. When the grain had a toasted aroma, she pulled the kettle from the embers and Taren gave her a large wooden pestle to pound the grain in preparation for making porridge.

By then, the sky had lightened. Disheveled, sleepy-eyed women left the soldiers' tents and went straight to work. Memni approached. "Is that grain ready to cook?"

"Almost," said Dar.

"I'll get the water," said Memni, grabbing a pair of buckets.

Taren came over after Memni left. "You two friends?"

"We served porridge to the orcs together."

"If you whore about like she does, you'll serve every night. Neffa's not blind."

Before Dar could speak, Taren walked away. Memni

returned shortly afterward. "Build up the fire," she said, "while I mix in the water."

Dar piled wood on the embers as Memni added water to turn the toasted and pulverized grain into a viscous paste. Then the two women dragged the kettle back over the flames. "Dar, would you stir?" asked Memni. "I'm beat. Sometimes I think Faus sleeps all day just so he can tup all night."

"And you submit to that for a handful of *roots*?"

"He gives me other things as well."

"Like those bruises?"

"They're not his fault; I shouldn't make him mad. Faus *loves* me."

Dar was about to reply, but changed her mind. *Her nights are probably easier if she thinks he loves her.*

The sun rose to the shouts of murdants rousing the men. Soon, soldiers carrying wooden bowls began to cluster about the cooking tent, waiting to be fed. Dar's job was to ladle out the porridge. She had served the orcs during the soldiers' evening meal, so this was her first encounter with most of the regiment's men. Though she expected crudeness, she was unprepared to be the focus of it. Word had spread that there was a "fresh birdie," and the men were eager for a look. Some didn't confine themselves to looking and made free with their hands. Even more were free with their tongues. Their frank appraisals of Dar's looks and whether she was "worth tupping" were made as if she were deaf or, at least, unfeeling.

Dar tried to ignore the comments and fend off the advances as best she could. They roused a mixture of anger and humiliation that showed on her face. That only increased the attention she received. Soon, she felt like a wounded animal harried by a flock of ravens. Finally, when one man grabbed her breast as she was serving him, she snapped and threw porridge in his face.

A soldier laughed. "Well, Varf, it seems that birdie pecks."

Varf's hand shot out and seized Dar's wrist so firmly she gasped. He pulled it upward while squeezing until she dropped the ladle. After it hit the ground, the soldier drew his knife and moved the blade toward Dar's face. "Let's see how well she pecks without a beak."

A hand gripped Varf's shoulder. "The girl was clumsy," said a steely voice. "I'm sure she's sorry. Aren't you, scabby?"

Before Dar could mumble "yes," Varf put his knife away. "I was just teasing, Murdant," he said.

The man who had intervened was older and harder-looking than the other soldiers. His leathery, sun-darkened face made his pale blue eyes seem more piercing. Those eyes fixed on Dar, but they didn't rove over her body. "Serve the man," the murdant said, "and this time mind you get it in his bowl."

Dar picked up the ladle and wiped it on her shift before serving Varf. Her hand shook so violently, she feared missing the bowl. Varf scowled, but the murdant's presence seemed to temper his anger.

"All right!" said the murdant in a loud voice. "Stop gaping and eat up. The lazy days are over. The Queen's Man has issued orders. I want all the murdants to report to me." He turned to Dar. "You're new. What's your name?"

"Dar."

"Well, Dar, watch where you serve the porridge from now on. The men will have their fun, and it's not wise to rile them."

"Yes, Murdant."

The murdant stepped away, then turned, as if seized by an afterthought. "Come to the Queen's Man's compound when you're done here. There's some work for you. Ask for me, Murdant Kol."

Dar finished serving. After the porridge-throwing incident, the soldiers were less free with their hands, and their comments were more subdued. From the way the other women regarded her, Dar suspected some regretted that Varf hadn't carried out his threat. She recalled the enraged look in his eyes and felt certain he hadn't been teasing. She touched her nose and silently thanked Murdant Kol that it was still there.

After the soldiers departed, the women grabbed hurried meals before beginning the next round of chores. Dar headed for the Queen's Man's compound. It lay at the edge of the encampment, for the general who commanded the regiment's orcish and human soldiers stayed apart from both. His compound reflected his high rank. The tents there were large and finely made. Each was sewn together and fitted over a frame so it resembled a cloth house with vertical walls and a pyramidal roof. Dar guessed the largest one belonged to the Queen's Man. As she approached it, a soldier barred her way.

"What are ye doin' here?"

"Murdant Kol told me to come. He said there was some work."

"Wait here. He's busy with the murdants."

As Dar waited, she thought she heard Murdant Kol's voice coming through the wall of a nearby tent. ". . . all shieldrons must be at the assembly point by the end of this moon. Take it easy; the Queen's Man wants the orcs rested for the campaign. Murdant Teeg, you'll have . . ."

"So birdie," said the soldier, "what does Kol want of ye?"

"I don't know."

The soldier grinned. "Can't ye guess?"

When Dar blushed, the soldier's grin broadened.

Dar's inquisition was interrupted when a group of men emerged from the closest tent. Dar recognized Murdant Teeg among them. Murdant Kol strode out last, with the assurance of a man with authority. He glanced in Dar's direction and smiled. "There are some hares in the cook tent," he said. "The officers got them hawking and want their pelts for helmet liners. You'll skin them and scrape their hides for tanning."

"I'll have to soak the hides for at least a day before scraping them," said Dar.

"A day is all you'll have," said Kol. "We'll be breaking camp day after tomorrow."

"Then I'll be sure to finish them by then."

"Good," said Kol. He led Dar to the tent where food was prepared for the officers. It was much smaller and better made than the one Dar worked in, featuring sides that could be rolled down in bad weather and a vent to let smoke out yet keep rain from entering. Two branded women were there, one tending the fires and the other pounding grain. Three men were preparing a meal. Kol addressed one of them. "Dar, here, will be skinning the hares. Give her a liver for her trouble."

Murdant Kol left, and Dar began to work. There were seven hares and she took extra care skinning and dressing them. When she was done, a cook took the carcasses. Dar reminded him that Murdant Kol had said she could have a liver. Irritation crossed the man's face, but he handed Dar one. "Take it, birdie, but don't cook it here."

Dar cupped the morsel in her hand and carried the pelts to the river. There, she waded out to a submerged boulder, spread the pelts on it, and weighted them down with rocks. That done, Dar skewered the liver on a stick and headed for the fire pit. It was crowded with women busy preparing another meal. Dar halted, imagining their reaction if she roasted her reward while they worked. Dar moved out of the women's sight, then removed the liver from the stick and ate it raw.

Dar was wiping her bloody fingers on the grass when she noticed Murdant Kol watching her. He sauntered over. "You're a fierce one," he said. "No wonder you rile the men." Kol eyed Dar's body as if he were judging a horse. Dar tensed under his scrutiny and Kol acknowledged her reaction by smiling. "Yes," he said. "I'm certain of it—your face looks better with a nose."

Dar frowned but did not reply.

"You show too much spirit," said Kol. "It causes trouble."

"So?"

Kol shook his head. "With that attitude you won't last long."

"So I should become a whore? I'd sooner die."

"You need do neither. Just don't provoke the men."

"And let them abuse me?"

"If they try, tell them you're my woman. They'll stop."

Dar stiffened. "*Your* woman?"

"Yes."

"So you're claiming me, as if I were plunder."

"No," replied Kol. "I'm offering my protection."

"Why?"

"Out of kindness," replied Kol. He smiled. "Is that so surprising?"

Dar thought it was. She studied Murdant Kol's face, trying to divine the reason for his smile, but his pale eyes offered no hint.

Six

After Kol departed, Dar headed to the cooking site. Passing the women's tent, she paused to peer inside. It was empty. Dar was tired after a troubled sleep, and the temptation to rest was irresistible. She slipped inside and lay down on the straw. *I've done everything I've been told. If Neffa wants me, she can find me.*

Not long afterward, Neffa did just that and woke Dar with a kick. Dar avoided a second one only by springing to her feet. "Lazy sow!" yelled Neffa. "There's no rest while the sun shines!"

Dar suppressed the urge to kick Neffa back. "What would you have me do?"

"Roast and pound grain," said Neffa. "And when you're done with that, I'll give you other work. Next time I catch you napping, I'll tell a murdant. He'll have you whipped. Understand?"

"Yes," said Dar.

Dar joined the women who were roasting and pounding the camp's entire store of grain in preparation for the march. Loral was there, and she helped Dar get set up. Each kettle of grain took a long time to process, and even Dar's work-hardened hands were blistered by the fifth batch. Dulled by the monotony of her work, she was caught off guard by the soldier. He seized her from behind, pinioning her arms. Then he lifted and swung her around. When Dar's feet touched the ground again, she was facing Varf. Another soldier grabbed her ankles. Dar struggled to break free, but the two men held her fast.

"Hello, birdie," said Varf. "Remember me?"

"Yes," said Dar. Then, swallowing her pride, she added, "I'm sorry about this morning."

"Not sorry enough." said Varf. He scanned the fire pit and pulled out a large stick. Its tip smoldered. "That porridge burned." Varf blew on the stick until its end glowed orange.

Dar glanced about frantically. The other women had stopped working. Their nervous stillness reminded Dar of fawns frozen by a hunter's approach. Some nearby soldiers looked on, also. They appeared amused. "What are you going to do?" she asked.

"Give you something to remember me by," replied Varf. He bent down and lifted the hem of Dar's shift.

"I'm Kol's woman!" blurted Dar.

Varf stopped. "What?"

"I'm Murdant Kol's woman. He told me to say that."

The soldier holding Dar's arms eased his grip slightly. "Varf . . ." he said in a cautionary tone.

"She's bluffing," said Varf.

"What if she's not?" asked the other soldier.

Varf stared into Dar's eyes, then tossed the stick away. "Then I'd say she's jumped from the pot to the fire." He spit, hitting Dar's foot. "Come on, men, the bitch learned her lesson."

The soldiers released Dar and retreated with Varf. She stood alone, feeling only partly relieved, for the expressions of the women made her uneasy. Dar hadn't planned to say that she was Kol's woman, and she feared the words that had saved her would have other consequences. As she pondered her situation, the women gradually resumed their work until only Loral glared at her. “That didn't take long,” she said in a cold tone.

“What do you mean?” asked Dar.

Loral turned away without answering.

Dar worked into the late afternoon surrounded by women, yet apart from them. Loral had ceased speaking to her, while the others had never started. Dar caught their surreptitious glances and sensed she was the subject of whispered conversations. Their behavior reminded Dar of her stepmother's after learning her new husband had abused his daughter. *Thess blamed me, not him. These women are acting the same way.*

As the afternoon wore on, the pace around the cooking tent picked up. Neffa ordered Dar to make porridge for the orcs and serve it to them as well. When the porridge was ready, Dar headed for the washing tent. There, she found Memni scrubbing off the grime from a day of lugging firewood. She looked exhausted, but smiled when she saw Dar. Dar smiled back, relieved she wasn't ostracized by everyone. After Dar washed and dressed, she joined Memni outside. “I've got porridge duty again,” Memni said with a sigh. Then she grinned. “I hear you got a man!”

“Who told you that?”

“Everyone. Word travels fast.”

“It's not what they think,” said Dar. “At least, I hope not.”

“Hurry,” shouted Neffa. “Don't make the orcs wait.”

Dar and Memni slid a pole through the kettle's handle,

lifted it, and joined the women bearing food. They had nearly reached the circle of straw shelters when they heard a drunken voice shouting, "Stop! Stop, ya bitches!"

Dar turned to see a soldier staggering up the slope, his bowl in hand. His comrades warned him to come back, but they kept outside the circle of branches. Dar thought they seemed afraid to enter it. The soldier with the bowl ignored their calls. Instead, he kept stumbling toward Dar and Memni.

"Can't ya hear me? Stop! Gimme some tuppin' porridge."

"You can't have this," said Memni. "It's for . . ."

The soldier swung at Memni, but missed. Memni dropped her end of the pole, nearly causing the kettle to tip over when it hit the ground. "Don't tell *me* what I can't do," said the soldier as he dipped his bowl into the steaming porridge.

Garga-tok appeared so quickly that Dar saw only a flash of movement before he gripped the soldier. The man gave a startled cry as he was lifted in the air and plunged headfirst into the kettle. What followed next was eerily quiet. The soldier's upper torso disappeared into the porridge and the orc held him fast as he thrashed about. Whatever screams or pleas the man attempted were silenced by the hot, viscous grain. All the soldiers and women were too cowed to speak; moreover, Garga-tok seemed beyond entreaty. He held the soldier, without apparent effort, until the man went limp. Only then did Garga-tok lift the soldier from the porridge to toss his corpse beyond the circle of branches.

Garga-tok turned his yellow eyes on Dar. "Pot dirty." He kicked the kettle, sending it rolling down the slope. "Make more."

Dar and Memni hurried to obey, glad to flee the murderer. Only when Garga-tok departed did the bystanders begin to talk. Most of the voices were hushed, but Dar heard one soldier laugh. "I always said drink would kill him."

The other women were asleep by the time Dar and Memni had more porridge. The moon had yet to rise, and the two women needed torches to light their way to the orcs who sat immobile in the dark. Dar called out the words Neffa had instructed her to say. "Saf nak ur Muthz la."

The night thundered with the orcs' response. "Shashav Muth la."

Torch in hand, Dar hurried to serve the orcs, reciting the words she had learned the previous evening. All the orcs received their food in silence until she came to one whose eyes reflected green in the torchlight. After she recited the phrase, he said, "Tava, Dargu."

Dar froze.

"Tava, Dargu."

It occurred to Dar that "Tava" might be a form of greeting, so she repeated it. "Tava."

The orc curled back his lips. "Theef maz nak Kovok-mah."

Dar stared at him, puzzled by his behavior. When she headed toward the kettle to refill her ladle, the orc said, "Vata, Dargu."

As Dar walked away she said "Vata" and heard the orc hiss.

Dar and Memni were tired and hungry, but they had to change out of their robes, wash them, and scrub the pot. Faus was absent, and dinner for both women consisted of scrapings from the kettle. As they ate, Dar asked

Memni, "Do orcs ever speak to you when you serve them?"

"Never."

"One does to me," said Dar. "Always the same one. He's tall with greenish eyes."

"Does he wear a short cape?"

"Yes."

"Then, he's sort of like a murdant. The soldiers call him Kovok-something."

"Kovok-mah," said Dar. "So *that's* what he said. He told me his name. I wonder why."

"I've no idea," said Memni, "but I'd avoid him. He's the one that killed a man with one blow. All orcs are dangerous and quick to anger. Remember what happened to that soldier tonight."

Dar shuddered at the thought. "Let's not talk about it."

"Tell me about Murdant Kol, instead," said Memni. "How'd you snag him so fast?"

"I didn't do anything, I swear by Karm's holy name."

"Didn't Kol say you were his?"

"Yes, but . . ."

"Then you are. Don't worry."

"I can't help but worry. I don't even know the man."

"All you need to know is that he's the high murdant. The Queen's Man and his officers give the orders, but the murdants run things, and Kol runs the murdants. He can have any girl he chooses."

Dar felt a chill in the pit of her stomach. "And I have no say in the matter?"

Memni gave Dar a puzzled look. "What's the problem? I'm happy for you."

"Loral didn't seem happy."

"Well, that's to be expected. It's *his* baby she's carrying."

"Kol's baby?" said Dar, her chill deepening.

"What does that matter? It's *you* he wants now."

Seven

Dar's father was sitting on her straw bed in the dark hut, his fingers softly traveling up and down her arm. Then his hand strayed elsewhere. Although they were alone, he spoke in a husky whisper. "Move over, honey. Let me lie beside you."

Dar woke with a start, her heart pounding. The dream of her father evoked thoughts of Murdant Kol. Sleeping women surrounded her, but she couldn't shake the feeling that the murdant was near. Dar envisioned him touching her, and dread prevented further sleep. She lay awake until Neffa called the women forth. At the cooking site, Dar made porridge for the soldiers and served it to them. This morning, the men made no crude remarks and kept their hands to themselves. Apparently, they knew she was taken.

After the morning meal, Dar went to retrieve the pelts and heard orcs in the river. Fearful that they might have dislodged the soaking pelts, she rushed into the water. Dar was relieved to see the orcs were bathing upstream and the pelts were where she had left them. She examined one and found it properly softened, though silt had lodged in the fur. While she rinsed it out, an orc swam closer. He stopped and stood chest-deep in the water a few paces away.

Dar recognized his green-gold eyes. Though nervous,

she thought it prudent to acknowledge him. "Tava, Kovok-mah."

The orc curled back his lips. "Tava, Dargu."

Dar had an ear for language, and having guessed the orcish word for "name," she replied, "My theef is Dar."

The curl of Kovok-mah's lips became more pronounced. "Theef nak Dargu."

"Dar."

"Thwa," said Kovok-mah. "No."

"Yes," replied Dar. "Hai."

"Dargu nak theef turpa ala ga."

"You said that before. What does it mean?"

"Dargu is proper name for you."

"Why? What does 'Dargu' mean?"

"Dargu is small animal. It hunts. Fur is brown in summer, white in winter."

"A *weasel*!" said Dar. She pretended to be insulted and made a show of scowling.

When Kovok-mah saw Dar's expression, he hissed, then said, "Dargu is small, but fierce."

The comment encouraged Dar to quip, "Especially when wet." The orc hissed again, and it occurred to Dar that he might be laughing. That gave her the courage to ask about what troubled her. "Why did Garga-tok kill that soldier?"

"He was angry because washavoki stole from Muth la."

Dar recognized the name. "Who is Muth la?"

Kovok-mah shook his head. "Washavokis understand nothing."

"How can I understand if you won't tell me?"

"Muth means 'mother.' Muth la is . . ." Kovok-mah paused, trying to think of the proper human word. "One Mother."

Dar shot him a puzzled look. "So the soldier stole from Garga-tok's mother?"

"Thwa. Muth la is mother of everything—world, stars, trees, animals, urkzimmuthi, even washavokis."

"So she's a goddess, like Karm," said Dar. "An orc goddess."

"I do not understand 'goddess.' Muth la is Muth la."

"And the food belongs to her?"

"Hai. When you say 'Muth la urat tha saf la,' you say 'One Mother gives you this food.' Washavoki soldier stole from Muth la."

To Dar, it seemed a poor reason to kill a man. "*I* made that food," she said. "That soldier only took it from me."

"You are muth," replied the orc.

Before Dar could respond to this cryptic remark, an orc called to Kovok-mah in Orcish. Kovok-mah replied in the same tongue, and the two briefly shouted back and forth. Dar thought their words sounded angry, but she knew too little about orcs to be certain. Then, without another word to Dar, Kovok-mah swam off.

Dar finished rinsing the pelts and went to the Queen's Man's compound to scrape them. The camp bustled with preparations for the march, and even the soldiers were busy loading wagons, slaughtering livestock, and sharpening their weapons. As usual, the women worked harder, and Dar thought it wise to pick up her pace as she walked.

The cooks were packing when Dar borrowed a knife, spread the pelts on the ground, and set to work. She was nearly finished when Murdant Kol strode by. He stopped when he noticed her. Despite wishing to appear calm, Dar tensed as he approached.

"How's my woman doing?" asked Kol, smiling slightly when Dar flushed red.

"I'm almost done with the pelts," she replied. "Where should I put them?"

"Give them to a cook to pack."

"They'll rot if not dried first."

Kol nodded, but seemed unconcerned. "Have the men bothered you?"

"No."

"Good," said Kol. "Still, you appear ill rested. A crowded tent makes for a fitful sleep."

"It makes for a warm one. Especially when I snuggle with Loral." Dar watched Kol for his reaction.

He was unperturbed. "How's she doing?"

"Perhaps you should ask her."

"Too busy," said Kol. "Keep an eye on her during the march. She's almost due."

"I'd think you'd do that. After all, she's . . ."

"She's what?"

Kol's sharp tone made Dar cautious. "She's under your command."

"I'm only a murdant," said Kol, his tone easy again. "Officers command the troops. I don't command anyone, least of all the women. I want you to watch over Loral because I can't. The regiment breaks up into shieldrons when passing through the king's lands—marching in smaller units makes it easier on the peasants. You and Loral will be with the advance shieldron, but I'll stay in the rear awhile to visit the other regiments."

"There are other orc regiments?"

"Yes, and I'm high murdant to all of them," said Kol. "My duties go beyond this unit."

Dar thought Kol's air of pride contradicted his assertion that he was only a murdant. "What will you be doing?"

"Ensuring the marches start smoothly. It's a long way to the assembly point."

"How long?"

"You'll be marching for nearly a moon."

Dar was relieved that Murdant Kol would be elsewhere during that time. Her face must have betrayed her feelings, for Kol asked in an ironic tone, "Does our parting make you sad?"

"You've treated me well so far."

"Tonight, I'll treat you even better. You want that, don't you?"

Dar's face reddened. "Do I have a choice?"

"With me, you always have a choice—I'm sure you'll make the smart one."

"Which one's that?"

"You know," said Murdant Kol as he left.

As Dar finished scraping the pelts, her feeling of helplessness grew stronger. Though Murdant Kol's protection was real, she realized it didn't spring from kindness. *He expects something in return*, she thought. *He wants it tonight*. That thought weighed on Dar's mind as she reported to the cooking site. The tent had been dismantled, but there was much activity about the fire pit.

"Where were you?" asked Neffa.

"I had to scrape pelts for Murdant Kol."

Neffa's eyes narrowed when she heard Kol's name. "Well, you missed the assignments. You'll be in Murdant Teeg's shieldron. Loral, Neena, Kari, and Taren will serve with you. Taren's in charge. That's only five women for thirty-six orcs and half as many men—hard duty. Slack off, and you'll be whipped, no matter who you're tupping."

"I'm used to hard work," said Dar.

"Then do some now," said Neffa. "There's meat to be dried."

Dar joined a group of women who were slicing thin strips of meat from goat carcasses and hanging them on a rack over a smoky fire. Taren was with them, quiet and aloof. Dar didn't know the names of the others. One handed Dar a knife and she began cutting strips, also. The imminent departure had charged the atmosphere, and everyone but Taren was talking about the campaign. Dar discovered that none of the women knew its cause or objective. Their interest lay elsewhere. One young, blond woman with a highland accent seemed particularly excited. "Muut says there'll be lots of booty."

"And he'll drink every drop of it," said a woman with a laugh. "You'll be lucky to get a shawl."

"That's not true," said the blonde. "Muut promised me a warm cloak and boots and jewels and . . ."

"*Jewels!*" said the first woman. "Neena, you're a bigger fool than I thought. Soldiers don't give jewels to the likes of us."

"Not when *some* will tup for a bowl of ale," added a third woman.

"You're no better."

"At least my man's a murdant," replied the woman. "At war's end, we'll see who's better dressed."

"War's not 'bout clothes," said Taren with such intensity that it silenced everyone. "It's 'bout killin' and dyin'."

"But there's booty, too," said Neena.

"Killin' don't make men generous," said Taren. "It makes them mean."

"Maybe mean to you," said a woman.

"Who's seen a real battle?" asked Taren, glancing sternly at each woman. None answered. "Well, I've lived through three. When things go wrong, the men fend for themselves. Mark me—some of you'll be crow's meat afore it's over."

"Muut says battles aren't so bad," said Neena in a voice sounding more hopeful than certain.

"Muut's no soldier—he drives a wagon," said Taren. "Hearken to the orcs tonight. They know 'bout war, 'cause they're the ones that do the real fightin'. When the moon rises, they'll sing their death song."

Taren's words cast a pall over the women and their conversation stopped awhile. Dar assumed the blonde was the same Neena who would be marching with her, and she studied her future companion. Dar noted the brand on her forehead was healed but still shiny pink. Like Leela, Neena appeared to have been sent off wearing her finest, though her shift and shoes showed the wear of camp life. Dar moved closer. "Neffa says you're marching with Murdant Teeg's shieldron," she said. "So am I. I'm Dar."

"I know," said Neena. She regarded Dar with an amused look. "Muut told me about your visit with Garga."

Neena's smile irritated Dar, but she tried to hide it. "It was my first sight of an orc. I thought I was going to be eaten."

"So you believed that story, too?" Neena laughed. "I was just as stupid, as a scabhead."

"When was that?" asked Dar.

"Last fall," said Neena, her smile fading. "I spent the winter at Taiben."

"Where the king has his palace?" asked Dar. "What's it like?"

"I never came near it, or the town either," said Neena. "We stayed outside its walls in the orcs' garrison. Being here's better."

"I take it Muut's your man," said Dar.

"One of them," said Neena with a breeziness that didn't seem genuine. "It's best to have more than one." Then she added, "Though not for you. Some men are possessive."

"And Murdant Kol's one of them?" asked Dar, who had ceased to be surprised that everyone knew her situation.

Neena nodded. "But his share of booty is greater than a soldier's. Please him, and you'll do all right."

Dar looked away and saw Loral struggling with a load of firewood. Neena caught her expression and whispered, "Are you worried about tonight?"

"Tonight? You know about tonight?"

"We're marching tomorrow, and men will be men," said Neena. "This night, even Taren may spread her legs."

"Karm help me!" said Dar.

"Haven't you ever tupped before?" asked Neena. "Well, don't worry. It's often pleasant."

"I saw my mother die in childbirth, and afterward . . ." Dar's face colored. "I know all about tupping. Don't tell me it's pleasant."

"You were just with the wrong man," said Neena.

"I don't want to talk about it!"

Neena looked annoyed. "I'm trying to help. You're not special, you know. We all do things to survive, willing or not."

As the day wore on, Dar grew ever more withdrawn. She dried meat until it was time to help prepare the evening meal. It consisted of all the foodstuffs that were too perishable to pack. As usual, Dar was detailed to serve the orcs. That night, she was glad to do so, for it meant avoiding the men a while. They were already milling around the fire pit. Most had been drinking, and drink had turned them bawdy. Even the few that were sober had a lewd glint in their eyes. Dar knew that look, and it made her apprehensive.

While she cooked, Dar kept scanning the crowd for Murdant Kol. By the time she left to bathe and serve, she still hadn't spotted him. Dar wasn't surprised. She imagined he would take his time, confident of her submission.

Waiting was torture. Dar kept envisioning Kol coming forward, expecting her to tup him. *It's either that or become fair game for anyone.* The women assumed she would submit to Murdant Kol. Dar knew it was the practical thing to do, but the thought of it evoked memories of her father's nocturnal visits. Her old feelings of humiliation and disgust welled up—emotions that only rage kept at bay. It was rage that had driven her at last to draw a knife and end the violations. That night marked the sole victory in Dar's life. *Now am I to submit again?* The idea ran counter to her very core. Dar thought of the women in the regiment: Loral, heavy with Kol's child. Memni, covered with bruises. All the others, so worn and haggard. *What has submission gained them?*

Yet Dar feared resisting. She recalled Varf raising her shift as he gripped the glowing brand, and she trembled. Despite her defiant words, she didn't wish to die. There was no triumph in that. Dar knew there would be no dignity either. All she wanted was to be left alone, and that was the one choice denied her.

Eight

Scrubbed and dressed in a clean robe, Dar walked with the other serving women. She bore a basket heavy with boiled roots. Hot water dripped from it, scalding her feet. Entering the circle of branches, she noted its interior had changed. The conical grass structures were gone and the top of the rise was bare, except for a huge pile of firewood and the seated orcs. For the first time, Dar saw them dressed for battle. Iron helmets covered their massive heads. Armor plates were strapped to their shoulders, arms, and legs. They wore heavy-soled sandals. Upon their laps, along with their metal bowls, lay massive weapons—battle-axes, wide-bladed swords, and iron maces, none of which bore the slightest hint of adornment. Everything she saw—helmets, armor, and weapons—was starkly utilitarian.

The Dark Path seems near, thought Dar, gazing at a bloodstained ax. *How quickly one steps from life onto the Sunless Way*. Throughout serving, Dar thought of death. It seemed inevitable unless she could bring herself to tup Murdant Kol. *I must. I have no choice.* She recalled the leering soldier's words on the day she was taken. *"Well, you're good for one thing." Was he right?* Dar recoiled at the thought. *Better good for nothing, than only that!* Yet, while Dar shrank from trading her body for safety, she realized resistance wouldn't save her. *No matter what I do, I'll lose.* She considered running away but knew her brand marked her for death. *And how might my captors sport with me before they took my head?* Immersed in such morbid pondering, Dar didn't recognize Kovok-mah in his battle gear. Perhaps the orc brooded also, for he didn't greet her.

The other women served quickly. A few seemed eager to join the men, and the rest appeared resigned to it. Dar dawdled, trying to avoid the inevitable. As raucous sounds grew louder in the camp, the silent orcs ceased to seem menacing. Instead, their camp felt like a refuge. *Men fear to come here.* She recalled how soldiers refrained from entering the circle even to save a comrade.

Though Dar stretched out serving as long as she could, she was done eventually. Reluctant and fearful, she headed to the bathing tent to change and confront Murdant Kol. She still hadn't decided what she would tell him. The noise of carousing had grown louder as the twilight darkened, making the prospect of what lay ahead seem more immediate and ominous.

The way to the bathing tent passed a pile of the shelters that had served the orcs as tents. Rolled up and bound with cord, they resembled cylindrical bales of hay, each longer than a man and several hand lengths in diameter. Dar halted when she reached them. The pile lay within the circle of branches—ground that men feared to tread. Dar realized it would be a perfect hiding place.

What will happen after Murdant Kol can't find me? Dar imagined all sorts of possibilities, but none more dreadful than what awaited her that night. *I'm just postponing things.* Yet postponing things meant remaining unmolested one night longer. *A night of peace,* she thought.

Dar made up her mind. She circled around the pile of

shelters so she was out of view of the orcs. It was getting dark, and she hoped that no one in camp would spot her as she burrowed between the cylinders. Although the bundles looked like bales of straw, they were not nearly as soft. Lying among them felt like resting in a woodpile. Nevertheless, Dar never considered leaving. She waited anxiously for some sign that she had been spotted, and when none came, she began to relax. *Don't think about tomorrow. Tonight, at least, no man will have me.*

A mournful sound invaded Dar's dreams, then woke her. It was a single, deep voice raised in song. The only words Dar understood were "Muth la," but there was no mistaking the song's solemnity. The camp was quiet, and the only other sounds were the snap and crackle of a bonfire. The fire must have been very large, for some of its light invaded Dar's hiding place. A second voice joined the first. It was equally somber. A third orc began to sing. Soon, he was joined by others until the air vibrated with voices that made sleep impossible.

This must be the death song Taren mentioned, thought Dar. She didn't understand its verses, yet was touched by them anyway. They had a pure and primal quality, like a child's wail or a wolf's howl in the empty night. Muth la's children were calling to her in the darkness, and Dar sensed their loneliness and yearning. The voices conjured visions of spirits departing life, leaving warmth and light behind forever. Perhaps, if Dar understood the words, she would have found comfort in them. Instead, she felt desolate and utterly alone.

The song gradually dwindled until only a single voice echoed in the dark. When it died away, the night was still. With muffled sobs, Dar cried herself to sleep.

* * *

A hand grasped Dar's ankle, jarring her awake and whisking her from her hiding place. Dar briefly glimpsed the orc that dangled her upside down; then her robe slid over her head, blocking her sight. Her captor began to shout angrily in Orcish, emphasizing each word with a violent shake. Dar recalled seeing a man grab a kitten by its hind leg and slam the helpless creature against the ground to break its body. She feared the orc was about to do the same to her.

Dar kicked at the orc with her free leg, but only hurt her bare foot against his metal armor. The orc began to swing her to build momentum for the first bone-shattering blow. Already, her leg felt as if it were being wrenched off. She gritted her teeth, expecting to die.

A second orc arrived, and the swinging stopped abruptly. It sounded as if the two were arguing. One orc began to growl, and when the growl approached the intensity of a roar, the hand let go of Dar's ankle. She dropped to the ground and lay there, stunned.

When Dar's eyes could focus, she saw that Kovok-mah stood over her. He was watching another orc retreat. Presently, he leaned down and spoke. "Dargu, you should not have slept there."

Dar was too dazed and shaken to do more than moan.

"Are you broken?" asked Kovok-mah.

Dar sat up and moved her leg. The red beginnings of a bruise encircled her ankle and there was a shooting pain deep in her thigh, but her bones seemed intact. "I'm still in one piece. Why did he do that?"

"He did not like your smell."

"I washed before I served."

"I told him that," said Kovok-mah.

"You also said 'Dargu nak muth,' that I am a mother."

Kovok-mah curled back his lips. "You understood that?"

"I understood the words, but not the meaning. I have no child."

"Washavokis have strange thoughts," replied Kovok-mah.

"We don't kill people for the way they smell."

"You find other reasons," said Kovok-mah. He gazed at the crowd of people standing outside the circle of branches. "You should leave," he said, lifting Dar to her feet. When Dar was standing, he strode away and disappeared into the ranks of orcs. They were staring at Dar, as were the soldiers and women. Slowly and painfully, Dar limped to her own kind.

Murdant Kol was waiting with the others. His eyes bore into Dar, yet his face remained a mask. Dar could see no way to avoid the murdant without being oblivious, so she walked directly to him. At the moment, he seemed as terrifying as any orc. When she left the circle, he gripped her arm. "Come with me," he said, his voice cool and official.

Kol set a quick pace, forcing Dar to hobble as best she could. The effort was agonizing. Dar noted that the crowd of onlookers hung back. When they were out of earshot, Kol halted, but he didn't release Dar's arm. "What was the meaning of that stupid trick?"

Dar had a ready answer. "I was afraid."

"Afraid?" said Kol, his hard voice almost mocking. "Afraid of what?"

"The men. They were drunk and rowdy. And you . . ." She forced some tears. ". . . you weren't there."

"You were perfectly safe," said Kol, his voice a bit softer. "You nearly got yourself killed."

Dar knew she should throw her arms around Kol, but she couldn't bring herself to do it. Instead, she grasped her leg with her free hand. "Ohhhh, my leg. It feels torn off!"

"Be grateful it isn't." Murdant Kol seemed to be making up his mind. After a moment, he released her arm. "You'll be fine when I see you next."

Dar attempted to look pleased at the prospect. "I know I've been silly. Will you forgive me?"

Kol smiled, shaking his head. "How could I not? You're only a scabhead. Now, join your shieldron—it's moving out."

Dar limped away to find Taren and, perhaps, get something to eat. The camp was in a state of chaos. Soldiers and women milled about, as oxen-drawn wagons moved toward the road. Only the orcs seemed organized. They stood on the rise, formed into six shieldrons, each six orcs wide and six orcs deep. Their bundled shelters were strapped upon their broad backs. In the end, it was Taren who found Dar. She handed Dar her ragged shift. "No time to change," she said. "You'll have to hurry."

"I'm not sure I can," said Dar.

"Murdant Teeg will let you ride in the wagon if you can catch it. Murdant Kol gave the word."

When Dar's effort to reach the wagon made her gasp with pain, Taren asked, "Why'd you do it?"

"Do what?"

"Hide like that," said Taren. "You were safe from the men. You're the high murdant's woman."

"I wasn't safe from the high murdant," whispered Dar. "I couldn't bear to . . . you know." She glanced at Taren and saw her expression had softened.

"Poor thing," said Taren. "What are you goin' to do?"

"He's staying in the rear, so I'm safe."

"But only awhile," said Taren. "I know little about men, but I do know this—delay feeds desire."

Nine

When Dar reached Murdant Teeg's wagon she was pale and gasping from the effort. Her thigh throbbed painfully, its skin already stretched tight by swelling. The murdant jerked her up to the driver's bench, which was the only place to sit. "Don't put on airs 'cause yer ridin', birdie. If it was up to me, ye'd walk."

"I can't walk," said Dar. "At least, not fast enough to keep up."

"Thoughts of bounty takers would speed yer steps." Teeg gestured to the roadside, where two heads were mounted on stakes. Dar turned away from the sight, but not before glimpsing Leela's long hair blowing in the breeze. Teeg laughed. "Ye'd keep up."

Once the wagon reached the main road, the shieldron looked more organized. A tolum and his sustolum led the way on horseback. The two officers were the only mounted men. With the exception of Dar, Murdant Teeg, and Muut, who drove the second wagon, everyone else walked. The soldiers and the women trailed the wagons. The orcs marched in the rear.

"So war's begun," said Dar.

"It never stopped," said Teeg, "though we rest in winter."

"Perhaps, this time, the king will regain his land."

"*His* land?" Teeg grinned. "Aye, why not call it his."

"Isn't it?"

" 'Tis worth takin', I know that. If a man wants to fight, he'll find cause. The king's no different."

"Why would he want to fight?"

"To fill his purse and pay his soldiers. That's reason 'nough for me. If ye wanted the long-winded one, ye should've asked Kol. He knows that stuff."

Thoughts of upcoming battles caused Dar to gaze at the marching orcs, who looked grim in their armor. She watched them awhile, both frightened and fascinated. "What army could face *them*?"

Teeg spit. "Piss eyes aren't real soldiers."

"They look fiercer than any soldier."

"Aye, they're fierce. Deadly, too," said Teeg. "I suppose ye know nothin' of huntin' boars."

"Not a thing."

"Them boars are dangerous. Their tusks can rip open any horse or man. To hunt a boar, ye need dogs to run it down and grip it till the spearman comes. Dogs hold fast even as they're torn apart."

"What does that have to do with orcs?"

"Piss eyes are like them dogs. They're strong and tough, but they lack guile. It's guile that wins battles. That's why a man's in charge of the regiments."

"Why would orcs obey a man?"

"They don't, really," said Teeg. "They obey their queen, though it's a man who gives her orders."

"The Queen's Man?"

"Aye, all his orders are in her name."

"I don't understand."

"Some treaty between her and our king."

"What do the orcs get out of it?"

"I've no idea. All I know is they don't serve from friendship. They hate us all. Remember that next time yer lookin' for a place to sleep."

"I was stupid last night," said Dar.

"Less stupid than tuppin' another man. Kol's not one to cross."

"I've already figured that out."

"Then yer not so stupid after all."

"When do you think I'll see him again?"

"Already pinin' for him?" Teeg grinned, making Dar wonder if he had guessed her true feelings. "Well don't worry. Kol likes to ride with the advance shieldron and his horse is faster than my oxen. He'll catch up quick enough. A week or two at most."

The wagons set the pace for the march and it was slow. The weather was pleasant, and under different circumstances, Dar would have enjoyed the ride. The fields they passed, though well tended, were empty. "Where are the people?" she asked.

"Hidin'," replied Teeg.

"Of course, the orcs."

"Even without piss eyes, soldiers aren't welcome."

"But you serve our king."

"We still need food, and peasants are stingy."

"Don't you pay them?" asked Dar.

Teeg laughed. "This is the king's land, and we're the king's men. Why should the master pay for what's his? Ye bear his brand. Did he pay for ye?"

Dar realized that a visit from soldiers might spell starvation. Teeg must have read her expression, for he said, "Miss a few meals, and ye'll not care where yer vittles come from. An empty belly's a great cure for a conscience."

* * *

The shieldron marched until late afternoon, when it halted at a ruined farmstead. A few roofless huts, their walls burned and crumbling, stood amid fields overgrown with weeds and saplings. Teeg looked around in disgust. "Slim pickin's tonight. Hop down, birdie, and get busy."

Dar limped to where the women were preparing a cooking area. "How's your leg?" asked Taren.

"Walking hurts, but I can work."

"Then help me with the tent and make porridge," said Taren. She dragged a tent from a wagon and unrolled it. "You need not serve the orcs tonight."

"It'd be better if I did," said Dar.

"Why?" asked Taren. "The orc that attacked you is here."

"I know," said Dar. "That's the reason I should serve. He mustn't think I fear him."

"Don't you?"

"Of course, but he shouldn't know it."

Taren shook her head, "How can you face an orc, but not a man?"

After the soldiers tended to the oxen, they pitched their tents and disappeared into them, leaving the women to set up the rest of the camp. Dar, Loral, and Taren unloaded wagons while Neena and Kari got water and gathered firewood. Before long, the evening's cooking was under way. The orcs' food, which was prepared separately from the men's, consisted solely of porridge.

While the women worked, the orcs set up their own camp. First, they marked off a large circle by sticking branches in the ground. When that was done, they erected their shelters. Afterward, most of the orcs shed their armor and clothes and headed for a nearby stream. Dar assumed they were going to bathe. Two remained in battle gear. One accompanied the bathers; the other remained at the camp.

Kovok-mah was the latter. When Dar had a free moment, she limped toward him until she was close enough to speak softly. "Shashav, Kovok-mah."

"How you know word for 'thanks'?"

"You say 'Shashav Muth la' when you get food, so I thought 'shashav' must mean 'thanks.' "

"Why you thank me?"

"For saving my life."

"Zna-yat did improper thing," said Kovok-mah. "I could not allow it."

Dar bowed her head. "Shashav. I would like to learn the words to tell Zna-yat I am sorry."

"Thwa," said Kovok-mah.

"Why not?"

"Dargu nak muth."

"You keep saying that. I'm not a mother. I have no child."

"Bowl is for food. When it is empty, it is still bowl."

Dar realized that "muth" must be Orcish for both "mother" and "female." "So, because I'm a mother, you won't teach me?"

"You should not say sorry to Zna-yat. Instead, say 'Kala muth verlav tha.' It means 'This mother forgives you.' This will not shame him, but it will help him see he was wrong."

Kovok-mah's reasoning struck Dar as strange. *No soldier would care if I forgave him.* Yet, apparently, an orc would. "Kala muth verlav tha," said Dar. "This mother forgives you."

"Hai," said Kovok-mah. "You speak good."

"Shashav, Kovok-mah." Dar saw orcs emerging from the woods. "I should go," she said. "Vata, Kovok-mah."

"Vata, Dargu."

As Dar limped back to the cooking area, she smiled when she realized that "vata"—Orcish for "goodbye"—was the reverse of "tava," which meant "hello."

"What are you smiling about?" asked Loral.

"Something the orc said."

"I've never heard of orcs saying anything funny."

"Have you ever talked to one?" asked Dar.

"No," said Loral, "and I don't intend to start. You, of all people, should know how risky that is."

Dinner was ready at sundown. Dar and Neena entered the sleeping tent to scrub the scent from their bodies and change into serving robes. The kettle held porridge for only thirty-six, and Dar was able to help carry it, despite her leg. It was she who addressed the orcs saying "Saf nak ur Muthz la"—*Food is One Mother's gift*. When the orcs replied "Shashav Muth la"—*Thanks One Mother*—she felt partly included.

That feeling gave Dar the courage to speak to Zna-yat. She limped over to her attacker, looking him squarely in the eye. His face was impassive, but Dar noted that his nostrils flared as she approached. She also noticed that every orc was watching her. Dar halted. "Zna-yat," she said, "kala muth verlav tha." *Zna-yat, this mother forgives you.*

Zna-yat's mouth twisted like Kovok-mah's did when he was surprised. He muttered something Dar didn't understand and turned his eyes away. Dar was unsure what effect her words had on Zna-yat, but merely uttering them made her feel bold.

Ten

♛

The woods were deep in shadow; yet, as Kovok-mah returned from bathing, he had no difficulty finding his way. He liked the night, when the washavokis were nearly blind but the urkzimmuthi saw clearly. The washavokis usually grew quiet after Muth la hid her golden eye, and Kovok-mah relished the peace. The only sounds were natural ones. Frogs peeped their springtime love song. The stream gurgled over its stony bed. Leaves rustled. It felt good to have shed death's hard clothes. Kovok-mah paused to let the breath of Muth la take the water from his skin. As he savored the tranquillity and the breeze, the day's last light left the sky.

Kovok-mah heard footsteps. He turned. Seeing Zna-yat approach, he greeted him in Orcish, the only language his cousin understood. "Tava, father's sister's son."

"Tava, mother's brother's son," replied Zna-yat. "Thomak-tok asks how many guards tonight."

"Only one. Muth la hides her silver eye. Washavokis will stumble and make noise if they come."

"Hai," agreed Zna-yat, "and we're still far from place for killing."

"Still, washavokis kill anywhere."

"Hai. Anywhere." Zna-yat lingered. When he spoke again, he used the intimate form of address permitted close friends. "Kovok, I'm puzzled."

"Why?"

"This morning, you called one washavoki mother and didn't let me kill it."

"Hai."

"I don't understand. Washavokis can't be mothers. They're animals."

"All animals come in two kinds, and one kind is like mother."

"Being like one thing isn't same as being it," said Zna-yat.

"One kind of washavoki called 'woe man' is enough like mothers that Muth la isn't dishonored when they serve food. Our queen says so."

"I'd rather receive it from true mothers," said Zna-yat.

"I would, too," said Kovok-mah. "But since I can't, I'll tolerate these woe mans. They'll act more like mothers if we treat them so."

Zna-yat pondered what Kovok-mah had said. "Is that why you call Weasel mother?"

"Hai."

"There's some sense in what you say, but only some."

"World has become strange," said Kovok-mah, "and we must learn to do strange things."

"That Weasel spoke to me this evening. It said 'This mother forgives you.' I was much surprised."

"How did you reply?"

"I said breath of Muth la would soon take its stink away."

"That was reasonable," said Kovok-mah. "Weasel is clean for washavoki."

"Perhaps so, but your interest in it is peculiar."

"Interest?"

"I've seen you speak to it. I know you taught it those words."

"Hai. It asked me to."

Zna-yat smiled. "Back home, you were always good to your goats. I think Weasel has become your new goat. That explains why you don't mind its smell."

Kovok-mah laughed. "Zna, you understand me too well. Weasel is like my goat."

"It's still washavoki."

"And mother," said Kovok-mah.

"Such thinking proves you've been away from home too long."

"Hai," agreed Kovok-mah, "far too long."

The women, except for Dar, were exhausted from marching all day. The soldiers were tired also, and by nightfall the camp was a quiet place. Dar's companions quickly fell asleep, but she was restless. No fatigue washed the worry from her mind or dulled the throbbing in her leg. Dar left the tent and peered into the night. There was no moon, and the obscure world seemed almost formless. Nevertheless, Dar limped into the dark, making her way as much by feel as by sight.

She entered one of the ruined huts and discovered it filled with weeds. Any trace of the people who had once lived there was hidden by the gloom. As she turned to leave, someone grabbed the skirt of her shift. "Can't sleep?" asked a man.

Dar recognized his voice. "Murdant Teeg?"

"Aye, 'tis me." Teeg was sitting by the doorway, his

back against the blackened wall. Dar could barely see him. Teeg's other hand moved, and Dar heard the sound of liquid sloshing in a bottle. She stepped back, but the murdant held fast. "Stay awhile."

Dar had little choice. She knelt down in the ruined doorway. Teeg let go of her shift, grabbed her torso, and pulled her toward him. Crushed against his armored doublet, Dar smelled the drink on Teeg's breath. She tried to break free. "Be still, birdie, yer safe. No man dare touch ye."

"You're touching me now."

"Just a hug. Ye can't begrudge that."

"I don't think Murdant Kol would like it."

"Huggin's not tuppin', so don't get yer piss hot. When Kol's done with ye, best be on my good side."

Dar grew still.

"That's more like it," said Teeg, not relaxing his grip. "Want some brandy?"

"No."

"Suit yourself." Teeg took a long swig from the bottle. "By Karm's ass, this place is a dung heap."

"It looks like it was nice once," said Dar.

"Aye, 'twas better than nothin'." Teeg spit into the darkness. "That tolum had shit for brains. 'Teach 'em a lesson,' he said. Well, we did, but who's campin' in the weeds?"

"The army did this?"

"Who else?"

"Why?"

"The peasants were hidin' food. The tolum found out and set the piss eyes on 'em."

Dar shuddered at the thought, causing Teeg to chuckle. " 'Twasn't pretty," he said, "but war never is."

"War? These were the king's own subjects."

"They should have thought of that when they hid the food."

Teeg shifted his arm and began to inch his fingers toward Dar's breast. When they reached it, Dar suddenly said, "I'd like a sip after all."

"That's more like it," said Teeg.

He passed Dar the bottle, and she tossed it into the weeds.

"Ye crazy bitch!" Teeg pushed Dar aside to grope for his brandy, allowing her to move into the shadows. Unable to run, Dar hid nearby and listened to Teeg curse and thrash in the dark. After a minute, he grew quiet. Dar remained still and waited. The ground was wet with dew before the murdant finally stumbled toward his tent. Only then did Dar creep away to join the sleeping women.

When the army was on the march, breakfast consisted of leftover porridge. The five women's morning duties were to serve the men, clean the kettle, and pack the wagons. Dar had managed to avoid Murdant Teeg at breakfast, but he found her as she was loading a wagon. He grabbed her arm and said, "Ye walk today." Then he went to hitch the oxen.

Taren overheard Teeg's statement. "Can you keep up?"

"I'll have to," said Dar.

"Don't lag behind," said Taren. "Not every head brought in for bounty comes from a runaway."

It was still early morning when the officers led their troops onto the road. The soldiers walked as a mob at the rear of the wagons. The women kept out of their way by tagging behind. The orcs followed at a distance, marching in orderly ranks. Only they and the two mounted officers gave the column a military appearance; the men looked more like brigands than soldiers.

From the outset, Dar had difficulty keeping pace. A shooting pain in her thigh caused her to walk with a stiff-legged gait that was both tiring and awkward. Despite determined effort, Dar soon lagged behind the women. Next, the orcs overtook her, parting their ranks so she walked among them—enveloped, yet apart. Gritting her teeth, Dar tried to walk faster, but her injured leg was incapable of the effort. The orcs passed her. The distance between Dar and the column increased until she could no longer see it.

As Dar trudged alone, she was alert to every sound. She had taken Taren's warning to heart, knowing her head would bring a windfall to anyone who took it. Peasants had cause to hate the army, and she expected no mercy. Thus, when Dar heard footsteps in the woods, she looked about for a means of defense. Spotting a large, pointed rock by the roadside, she grabbed it. It would be a clumsy weapon against a sword or knife, but it was better than nothing.

Thick, high greenery flanked the road, screening her view. Whoever was approaching took no effort to move quietly. When the noise sounded close, Dar used both hands to lift the rock above her head. She assumed an aggressive pose and expression. Then the shrubs parted, and Kovok-mah stepped onto the road.

Dar regarded him warily, uncertain of his intentions. Then Kovok-mah's lips curled back in what Dar realized was an orcish smile. "Dargu is very fierce."

Dar let the rock drop. She began to laugh, partly from relief and partly from awareness of how ridiculous she looked. When it became obvious that Kovok-mah didn't understand her laughter, she laughed even harder. She was gasping for breath by the time she stopped.

"Why were you barking?" asked Kovok-mah.

"I wasn't barking. I was laughing." Dar hissed in imitation of orcish laughter.

Kovok-mah smiled. "You are . . ." He paused. "I do not know washavoki word. Ga nat gusha."

"I'm gusha? What does that mean?"

"You do strange things, things that make me hissav." Kovok-mah hissed with pretend laughter.

"So I'm funny?"

"Perhaps that is word."

"I'm glad you're amused."

If Kovok-mah caught Dar's sarcasm, he showed no sign of it. "It is not wise to walk alone."

"I walk alone because I can't keep up. Zna-yat nearly tore off my leg."

"Lie down," said Kovok-mah.

"Why?"

"Nat thwa gusha."

Be not funny? thought Dar. It occurred to her that "gusha" probably meant "silly," not "funny." She hesitated, then lay on the road. Kovok-mah knelt beside her and began to pull her shift up to her waist. Alarmed, Dar tried to stop him, but Kovok-mah seemed unaware of her attempt at modesty. Dar ceased struggling and hoped her body held no attraction to an orc. Kovok-mah's hands were huge and clawed, but his fingers probed Dar's swollen thigh gently. Gradually, Dar relaxed.

"Nothing is torn," he said after a thorough examination. From a pouch, he produced a freshly uprooted plant with large, fuzzy leaves. "This is nayimgat. Chew leaf, but do not swallow it."

Dar took a leaf and sniffed it. It was strongly aromatic. She stuffed the leaf into her mouth and chewed. Its bitter taste caused her mouth to water. Her tongue became numb, and she swallowed her saliva with difficulty. Dar wondered if herbs that would heal an orc might sicken a human. *Too late to worry about that.* The numbness spread. She was dizzy by the time she spit out the leaf.

"Come," said Kovok-mah. "Rest in shade."

"I can't rest. I must keep walking." Yet, as Dar spoke, she doubted walking was possible. Her eyes were having difficulty focusing and it took great effort even to rise. She attempted a step and pitched forward, barely aware of the hands that caught her.

It was dusk when Dar opened her eyes. The road was different. She smelled smoke and heard the lowing of oxen mingled with men's voices. Dar sat up. She was lying in a roadside copse of birches.

Kovok-mah was gone. *He must have brought me here.* Dar wondered why. *Is he in charge of strays?* She doubted it. Her ribs felt bruised. *He probably hefted me on his shoulder.* Her injured leg ached as if it had been pummeled, but it was no longer stiff. Dar rose. There were no shooting pains in her thigh.

Dar walked—limping only slightly—toward the voices. When the road turned, she saw the encampment. Neena and Kari were returning from serving the orcs. Taren spied Dar and hurried over to her. "We thought you were gone for good. How did you make it?"

Dar decided not to mention Kovok-mah. "I rested, and my leg got better."

"Karm surely guarded you. Come eat somethin'. You look exhausted."

As Dar ate some porridge, she caught Murdant Teeg staring at her with a surprised expression. She pretended not to notice. Afterward, she went into the sleeping tent. Loral was lying there, moaning softly.

"Are you all right?" asked Dar.

"Just a backache," said Loral. "I thought I'd never see you again."

"I'm here. I made it."

"I've been thinking all day about how I treated you," said Loral. "I'm sorry. It's not your fault Kol likes you."

"He doesn't like me," said Dar. "He just wants me. There's a difference."

"Don't avoid him for my sake."

"I've other reasons."

"You can't cross a murdant! Teeg didn't lift a finger, but he nearly caused your death. You've got to . . ." Loral gasped and moaned.

"Roll over on your side," said Dar. "My mother had pains like yours. I know what helps." Loral moved and Dar knelt beside her.

"I'm glad we're friends again," said Dar as she began to massage Loral's back. "Is this helping?"

Loral sighed. "Yes."

"Good. These pains usually go away. If they don't and get stronger, it means you're going to have your baby."

"If that happens, will you know what to do?"

"No," said Dar.

Eleven

Rain arrived before sunrise. It found holes in the tattered tent and dripped on Dar until she woke. It felt too early to rise, but her discomfort was greater than her drowsiness. Dar sat up and moved her leg. It seemed better. The other women stirred.

The rain fell harder, and everyone grew wet as water invaded the shelter. When the black sky turned pale, the women left the tent to be drenched in earnest. Their breath condensed in the cold, damp air as they waited to serve the men soggy breakfasts. Everyone was in a dismal mood.

On the march, the muddy road mired men and oxen, and Dar had no problem keeping up. The miserable weather turned the marchers inward. Everyone seemed sullen and absorbed in his or her misery. Yet, as Dar sloshed barefoot in the mud, her thoughts were not on her cold feet or her waterlogged cloak. Instead, she pondered her plight.

Dar was trapped, and she knew it. Marked as she was by her brand, escape was suicide, while life in the regiment seemed only a slower path to death. Dar saw how quickly the army wore women down; even Neffa wasn't much older than she. Women were easy to replace and valued accordingly. In such an atmosphere, men's "generosity" and "protection" were hollow promises. Though Dar racked her brain, there seemed no refuge. Then she had an inspiration.

Dar lagged behind until the orcs overtook her. Soon she was walking in their midst. Spying Kovok-mah at the rear of the column, Dar slowed down until they were walking abreast. "Tava, Kovok-mah."

Kovok-mah didn't reply or even turn his head.

"Tava, Kovok-mah," said Dar, louder this time.

The orc regarded Dar. An iron helmet enclosed his head and his green eyes peered out from it like a beast's from a hole. With a sinking feeling, Dar realized the vastness of their differences, and her plan seemed as risky as it was desperate. Nevertheless, she persisted.

"Kovok-mah, can we speak together?"

The orc didn't respond, but he slowed his pace until the two of them trailed the marching column. When Kovok-mah still didn't speak, Dar took the initiative. "I would like to learn your language."

"Kam?"

That must mean "why," thought Dar. She gave what she hoped was a lighthearted answer. "Dargu nak gusha." *Weasel is silly.*

"Hai. Gusha."

Wrong approach, thought Dar. "Dargu nak muth." *Weasel is mother.*

Kovok-mah stopped walking. "Why wants this washavoki to talk like urkzimmuthi?"

"Thwa washavoki," said Dar. *Not washavoki.* "Dargu nak muth."

"You have not answered my question."

Dar pointed to the scab on her forehead. "See this? I was marked so I can never leave. I will live among urkzimmuthi till I die."

"So? You have your own kind."

"Washavokis do not respect mothers."

"Many urkzimmuthi say washavokis are not mothers."

"But you think differently."

Kovok-mah stared at Dar with an expression she was incapable of reading. It made her wonder if he had guessed her motive. Men feared orcs, and Dar hoped to learn Orcish so she might use that fear to her advantage.

Kovok-mah took his time deciding. At last, he waved his hand about. "Hafalf. Rain."

Dar smiled, realizing Kovok-mah had agreed to teach her. "Hafalf."

Kovok-mah cupped his hand, dipped it into a puddle, and held it before Dar. "Falf."

Dar peered at the liquid in the orc's palm. "Falf. Does that mean 'water'?"

"Hai." Kovok-mah lifted a lock of Dar's dripping hair. "Dargu nak falfi."

"Dargu nak falfi. I'm wet."

"Hai." Kovok-mah touched his chest. "Ma nav falfi."

Dar did the same and repeated the phrase.

"Thwa. Kovok-mah pahak 'Ma nav falfi.' Dargu pahak 'It nav falfi.' "

Dar thought for a moment. *"Pahak" probably means "say." Does he mean that orc women say "I" differently than orc men?* She responded using the little Orcish she knew. "Mer nav Dargu. Mer nav muth."

"Hai. Dargu nak qum."

Qum? thought Dar. She wondered what it meant, then made a hopeful guess. "Does that mean I'm smart?"

Kovok-mah's lips curled into a smile. "Hai. Dargu nak zar qum."

Engrossed in learning, Dar forgot the foul weather.

Her enthusiasm intrigued Kovok-mah. As he walked down the muddy road naming things to the strange and inquisitive washavoki, Kovok-mah didn't heed his comrades' disapproving glances, but he did notice them.

Dar's lesson ended. Kovok-mah returned to the marching column and Dar rejoined the women. "I was worried 'bout you," said Taren. "How's your leg?"

Dar realized that the orcs had screened her and Kovok-mah from view. "It's all right," she replied. "I slowed down awhile and got a second wind."

"That's what I need," said Loral. "My back's hurting again."

Dar saw the pain in Loral's eyes and recalled her mother. "You shouldn't be walking."

"We won't march much longer," said Taren. "The tolum hates ridin' in the rain."

Dar surveyed the landscape, wondering where they would halt. The woods had given way to small fields and clustered huts. To her eyes, many sites looked suitable, but the shieldron marched past them. A while later, the sustolum—a lad scarcely out of his teens—rode to the rear where he spoke a command in Orcish. A dozen orcs left the column and followed him as he returned to the head of the march. The shieldron halted, and Dar watched the two officers and the twelve orcs leave the road. A few huts, clustered about a large barn, lay a short distance away. The officers led the orcs in their direction. The soldiers followed at a greater distance.

Some of the orcs entered the largest hut while the officers remained on horseback. They brought out a man, two women, and numerous children. Then the orcs entered the other buildings and collected more people. When the peasants were assembled, the tolum spoke. Dar was too distant to hear what he said. When the tolum finished speaking, he raised his arm. The soldiers advanced and the wagons headed toward the barn.

Taren turned to Loral. "You'll sleep dry tonight."

Loral, her face screwed up in pain, only nodded.

The women approached the buildings. By the time they reached them, soldiers were engaged in carrying off food. Two held a struggling pig while a third dispatched it with his sword. He grinned at Dar. "Ye'll be roastin' pork tonight!"

Taren sighed. "We'd best get a fire goin'. Let's find the kitchen."

Having grown up in a one-room hut, Dar had no idea what Taren was talking about. She assumed every building was a separate home. Yet not wishing to appear ignorant, Dar looked about and pushed open the door of a small, windowless structure. Its interior was black and filled with the aroma of smoked meat, though all the meat hooks were empty. An ancient woman sat slumped on the floor. She was sobbing. "Is this the kitchen?" asked Dar.

The woman slowly rose and hobbled over to Dar. Her teary eyes bore a venomous look. Dar felt paralyzed by it and seized by the compulsion to explain that she was different from the men who had plundered the larder. She never got the chance. The woman spat in her face, then slammed the door.

Taren found the communal kitchen, which had an ample supply of dry wood. The women lit a fire in preparation for cooking. Dar was glad they need not gather firewood, though she felt guilty taking it. The soldiers shared none of her qualms and brought an excess of food to cook. They had already moved into the barn after driving the livestock into the rain. The officers commandeered the largest hut for their use. A few orcs were stationed about to ensure the peasants remained docile. The rest encamped in a field, as if to distance themselves from the looting soldiers.

Despite her conscience, Dar was happy to be out of the rain and cooking in a warm building. There was a pig to roast, a dozen chickens to pluck and stew, roots to boil, and porridge to make. The pig took a long time to cook, and dinner was served near dusk. Dar and Neena served the orcs, who ate outside in the rain. It seemed strange to Dar that the orcs would endure the weather while procuring shelter for the men. She wanted to ask Kovok-mah about that, but decided to wait. When they finished serving, Neena joined Kari, who was with the soldiers in the barn. Dar returned to the kitchen.

Loral was asleep on the floor.

"Taren," said Dar in a low voice, "I'm worried about her. I don't think she should march all day."

"There's nothin' to be done for it," said Taren.

"I rode in a wagon. Why can't she?"

"Teeg would not abide it."

"Why not?"

Taren shrugged. "I don't know the reason, but I know the man. Loral must walk."

Dar gazed at Loral curled up on the hard-packed dirt. She was pale. Even slumbering, she looked exhausted. Dar thought a minute, then stepped out into the rain. She walked over to the officers' hut and entered it. The tolum and the sustolum were seated at a table strewn with the remains of an ample dinner. Each had a bottle. The tolum, a porky man in his early twenties, eyed Dar coldly. "By Karm's ass, what are you doing here?"

"Sir, a woman needs your help."

The tolum turned to the sustolum. "That's why I hate this regiment—women."

"She's with child, sir. She's due any day."

"So?" said the tolum. "That happens when you spread your legs."

"She needs to ride in a wagon."

"She needs to ride in a wagon," repeated the tolum in a high-pitched, mocking tone. He slammed his fist on the table. "Am I to be lectured by a whore?"

Dar's face colored. "I'm not a whore, sir."

"Perhaps not," replied the tolum. "Real whores leave after they've been tupped."

"We don't stay by choice," said Dar.

"Nor mine," said the tolum. "It's the piss eyes' fault. If it were up to me, I'd dump the lot of you."

"We're here because of the orcs?"

"Only women may serve them. Their rule, not mine. Now, get out."

Dar remained put. "But Loral may die if she has to walk."

The tolum's face flushed crimson, but his voice was cold. "I gave you an order." He leaped up from his chair, seized Dar's arm, and dragged her to the open door. "Teeg!" he bellowed.

When the murdant came running, the officer shoved Dar toward him. "Murdant, flog this bitch for insubordination. Three stripes."

Teeg grinned. With a quick motion, he grabbed Dar's arm and twisted it behind her back. "Well, birdie, ye have a knack for trouble." He pulled upward on Dar's arm until she winced. "Come quietly."

Teeg ordered a soldier to bring him rope and a whip, then marched Dar to a fence behind the barn. The soldier who brought these items was followed by men who were glad for a bit of entertainment. Teeg released Dar's arm. "Will ye bare yer back, or need I tear yer shift?"

Dar meekly removed her shift. Teeg turned to the soldier who brought the whip and rope. "Tie her wrists to the fence post."

The soldier stopped ogling Dar's nearly naked body and bound her wrists. Then he held a loose end of the rope before her mouth. "Bite down on this," he said. "It helps."

Dar clamped the rope in her teeth and waited. Frigid rain hit her bare back. Teeg waited until she was shivering from fright and cold before he let the whip fly. The studded thongs bit into Dar's flesh, combining the shock of a blow with the pain of broken skin. Having tasted the lash, Dar found waiting for the second blow more agonizing than waiting for the first. Teeg, a master of torment, understood the terror of anticipation and delayed the second lash. When it finally fell, its mark crossed the first one. The third lash completed the bloody star on Dar's back.

"I do nice work," said Teeg, "if I say so myself. Leave her there awhile, then have Taren untie her."

By the time Taren arrived, rivulets of bloody rainwater flowed down Dar's back and legs, and she was shuddering from pain and cold. Dar couldn't see the extent of her injuries, but she got a clue from Taren's sickened expression. She untied Dar, picked up Dar's shift, and led her to the kitchen. "I'll wash your stripes," she said. "You should leave them uncovered tonight."

"Thanks, Taren."

"Dar, what did you do?"

"I asked the tolum if Loral could ride in a wagon."

"That was stupid."

"I know that now."

"Karg's worse than Teeg."

"Not worse," said Dar. "Teeg enjoyed doing this."

"I should poison them all," said Taren.

Twelve

Dar lay awake most of the night, consumed by despair. *What good will speaking Orcish do me? Words can't protect me.* She could think of nothing that could.

When dawn approached, Taren gently touched her shoulder. "When men are flogged, they go bare-backed until the stripes heal. Since you cannot, wear this under your shift." She held out one of the robes the women wore to serve the orcs. Its skirt had been torn away. "It's clean, so perhaps your wounds won't fester."

Dar dressed, wincing when the cloth touched her raw flesh. It was still raining, and she ate her cold porridge huddled with Taren by the fire. They let Loral sleep.

Kari and Neena arrived from the barn, looking tired. "The men will be coming soon," said Kari. "Take care, they're all hungover."

"There's a rumor we won't march today," said Neena.

"If it keeps rainin' and the vittles hold, Karg might stay put," said Taren. "If so, Karm help us. Idle men make work for women."

Kari noticed Dar's drawn face. "They said you were whipped."

"I was."

"Why?" asked Neena.

"She stuck up for Loral," said Taren, "and the bastards flogged her for it."

Loral woke at the mention of her name. "Is it time to get up?"

"Rest until the men come," said Taren.

Loral sat up. "I'm fine. I really am. The pains are gone."

"I'm glad," said Dar, although she had hoped Loral would give birth while they were sheltered.

The men staggered in to eat. Their leisurely pace suggested the rumor was true and there would be no march that day. Teeg arrived last. Holding his bowl for Dar to fill, he looked satisfied. "How's yer back?"

Dar acted serene. "A night's rest worked wonders."

Teeg searched Dar's face for signs that he had broken her, but she was inscrutable. "If ye could rest, perhaps I went too easy."

"I learned my lesson."

"Aye," said Teeg, wondering what lesson that was. He turned to Taren. "No march today, so the tolum wants proper food. Make chicken stew, roast veal, and bread."

"Bread!" said Taren. "None of these girls can bake bread."

"Tell it to the tolum, if ye think he'll listen," said Teeg. He grinned. "Ye could send Dar with the message."

Taren's prediction of a hectic day proved true. The soldiers' sole assistance was to fetch a calf and kill it. The women did everything else, from butchering the calf to catching the chickens. Every movement brought Dar pain that exhausted her. Taren noticed and retrieved a metal box from a wagon. "Dar," she said, "I have a job for you."

"What?"

"Since orcs don't scare you, I thought you might take

them these." She opened the box. It contained black seeds that were the shape of dried peas, though slightly larger. "They're called wash-something. Orcs fancy them in foul weather."

"What do I do?" asked Dar.

"Just visit each one's grass tent, say the words you do at supper, and give them some seeds—about five each." Then she whispered, "Take your time doin' it."

Dar flashed a thankful smile. She washed and changed in the smokehouse, where she discovered the robe beneath her shift was soaked with blood. When she was clean, Dar filled a small bag with seeds and went about her errand. She gave seeds to the orcs standing guard first, then headed for the orc encampment. It lay encircled by upright branches in the middle of a meadow. The orcs were inside their conical shelters. Dar approached the nearest one and said the required phrase. Hands parted the shelter's reed wall and emerged to receive the seeds. After thanking Muth la, the orc closed the gap.

At the apex of each shelter was a woven band that bound the reeds together. Each band was distinctive. The shelter that had a green and yellow band turned out to be Kovok-mah's. After receiving his seeds, he said, "I smell blood."

"I was flogged last night."

"I do not understand 'flogged.' "

"Men hurt my back."

"Turn around," said Kovok-mah. When Dar did, he saw spreading bloodstains on her wet robe. He sniffed the damp air. "Come back when you finish."

"Kam?" *Why?*

"I smell bad things. You could get sick."

Dar finished handing out the seeds, then headed for Kovok-mah's shelter. He made an opening as she approached. "Take off robe and come inside."

Dar hesitated.

"Come. I know healing magic."

Dar's fear of festering wounds overcame her apprehension. She whisked off the wet, bloody garment and crawled into the shelter.

There was barely room for the two of them. Sitting cross-legged, Kovok-mah took up most of the floor space. His helmet and a few possessions occupied the rest. Dar found herself kneeling awkwardly on Kovok-mah's lap, her face inches from his. "Bend down," said Kovok-mah. "I must see your back."

Dar hunched crosswise in Kovok-mah's lap. A cloak covered his legs, so it wasn't an uncomfortable position. Kovok-mah gently felt the outlines of Dar's lashes without ever touching the wounds themselves. Next, he leaned over and sniffed them. Then he opened a bag that had several compartments, each containing dried leaves, roots, or seeds. Kovok-mah took things from several different compartments and put them in his mouth. He chewed them awhile, then leaned over and spit on Dar's wound.

"What are you doing?" asked Dar with disgust.

"Mmph," replied Kovok-mah, placing a hand on Dar's neck to hold her still.

The place where Kovok-mah had spit burned and tingled at first, then became numb. Dar relaxed. Kovok-mah spit again. When every lash stroke had been covered with herb-laced saliva, Kovok-mah spit out the chewed materials and blew upon the wounds to dry them. The herbs affected Dar like drink, and she was warm despite being undressed. If Kovok-mah hadn't spoken, she probably would have fallen asleep. "Why did they do this to you?"

"I made the tolum angry."

"How?"

"I wanted him to help a woman."

"And they hurt you for this?"

"Hai."

"Urkwashavoki nuk tash," muttered Kovok-mah.

"What?"

"Washavokis are cruel."

"Then why do you fight for them?" asked Dar.

"This is our queen's wisdom."

"The tolum said women are here for urkzimmuthi. Is that your queen's wisdom, also?"

"Hai."

"Why?"

"I already told you. Food belongs to Muth la. Mothers should give it to us."

Her inhibitions dulled by the herbs, Dar spoke her feelings. "*That's* why I was taken and branded? My life was ruined just so I could serve you food?"

"Washavokis branded you."

Kovok-mah's reply only increased Dar's ire. "Because of *you*! I'm here because of *you*!"

"You make no sense. Mothers always serve."

"That's not true."

"Washavokis understand nothing."

The calm Dar had felt only moments before was shattered. She felt abused and angry. She grabbed her wet robe and managed to slip it on. "I should go," she said.

"I also think this," said Kovok-mah.

* * *

In the evening, Dar returned to the orc encampment with Neena to serve. Though rain still fell, the orcs were seated outdoors. When Dar gave Kovok-mah his food, he didn't acknowledge her beyond the usual formalities. After he finished eating, Zna-yat approached him. "Mother's brother's son, it's good time to walk beneath trees."

Kovok-mah glanced at the grove beyond the meadow's edge and understood his cousin wished to speak privately. "Hai," he said. "It would be pleasant to walk."

The two orcs strolled off. Zna-yat waited until they were far from the keen ears of the others before he spoke. "I smelled strange thing—one washavoki with scent of healing magic. Others smelled it, too."

"I gave Weasel this magic."

"I thought so."

"I saw wisdom in it," said Kovok-mah.

"Most do not," said Zna-yat. "You're losing respect."

"If that's so, then it's so."

"That's selfish answer. When time for killing comes, you must lead. Don't let someone lesser do it."

"They would choose another?" asked Kovok-mah.

"Sons won't follow someone they can't understand. They think you're acting foolish."

"And you, also?"

"I can't understand why you teach our speech to Weasel, or why you gave it healing magic."

"I don't fully understand, myself," said Kovok-mah. "Perhaps it's because she's different."

"*She?* You call it *she* now?"

"You think that strange?"

"Of course!" said Zna-yat. "I've never heard such talk. To call one animal 'she.' It's reckless."

"How?"

"It will destroy your authority. We need your leadership. For Muth la's sake, avoid this Weasel. Washavokis don't care for us; it's foolish to care for them."

"She's like favorite goat, nothing more."

"If your comrades were starving, would you spare that goat?"

"Thwa," said Kovok-mah.

"You must think of your own kind first. Washavokis aren't like us. They're dangerous and unpredictable."

Kovok-mah thought of Weasel's anger coming so quickly after he had healed her. "I see wisdom in what you say."

"Will you cease your strange behavior?" asked Zna-yat.

"Hai."

Zna-yat smiled. "You've always put others before yourself, that is why you're strong in their chests. I'm proud to be your kin."

"Such words warm my chest," said Kovok-mah. "I'm glad you spoke to me."

Thirteen

The following morning, Taren examined Dar's back. She was amazed to find that the lashes had scabbed over and the skin surrounding them was no longer swollen. "This is Karm's grace," she said. "Many a girl's died from flogging. You'll have scars, though."

"Murdant Kol won't mind," said Neena. "They won't even show when she's on her back."

Dar shot Neena an annoyed look. Neena smiled back.

The rain had ended and the soldiers broke camp early. As Dar headed to the muddy road, she saw the peasants returning to discover what remained of their food stores. They faced a hard summer and a harder winter. Yet, because they hadn't resisted, their other possessions remained untouched. Thus, Neena and Kari had only sausages to show for their favors.

Dar walked with Loral. Though their friendship was renewed, Dar often found conversation difficult. Too many topics stirred up heartache. Dar refrained from asking about Loral's home and family, for they were lost forever. The upcoming birth seemed an ominous—not a blessed—event. The high points in both their current lives were food and rest, and they had little of either. Yet the bond between them could be expressed silently, and that's what Dar mostly did.

By noon, the march had taken its toll on Loral.

When her friend became oblivious of everything except the necessity to keep walking, Dar lagged behind to speak with Kovok-mah. She regretted her last words to him and wanted to thank him for healing her lashes. This time, he marched toward the front of the column, and Dar was surrounded by orcs when she said, "Shashav, Kovok-mah." *Thanks, Kovok-mah.*

"Speak to me like washavoki, not in speech of mothers."

"Dargu nak muth." *Weasel is mother.*

"Do not say that!"

"Kam?" *Why?*

"You are different thing. You are washavoki."

"Why are you saying this?"

"Because it is so. I was foolish to talk to you, foolish to give you magic. I am finished speaking. Go away."

Dar stared at Kovok-mah in disbelief, while he resolutely ignored her. When she saw he wouldn't speak to her, she rejoined the women. Only then did Kovok-mah sigh softly to himself.

The march continued into late afternoon, when the shieldron halted near a hapless peasant's hut. The family was either very poor or had been warned of the army's approach, for their larder was nearly empty. Only the officers ate well that evening; everyone else had porridge. It was twilight when Dar and Neena approached the orcs' encampment bearing dinner. As they entered the circle of branches, Dar whispered, "The orcs are acting strangely. Be prepared to run."

The two women halted before the seated orcs. "Saf nak ur Muthz la," said Dar. *Food is Muth la's gift.*

"Shashav Muth la," said the orcs in unison. *Thanks Muth la.*

Dar whispered to Neena, "Don't serve them yet, I have something else to say." Then Dar addressed the orcs in their own tongue. "Urkzimmuthi say me no mother. Then no mother gives you this food. No Muth la. No mother. No food." Dar whispered to Neena. "We must go now."

"Why?"

"They're angry. Now come along."

When the two women turned to leave, Kovok-mah shouted, "Stop!"

Dar shouted back, "Thwa muth. Thwa saf." *No mother. No food.*

Kovok-mah rose, puffed up his chest, and roared. "Run!" shouted Dar to Neena, who required no further encouragement. She dashed off. Dar stood her ground. As Kovok-mah strode up to her, she thought he might kill her.

"Serve us!"

"Steal this food!" answered Dar. "I will not give it to you."

Kovok-mah raised his sword, and Dar closed her eyes, expecting to gaze next upon the Dark Path.

"Why?" asked Kovok-mah. "Why are you doing this?"

Dar opened her eyes. Kovok-mah had lowered his sword. "Because you cannot have it both ways. You want me to serve, yet say I'm no mother. If that's true, then the hairy-faced washavokis can serve you. I'm tired of it."

Kovok-mah asked quietly, "What do you want?"

"All must say I am mother. Then I will serve."

For just an instant, Dar caught a hint of a smile on Kovok-mah's face. He turned and spoke to the orcs in their language. Dar could follow little of what he said, but she assumed by the length of his speech that he wasn't commanding his comrades, but rather trying to persuade them. When he finished speaking, the orcs said in unison, "Ther nat muth."

Kovok-mah turned to Dar. "They have said you are mother. Now, will you serve?"

"Hai."

As Dar dipped the ladle into the kettle, she felt the eyes of the orcs upon her. She wasn't naive; she knew her victory was a small one. *But it's still a victory.*

When Dar returned lugging the empty kettle, she was met by Taren. "What happened with the orcs? Neena was scared out of her wits."

"What did she say?" asked Dar.

"That you said somethin' that riled them." Taren shook her head. "Dar, your tongue stirs up trouble."

"Not this time."

"How can you say that? Neena said they almost killed you."

"They wouldn't do that. Orcs respect women."

"I've seen them slay plenty," said Taren. "Maybe they're fond of their mothers, but they're not fond of us. If you hang around them long enough, you're goin' to get killed."

"You don't understand."

"I do," said Taren. "You're scared of men, so you run to the orcs. You'd be safer with your own kind. Murdant Kol's not so bad."

"I can't believe you're saying that!"

"Maybe you don't fancy men, but don't jump from the pot into the fire. If you're careful, you won't end up like Loral."

"Care is useless when others run our lives."

"So men look to their own wants first," said Taren. "Why would orcs be any different?"

"I'm sure they're not," said Dar. "But they want different things."

"And what might they be?" asked Taren.

"Not our bodies," said Dar. She looked thoughtful. "Perhaps it's our blessing."

Taren snorted. "You're daft!"

Fourteen

♛

It was mid morning when the thunderstorm hit, instantly drenching everyone. The road filled with water, but the march continued. Dar scanned the sky. It was uniformly dark, and she guessed it would rain for a long while. The heath they were traveling through offered no shelter. There were only a few stunted trees and no habitations at all. It was easy to see why people shunned the place. Springtime had barely touched it, and the bleak landscape remained a somber brown.

Dar heard heavy footsteps and turned to see Kovok-mah splashing up the road. He slowed when he reached her. "Tava, Dargu."

"Tava, Kovok-mah."

"This weather makes us think of washuthahi," said Kovok-mah, who then turned and rejoined the orcs.

Taren watched him go with a surprised expression. "Well, that's a first."

"What's washuthahi?" asked Dar.

"Those black seeds," said Taren. "I think that orc was hintin' they'd fancy some."

Dar considered Taren's idea. *If orcs believe mothers own the food, they may think it's improper to ask for it directly.* "I'm sure you're right," she said. "I'll give them some."

Dar jogged up to a wagon and found the box of seeds. She placed some in a bag and waited for the orc column to march up to her. When it did, she gave each orc some washuthahi. Kovok-mah was marching at the column's rear and when Dar approached him, he slowed his pace so they walked apart from the others.

Dar held out the seeds. "Muth la urat tha saf la."

Kovok-mah's large, clawed fingers delicately plucked the small black spheres from Dar's palm. "Shashav Muth la," he said. Then he added in a softer voice, "Shashav, Dargu."

Dar didn't know what to say next. She looked at the huge orc walking beside her, his frame made even more massive by rusty iron plates, and she thought of how alien he was. An iron helmet hid most of his face, and the portion she saw was unreadable. Yet she knew that she must make some connection. Dar racked her brain for something to say. Eventually, she said, "Mer nav falfli." *I am wet.*

Kovok-mah looked at her. "Hai, zar falfi." *Yes, very wet.* After a silent moment, he spoke to Dar in her own tongue. "I think we should speak of things other than weather."

"Hai," said Dar. "You were angry with me last night. Are you still angry?"

"I do not know washavoki word for how I feel. You are very strange."

"You are strange to me, also," said Dar. "Perhaps when I learn your speech, you will be less so."

"I think not," said Kovok-mah. He paused. "You spoke wisdom last night. There is difference between woe mans and hairy-faced washavokis."

"Do the others believe that?"

"They said you are mother."

"Saying something and believing it are different things."

"How could that be so?" asked Kovok-mah. "Such speech would have no meaning."

"People lie all the time."

"What is 'lie'?"

"It's saying something you know is not so."

"On purpose?" asked Kovok-mah.

"Of course on purpose."

"Washavokis do this thing?"

The question seemed so naive that Dar thought Kovok-mah was teasing. Yet he wasn't smiling, and it dawned on her that he was serious. She was so surprised, it took a moment for her to reply. "Why, yes . . . we lie all the time."

"Do you do this?"

"I've never lied to you," said Dar, hoping that answer would satisfy him.

Kovok-mah lapsed into silence, as if he needed to ponder what Dar had said. He put one of the washuthahi seeds in his mouth and chewed it. Eager to change the subject, Dar asked him, "What are those seeds for?"

"Washuthahi is very good. It makes warmth."

Dar reached into the bag and pulled out one of the black, wrinkled spheres. After turning it in her damp fingers and sniffing it, she popped the seed into her mouth and bit down gently. Its shell cracked, releasing a pleasantly spicy flavor that gave the impression of sweetness. "This isn't bad," she said. "Do you eat it?"

"Keep in mouth and chew."

As Dar chewed the seed, its flavor grew more pronounced and was accompanied by a sensation of warmth. The colors around her became more vivid, and the damp air smelled rich and fragrant. The rain no longer bothered her. She grinned broadly at the orc. He curled back his lips in return. "You not washavoki now."

"Hai. Dargu nak thwa washavoki," said Dar, showing off her limited Orcish.

The conversation turned to language, and as Dar walked with Kovok-mah, he pointed at things and named them. Dar repeated the words, then Kovok-mah corrected her pronunciation. After a while, he began a new lesson. "We put words together to make new ones. Here is sense of 'urkzimmuthi.' 'Zim' is child. 'Urkzim' is more than one child."

"We'd say 'children.' " Dar looked puzzled. "You call yourselves childrenmother?"

"Thwa," said Kovok-mah. "Muth is mother. "Muthi means . . ." He paused to think. ". . . 'of mother.' We add sound at end of one word to show it speaks about another word."

"So 'urkzimmuthi' means 'children of mother.' "

"Hai." Kovok-mah held out a washuthahi seed. " 'Wash' means 'teeth.' 'Uthahi' means 'pretty.' "

Although Dar thought the seed looked somewhat like an orc's black tooth, she was amused that it was called "teeth-pretty." She suspected that chewing these seeds had affected her mood, for she felt lighthearted despite the foul weather.

That mood persisted when the lesson was over and Dar headed to rejoin the women. She grinned broadly as she splashed up the road. Taren, Kari, Neena, and Loral didn't share Dar's cheerfulness. They looked bedraggled and dispirited as they slogged along. Neena was shocked when Dar smiled at her. "Dar!" she said. "What happened?"

"Nothing. Why?"

"Your teeth are black!" said Neena.

"Let me see," said Taren. Dar opened her mouth and Taren peered inside. "They're as black as any orc's. You must have done something."

"I chewed a few of those seeds," said Dar. She suddenly understood why "washuthahi" meant "teeth-pretty" and laughed.

"I don't see what's so funny," said Neena, "You look awful."

"Not very kissable," said Taren, "though I guess that doesn't bother you."

"Not in the slightest," said Dar.

"Ugh!" said Neena. "Why would you eat orc food?"

"Those seeds aren't food," said Dar. "They're something else. A kind of magic."

"That's even worse," said Kari. "Maybe you'll turn into an orc."

Dar playfully flashed a broad, black-toothed grin. "Maybe. I should ask about that." She turned about and headed toward the marching orcs. When she reached Kovok-mah, she curled back her lips in an orcish smile. "Nuk merz wash uthahi?" *Are my teeth pretty?*

Kovok-mah seemed pleased that Dar had returned. He smiled back. "Therz wash nuk zar uthahi." *Your teeth are very pretty.*

"If 'washuthahi' means 'pretty teeth,' what does 'washavoki' mean?" asked Dar.

" 'Avok' means 'dog.' "

"So washavokis have the white teeth of dogs?" asked Dar.

Kovok-mah hissed with orcish laughter. "Dargu nak thwa washavoki. Darguz wash nuk uthahi." Some of the other orcs joined in laughing.

Dar mentally translated. *Weasel is not dog-teeth. Weasel's teeth are pretty.* She smiled. *Maybe they are,* she thought, *to an orc.*

The rain stopped falling in the afternoon, but the sky remained dark. By then, Dar's buoyant mood had faded, and she was as tired and miserable as the other women. Loral suddenly gasped. "My pains are worse!"

"How long have you had them?" asked Dar.

"Since this morning," said Loral.

"And you've been walking all this time?" asked Dar.

"They're not going to stop the march for a woman," said Loral.

"Can you hold out a little longer?" asked Taren. "We'll probably be haltin' soon."

"I don't know," said Loral. "I'll try."

Taren regarded the others. "Who of you knows 'bout birthin' babes?"

No one answered.

"Come on, all of you had mothers," said Taren. "Did you ever see her give birth?"

Both Neena and Kari shook their heads.

"How about you, Dar?" asked Taren.

Dar didn't want to say in front of Loral that she had watched her mother die. "It was a long time ago."

"Then you're the closest thing we've got to a Wise Woman, here. You'll have to do."

"But I won't be any help," said Dar.

"At least you can stay with her if she gets left behind. She shouldn't be alone."

"Yes, I can do that," said Dar, fervently hoping it wouldn't be necessary.

"Come with me," said Taren. "I want to show you something." She led Dar to the supply wagon and pulled out a kettle the size of a bucket. Packed inside were a flint and iron, the cloth Taren had torn from the serving robe, two full water skins, and a loaf of bread. The bread, which had been baked on the tolum's orders, was burned and nearly flat. At the time, Dar had taken vindictive satisfaction at the failure of their baking. The prospect of eating that same bread was less pleasing. "If Loral's time comes while we're marchin', take this kettle."

"I see you've planned in advance," said Dar. "Why don't you stay with Loral?"

"Because I've never watched a birth. At least you've done that." Taren scanned the desolate countryside. "What a Karm-forsaken place to have a babe. Let's hope it doesn't happen here."

"Yes," said Dar.

"If it does, move away from the road and hide your fire."

"I will."

"If it goes poorly, and you come back alone, burn the brand from her forehead first. That way, no bounty taker will disturb her body." Taren sighed. "That's all the advice I can give."

Dar and Taren rejoined Loral and the others. They had walked but a little farther when clear liquid suddenly flowed down Loral's thighs. Loral halted, staring at her dripping legs with consternation. "Dar! What's happening?"

"It's time to leave the road," said Dar. She grabbed the kettle Taren had packed from the wagon, then took Loral's hand. "Come."

Loral's eyes widened with panic. "No! I can't do it!"

"Yes, you can," said Dar.

Loral burst out sobbing as Dar led her into the damp, waist-high heather. The soldiers kept marching, ignoring the two women. Dar and Loral moved slowly, for there was no path and Loral's pains forced frequent stops. The terrain undulated, and the low parts were boggy. Skirting the damp areas, Dar headed for a clump of scrubby trees far from the road. They were in leaf and promised some shelter if it rained again. After what seemed forever, the two finally reached the trees. Dar pulled up bracken, shook it as dry as she could, and laid it by the largest tree trunk. Then she turned to Loral. "Lie down here."

Loral lay on the makeshift bedding. "What's going to happen, Dar?"

"Your baby's coming out."

"Don't I have to do something?"

"I don't think so," said Dar. "The baby does it on its own."

"How? How can a baby get through my womb-pipe?"

"I don't know. It just does."

"But it hurts. It hurts a lot."

"Yes," said Dar. "It hurt my mother, too." Dar glanced at the sky. "I should gather firewood before it gets dark. Will you be all right?"

"Don't go!"

"I'm not going far. You'll want a fire later."

Loral pleaded further, but Dar ignored her and left.

As she headed for some dead trees deeper into the heath, she felt relieved to get away and guilty that she had those feelings. When Dar reached the top of a slight rise, she saw the trees were standing in water, their trunks and branches silver gray against the bog that had killed them. Dar descended the rise and waded into the black pond. "Oh well," she said to herself, "at least the wood will be dry."

Dar pulled off branches and carried them to dry ground. After she had broken off all the branches she could reach, she took an armload back to the campsite. Loral sat against the tree, her face a mask of pain and fear. Dar dropped the wood and rushed to her side. Loral grabbed her hand and squeezed it so tightly that Dar's bones ached. Gradually, Loral relaxed her grip. Her face relaxed also. "When will this end?" she asked.

"Soon, I hope."

It did not end soon. Dar tried to get the remaining firewood during the intervals between Loral's birthing pains and was forced to run as the intervals grew shorter. By the time Dar had a fire lit, the pains were coming frequently. It grew dark. Though the pains continued and grew more intense, nothing else happened. Dar felt completely useless.

As the night wore on, Loral broke into a sweat, though the air was chilly. She moaned, "Oh my back!" She hiked up her shift and assumed a squatting position. Blood trickled from between her legs.

"What are you doing?" asked Dar.

Loral glared at her irritably. "I'm trying to get comfortable." She grimaced and her face turned red.

"Loral . . ."

"I'm pushing. I need to push!"

"Push what?"

"Will you shut up? Go away!"

Dar remained. She hoped that Loral's urge to push was a sign that something was about to happen. Nothing did. The urge to push continued to come at regular intervals. Though Loral strained with each effort, as far as Dar could see, the only result was to spend her strength.

As time passed, Loral's legs trembled, and her eyes grew wild. Loral's moans took on a sharper note. She had hiked her shift above her waist, and the space between her legs began to part. A bulge of dark, wet hair appeared. A moment passed, and the bulge became a hemisphere and then a little head. Shoulders came next. Dar cradled the head as the wet body followed, dark in the firelight.

Dar had forgotten there would be a cord attached to the child's belly. For a moment, she didn't know what to do. Dar held the baby, not wanting to tug at the cord. Finally, she recalled that someone—she had forgotten who—had cut the cord when her mother had given birth. Lacking a knife, Dar grabbed the flint Taren had given her. It had no sharp edge, and she was reduced to gnawing the cord until it parted. Blood poured from the severed end. Dar briefly panicked, then tied a knot in the cord.

Though the baby was born, Loral wasn't yet finished. After a little more effort, a strange object emerged. It was attached to the other end of the cord and resembled a piece of raw liver. Dar had no idea what it was. With its appearance, Loral relaxed and lay back on her weedy bed. "Is it a boy or a girl?" she asked.

Dar looked. "A girl."

Loral seemed disappointed, but she said, "Let me hold her."

Dar used the scrap of cloth to wipe the child clean before placing her in Loral's arms. The tiny girl seemed to stare at her mother. Loral gently touched her little face, then burst out crying. "What's going to happen to her?" she said between sobs. "What's going to happen to me?"

Dar was wise enough not to venture an answer.

Fifteen

Dar did what she could to make Loral comfortable. She cleaned her, gave her the baby to nurse, and wrapped mother and child in her own cloak. Then she built up the fire with the remainder of the wood. When she finished, Dar lay against Loral on the side away from the fire. Soon, both women were asleep.

Loral's shivering woke Dar when there was only a faint glow in the eastern sky. "Are you all right?"

"I'm c-cold," said Loral in a groggy voice.

Dar got up. The fire had died to embers. She pushed the unburned ends of the branches together and blew on them. A yellow flame appeared. Then she uprooted some heather and tossed it on the flame. The fire flared up. "Is that better?"

"I'm still cold and wet."

In the firelight, Loral's lips looked dark. Dar bent over to stroke Loral's brow. It was clammy. "You've been lying on damp ground," Dar said. "It's dry closer to the fire."

Loral said nothing; she simply stared at Dar, looking confused. Dar took matters into her own hands and dragged Loral to drier ground. The place where Loral had lain appeared black in the dim light, like a permanent shadow. Dar touched the large, dark spot and drew back her fingers. *Blood!* Loral had been lying in a pool of it.

The discovery plunged Dar into despair. *She's been bleeding half the night.* Judging by the quantity of blood, she guessed that Loral was dying and wondered if Loral had guessed it, also. *Should I tell her?* Dar couldn't bring herself to say the words. "Loral."

"What?" said Loral, her voice as distant as a sleeper's.

"I'll take care of your baby."

A faint smile came to Loral's dark lips. "Thanks."

"Do you have a name for her?"

"Frey."

"That's a pretty name."

Loral said something that Dar couldn't understand, then closed her eyes. For a moment, Dar thought Loral had died, but she still breathed. Dar lifted the cloak and took Frey from her. The infant woke and began to cry. Dar tore the neck of her shift until she could slip the baby down its front and guide her to a breast. The child began to suck and calmed down. "I'm nursing you with empty breasts while I watch your mother die," Dar whispered to her. "What good am I?"

Light came to a gray sky, revealing that Loral's dark lips were a shade of blue. They contrasted with skin that was almost white. Loral's breathing was barely perceptible. By the time the sun rose, it had ceased altogether.

With a brand from the fire, Dar burned away the scar that had marked Loral as the king's property. Dar took back her bloodstained cloak, for she needed it too much to leave it behind. She covered Loral's ruined forehead with sprigs of heather, then arranged her corpse so she looked peaceful and dignified. That was the best Dar could do; she had no means to bury her friend, nor were there stones to build a cairn.

Dar held Frey so she might view her mother. "She gave you life," Dar said to the fussing baby, "though she bought it with her own."

Dar returned Frey to the warmth of her shift and sat down to eat some bread, soaking it in water so it was chewable. She briefly considered remaining to lead a solitary and feral life. *A baby wouldn't last long in the wild*, thought Dar. *Returning to the regiment at least gives her a chance.* Though that chance seemed a slim one, Dar felt compelled to do whatever she could.

Tired as she was, Dar knew she must hurry to catch up with the soldiers. *They're probably already on the march.* Dar wrapped a strip of rag around her head to hide her brand from anyone she encountered. Then she grabbed the pot and its contents, donned her cloak, and headed for the road, carrying Frey beneath her torn shift.

The road snaked through the empty landscape, bearing the marks of the army's passing. Dar walked as quickly as she could; yet it was mid morning before she came upon the remains of the previous night's encampment. By then, she was concerned about Frey, for she doubted Loral had been able to nurse her. Dar poured water into the kettle, wetted a finger, and pushed it into the infant's mouth. The child sucked it vigorously. "You're thirsty, aren't you?" said Dar. She continued to give the baby water, one drop at a time.

With her attention focused on Frey, Dar didn't notice the man walking on the road until he was fairly close. She was alarmed to note that, despite being dressed as a peasant, he carried a sword. Dar slipped into the heather, crouched down, and retreated into the tangled brush. She hid twenty paces from the road and waited for the man to pass. With hearing heightened by fear, she listened to his footsteps. They grew louder, then stopped.

"I saw you," called a voice. "What cause have you to hide?"

Dar remained silent and still. She heard the sound of someone moving in the heather.

"I mean no harm," said the voice. "Perhaps I can help you."

Frey began to cry. Dar was trying to calm her when a man bearing a small knapsack stepped before her. His weather-stained clothes were ragged, and his bearded face was as grim as any soldier's. He smiled at Dar, but the smile didn't reach his wolfish eyes, and she noticed his hand gripped his sword hilt.

"You look worse for your journey," he said, taking in Dar's muck-blackened legs and feet. "Where are you headed?"

"That's my own business," said Dar, rising.

"And so it is. I never claimed otherwise." The man gazed at the lump in Dar's shift. "You got a babe in there?" He stepped closer. "Can I see? I'm fond of babes."

Dar glanced down at Frey. As she did, the man tore the rag from her head. He grinned when he saw her brand. "That's worth five silvers."

The stranger seized the top of Dar's shift as he drew his sword. Dar swung the kettle, striking the man's forehead. He moaned, wobbled, and released her. She swung again, this time with such force that the kettle's handle snapped. The man pitched face-first into a bush. Dar grabbed his sword, then turned him over. His eyes stared blankly beneath the crater in his forehead.

Frey wailed, having slipped farther down Dar's shift. Dar tended to her, then decided to search the dead man's knapsack for food. She rolled him over and untied the drawstring. Locks of human hair fell out. Dar investigated no further.

Armed with the bounty hunter's sword, Dar traveled unmolested. The few people she encountered gave her a wide berth, for she had a dangerous and desperate air. If anyone guessed her rag hid a brand, they took care not to show it. Throughout the day, Dar trudged after the army and caught up with it at dusk. The women had already served the evening meal and were cleaning up.

Neena spotted Dar first. "Dar! Where's Loral?"

"She walks the Dark Path."

"And her baby?"

"I have her here." The women rushed over, and Dar produced Frey.

"Too bad it's a girl," said Taren. "Peasants are more likely to take a boy."

"We could keep her here," said Kari.

"None of us can nurse it," said Taren. "Even if we could, this is no place for a child."

Neena gently touched Frey's hand. "She's so tiny."

"Aye, she's that," said Taren. "Helpless, too. Go tell the murdant that Dar's returned with a babe."

As Dar gazed at the baby in her arms, she was overwhelmed by melancholy. The injustices in Loral's life had passed to her child. "It's so unfair," she whispered.

A hand touched Dar's shoulder. "Is this the babe?" asked a voice.

Startled, Dar whirled about.

Murdant Kol glanced at the child. "She favors her mother."

Sixteen

Murdant Kol spurred his horse to a gallop as he rode from camp at daybreak. Speed was unnecessary, but haste gave the right impression. He slowed his steed to a trot only when he cleared a rise and was hidden from view. The bouncing gait had disturbed the baby in his arms, who continued to wail after the horse slowed down. "Hush!" said Kol in a tone more effective on soldiers than newborns. The baby did not obey.

Wrapping one arm about the child required guiding the horse single-handedly. Kol, an accomplished rider, made it look effortless. Soon he was riding in familiar territory where heath gave way to pastures. The green hills were sheep country, and the wool trade supported a small, walled town on the Lurven River. The Lurven divided the valley, and the road headed for the only bridge, a stone arch about a mile upstream from the town. It was still early morning when Murdant Kol reached it.

The rains had swelled the river, and its dark waters flowed swiftly beneath wisps of mist. Kol halted his horse in the middle of the span. In the distance, the mist took on a golden hue. It was a tranquil sight. Kol lifted Frey, who had finally dozed off, so she faced the vista. The baby was light in his hand, and he easily tossed her in a high arc. A short cry preceded the splash. Silence followed. The blanket drifted toward the surface of the black water. Then the current bore it away.

Murdant Kol turned his horse toward town and the pleasant prospect of a proper breakfast.

The women were marching even before Murdant Kol entered the town. "Dar," asked Kari. "What were you doing in the tent this morning?"

"Washing."

"Whatever for?"

"She's picked up orcish habits," said Taren with a note of distaste. "First the black teeth. Now bathing."

"Do you think Murdant Kol will find a home for Frey?" asked Dar, trying to change the subject.

"Perchance," said Taren. "An orphan leads a hard life, though."

"It'll be less hard than her mother's," said Dar.

"Aye," said Taren. "The men saw to that."

As Dar trudged along, her sadness over Loral's death fought with her concern for Frey and the dread caused by Murdant Kol's reappearance. His sudden return had been a shock, although she had expected it. Their reunion had a strangely official quality, more like a meeting of a murdant and his subordinate than a man and his woman. Kol had briefly questioned her about the birth and Loral's death, but he had been more interested in how Dar acquired the sword. Frey seemed of little consequence to him. He had taken the sword that evening, and the baby at first light.

The clear sky and mild weather did nothing to lighten Dar's spirits. Her pace lagged, and soon she was walking among the orcs. "Dargu gavak nervler," said a voice.

Dar looked about and saw Kovok-mah had spoken. "What?"

"I said you look sad."

Dar, who still had trouble reading Kovok-mah's facial expressions, was surprised he could discern hers. "Mer nav," she said. *I am.*

"Kam?" *Why?*

"Loral walks the Dark Path."

Kovok-mah regarded Dar with an expression she assumed was puzzlement. "What road is this?"

"The one spirits travel after they leave the body. Loral is dead."

"She has returned to Muth la," said Kovok-mah. "It is sad for you, but not for Loral."

"I left her lying on the ground," said Dar, her voice cracking.

"We would say 'te far Muthz la'—'on Muth la's breast.' It is good place. Think of your own mother."

The remark caused Dar to cry softly. Kovok-mah watched her, then said, "You have made this sound before. On day we met."

"Mer nav nervler." *I am sad.* Dar ceased sobbing and let out a wrenching sigh. "How do you say 'real mother'?"

"Real mother? I do not understand."

"Loral had a baby, doesn't that make her a real mother?"

"We would call her 'muthuri.' It means 'giving mother' in your speech."

"I see," said Dar. "Loral gave life. I give only porridge." She sighed again.

"You are still mother," said Kovok-mah, "and your teeth are pretty."

Dar smiled at his transparency. "Hai. Will they ever look like a dog's again?"

"Not if you are careful to chew washuthahi."

"I'll try to keep up my appearance."

"It is pleasing to see pretty teeth."

Dar walked silently awhile, then she asked, "What do urkzimmuthi mothers look like?"

"They are smaller than sons, their heads are smooth, and all their teeth are little," said Kovok-mah. "They look somewhat like you, but much prettier."

Dar smiled. "Don't you believe in flattery?"

"What is flattery?"

"You wouldn't understand. It's a kind of lie."

"You mean saying words without meaning?"

"Hai. Like saying I'm pretty."

"Your teeth are pretty."

"You told me that before."

"And you have big chest."

Dar looked down. "My breasts aren't big."

Kovok-mah smiled. "Thwa urkfar—not breasts. 'Big chest' means big feelings, courage."

"Washavokis would say 'a big heart' or perhaps a brave one," said Dar.

"Maybe same thing," said Kovok-mah, who didn't seem sure. "It is good to have big chest. I give you no flattery."

Dar had rejoined the women by the time they marched past the town. Until then, the largest settlement she had ever seen had been the village near her home. Compared with that collection of huts, the small town seemed imposing. Dar gaped at the structures visible above its wall, astonished by their size, cut-stone masonry, and tiled roofs. Her amazement amused Kari, who was teasing Dar when Murdant Kol rode out from the town's gates. Dar strained to see if he still had Frey and would have spoken with him if he hadn't joined the officers at the front of the column. For the rest of the day, she anxiously waited for a chance to learn if Kol had found the baby a home. When the army finally halted for the night, Dar hurried to see him. "Murdant Kol," she said. "What news? Were you successful?"

Kol smiled. "Karm has favored the child. I found a family that took her in as one of their own. They're weavers who prize a girl's nimble fingers."

"Do they have other children?" asked Dar.

"Three daughters. They were already doting on the babe when I left."

Dar beamed, but then her face took on a different expression. "You must be happy for your daughter."

Kol feigned puzzlement. "My daughter? Did Loral tell you that?"

"No, someone else did."

"Well, you shouldn't credit gossip. The child's not mine. Loral would have told you herself if you had asked her."

"It's too late for that."

"Aye, and it's a shame. She was a fine lass." Murdant Kol paused, as if lost in thought. "Do you know anything about horses?"

"No," said Dar.

"I've heard you get on with the piss eyes. Someone like that would be good with horses."

"I don't see why."

"Both beasts are dangerous, but you strike me as the fearless type."

"You're wrong."

"Then brave, instead." Kol smiled. "Not many would attack a swordsman armed only with a kettle."

"I was protecting Frey."

"I fancy you'll show the same devotion to my horse. I need someone to care for Thunder."

"I wouldn't know how."

"I'll teach you."

Dar regarded the murdant uneasily. "We're already short a woman, and . . ."

"You'll do what's required," said Murdant Kol in a sharp tone.

Dar's face colored, but she kept her voice meek. "Yes, Murdant."

"I left my groom behind," said Kol, his voice easy again, "and these soldiers are a ham-handed lot. I sense you have the proper touch. The rest you can learn."

"When do you want to teach me?"

"Now. Thunder must be groomed after being ridden."

Dar glanced toward where the women were lighting the cooking fires. "Now?"

"Yes." Kol touched Dar's arm and felt her tense. "You seem skittish. That won't do. Thunder can sense fear."

"Your horse doesn't frighten me."

"Then what does?" asked Kol. When Dar didn't answer, he grinned. "Surely not me."

"I told you I'm not fearless. I was frightened when I killed that man."

Kol's grin broadened. "But you still killed him."

"I did."

"I ride Thunder because the horse has spirit," said Kol. "I appreciate spirit. Come, it's time you two met."

Kol led Dar to where Thunder was tethered and showed her how to rub him down. Then he watched Dar work, noting how her gentle touch calmed the horse. *She has good instincts*, he thought, recalling that Thunder had killed a groom. *The fool tried force and got trampled for it.* As high murdant, Kol knew mastery was achieved by many means. Violence was only one of them.

Seventeen

Taren looked at Dar crossly when she approached the cooking fires. "Dallyin' already? I thought you wanted no part of Murdant Kol."

"I don't," said Dar. "He made me take care of his horse."

Taren scowled. "As if we weren't shorthanded already. Help me with the porridge. I can't do everything."

"Where are the others?"

"Gatherin' wood. There's precious little. I must speak to Murdant Teeg about gettin' a new girl."

"Please don't," said Dar.

"What's it to you?"

"I keep thinking of Loral," said Dar. "Why ruin another life?"

"What about *our* lives?" said Taren. "Many backs make burdens light."

"I'll work twice as hard to make up the difference," said Dar. "At least, let me try."

Taren looked skeptical. "Murdant Teeg can decide to take a girl on his own, or Murdant Kol, for that matter."

"I know," said Dar. "Just don't ask them to do it."

"But how can you do this added work and spend nights with your murdant?"

"Maybe there won't be any nights."

"I thought you were his woman, or has he lost interest?"

"I don't understand what's going on," said Dar. "He hasn't . . . you know."

"I don't know," said Taren.

"He could drag me to his tent anytime he wants, but he hasn't. He's only touched my arm. And yet . . . the way he looks at me . . ."

"Have you changed *your* mind?" asked Taren.

"No."

"Then what will you do? You can't fight him."

"Probably not, but he seems to know how I feel."

"Aye, and he could be playin' with you," said Taren.

"How did he treat Loral?"

"I'm not the one to ask, but I think it's plain."

"He told me Frey isn't his child."

Taren snorted. "Aye, and Loral died a virgin, just like Karm's mother." Mentioning Loral's death made Taren think. "All right, Dar. I won't ask Teeg for another girl. We'll make do until the regiment joins up."

The following day, the army left the Lurven Valley and Dar first glimpsed the broad Therian Plain. Taren had marched across it twice and Loral once, and they had told her about what lay ahead. Far to the west, beyond Dar's sight, flowed the Turgen River, which marked the border of the kingdom. The Urkheit Mountains were to the north, also too distant to be seen. The Turgen originated there, and its only bridge lay close to the mountains. It had been taken two years ago, and the army would assemble there to invade the neighboring kingdom. Reaching the bridge would take two weeks of hard marching.

As the shieldron crossed the plain, it sometimes

camped in the open, but usually commandeered a peasant holding. Dar grew accustomed to living off others' possessions, though she was never comfortable with it. Her existence settled into a routine. She rose early each morning, served the soldiers, hurriedly ate, then fed and saddled Thunder. Murdant Kol had been right about her and the horse. Dar soon bonded with Thunder. Once she was able to sense his moods and needs, she felt relaxed around him.

Thunder's master was another story. Murdant Kol continued to perplex Dar. He made no advances, yet she remained fearful he would. The other soldiers didn't bother her, and that was the only benefit of being "Kol's woman," for the murdant wasn't generous. Dar still marched barefoot in her ragged shift, its torn front crudely stitched together. His only gift had been a puzzling one—a dagger to replace the sword he had taken from her. Dar thought Kol gave her the weapon either for reassurance or to show that she was no threat to him, even armed.

During a portion of every day, Dar marched with the orcs. She spoke mostly with Kovok-mah, but as her fluency in Orcish increased, she sometimes spoke to other orcs as well. Those were the ones who tolerated her as a kind of pet. Most ignored her. A few seemed annoyed by her presence. Because of them, Dar preferred to walk apart with Kovok-mah when he taught her his language.

The end of Dar's day was always the most hectic part. The women were as tired and hungry as everyone else, but they alone had to collect fuel, build fires, cook, serve both men and orcs, and clean up. In addition to those chores, Dar also had to rub down and groom Thunder. She was always exhausted by evening.

By the time Dar adjusted to the rhythm of the march,

she was no longer a scabhead. The crusts on her forehead had fallen away, leaving a bright pink outline of a crown in their stead. Her back had also healed; though, each time Dar touched her scars, she felt resentment.

The weather turned hot and dry, baking the road. For days, the army marched in a cloud of dust. When rain finally came, it was welcome at first. Yet the drops that cleared the air quickly turned the road to muck. Soon, men were cursing and hoping the tolum would call a halt for the day.

When the shieldron neared a cluster of buildings, the sustolum rode back and called for orcs to follow him. A dozen, Kovok-mah among them, followed the young officer. Dar knew the drill: The officers would ride to the peasant holding and demand food and shelter in the king's name. The orcs' presence ensured submission. Afterward, the soldiers would descend like locusts, commandeering accommodations and supplies. Afterward, the women's work commenced.

On that rainy day, the only variation was that Dar followed the officers as they entered the holding. She needed to start grooming Thunder immediately, for the horse was mud-spattered and would require extra attention. Dar glanced about the compound as she entered. Small stone buildings were grouped to form a rough courtyard in front of a barn. Within this space, a knot of peasants stood sullenly in the rain, warily eyeing the orcs. Murdant Kol was still on horseback, as were the two officers.

Dar was waiting for Kol to dismount when a boy ran out of the barn. Barely into his teens, he wasn't an imposing figure, despite the pitchfork he brandished. Yet his reckless hatred made him menacing. He jabbed the pitchfork toward the tolum's horse. "Leave us be!" he shouted.

Dar looked at the tolum to see what he would do. Tolum Karg's face reddened, but his voice was cold. "This is treason," he said. Keeping his eyes on the boy, he shouted a single word in Orcish—"Tav!"

An armored orc bounded forward and splintered the pitchfork's shaft with the downward stroke of his sword. The blade continued moving, looping upward before descending again. It bit into the boy's shoulder and sliced to the middle of his chest. It happened so fast, the boy had but an instant to react. He opened his mouth to scream, but there was no breath in him; it had departed in a rush of blood. As the boy slumped to the muddy ground, a woman screamed and ran toward him. The orc whirled and cut her down. Then, to Dar's horror, the orcs descended on the other peasants and began slaying them with efficient butchery.

Dar closed her eyes, and covered her ears, but her brief glimpse of the attack was seared into her mind. Its quickness and savagery stunned her like a physical blow. She wanted to scream and sob at once, but lacked the strength to do either. Instead, she stood paralyzed by feelings of horror, disgust, and nausea. When she opened her eyes again, all the peasants were dead. Three were women. Four were children. As their blood mingled with the rain and spread over the wet courtyard, their slayers were transformed in Dar's eyes. *They're worse than beasts.* Recalling how she had served them, spoke with them, and even let one touch her, she felt ashamed and befouled.

By the time Taren, Neena, and Kari arrived, the orcs had dragged the corpses away and departed. Yet, evidence of slaughter lingered. Blood stained the ground.

The damp air smelled of it. The soldiers were busy looting possessions made forfeit by the boy's treason. Dar stood alone in the rain, holding Thunder's bridle. Taren surveyed the scene, then walked up to her. "You saw what happened?"

"A boy ran out with a pitchfork. Just a boy," said Dar. "He didn't stand a chance. None of them did. Unarmed women. Children. It made no difference. The orcs . . . they just . . . Oh Karm! It was awful!"

"They're orcs," said Taren. "Killin' comes natural to them. Don't say I didn't tell you."

"But I . . . I never thought that . . . that . . ."

"Well, open eyes see truth," said Taren.

Dar was in the barn brushing Thunder when Murdant Kol entered. "That was a terrible thing to see," he said in a gentle voice. "It's especially hard to watch children die." He came closer and saw Dar's face was streaked with tears. Kol delicately stroked her cheek and was pleased when she didn't pull away. "I should have warned you," he said.

"Warned me?"

"I've seen you walking with the piss eyes and talking to them," replied the murdant. "There are times when you think they're almost human. That's always a mistake."

"Why would the king have such soldiers?"

"War's a hard business."

"These people weren't at war. They were the king's own subjects."

"True," said Murdant Kol. "The tolum should have said 'Kill him,' not just 'kill.' Piss eyes are too literal."

"The proper phrase is 'Tav gu'—'Kill it.' We're 'its' to the orcs."

"That doesn't surprise me," replied Kol. He sensed Dar's vulnerability and added, "I can protect you from most things, but not from orcs. I'd feel better if you stayed clear of them."

"Why do you protect me at all?"

Kol flirted with the idea of embracing Dar, but decided not to push his advantage. Instead, he spoke in a sympathetic tone. "If this day proves anything, it's that life's fragile. When you've seen as much killing as I have, you want to stand against the storm and give some shelter."

"I'm grateful," said Dar.

For the first time, Kol believed she meant it. He silently watched Dar brush his horse and reflected how the two had much in common. Dar's body possessed grace and strength. Like Thunder, she also had spirit. When he had met Dar, she was as wary and skittish as any colt, but he had been patient and clever. *Soon*, Kol thought, *she'll be ready for the bit.*

Eighteen

♛

The slaughter in the courtyard shook Dar profoundly, and when she served the orcs that evening, all her original trepidation returned. Once again, they seemed like monsters. The following day, Dar avoided contact with Kovok-mah and the others. She didn't even look in their direction. The mere sound of their footsteps assumed an oppressive note. As Dar marched, she felt trapped between the soldiers and the orcs and threatened by both.

The shieldron halted for the night far from any habitation. Dar groomed Thunder, then helped search for firewood. It was scarce until she found a dry stream. She was following its bed, gathering driftwood, when Kovok-mah spoke her name. Startled, she gazed at him uneasily, surprised that he could move so quietly and wondering why he felt the need to do so.

"You are frightened," said the orc.

"I'm not," replied Dar.

"What you say makes no sense. I smell your fear."

Dar wondered what fear smelled like. "Hai. I'm afraid. I saw you kill those peasants."

"Washavokis are cruel," said Kovok-mah.

"*We're* cruel? You slaughtered innocent people."

"I do not understand this word 'innocent.' What does it mean?"

"It means they didn't deserve to die. They did nothing to you."

"But tolum said we must kill them."

"He said 'tav.' That's all."

"Tav means 'kill.' We did what washavokis wanted us to do."

"But . . ."

"Washavokis want us to kill because they are cruel," said Kovok-mah.

"You don't understand," said Dar. "There should be a reason for killing someone."

"If woe man goes away, washavoki brings head and gets gift. I have seen this, but I do not understand. What is reason why woe man is killed?" Kovok-mah waited for an answer and when he got none he said, "All washavokis seem alike. I do not know which should live and which should die."

"Then you shouldn't kill any of them," said Dar.

"I will obey tolum."

"Why?"

"Your king gave our queen strong healing magic, and great gifts require great gifts in return."

"What does that have to do with it?"

"Your king desired us to kill for him," said Kovok-mah. "Our queen promised this gift."

"So you're here because of your queen?"

"Hai. Our queen swore urkzimmuthi would kill, so I do it," said Kovok-mah. "Still, I think your king desired cruel gift."

When Dar tried to imagine the diplomacy of kings and queens, she felt confident it dealt with enemies, not frightened peasants in rainy courtyards. Yet, the peasants were the ones who had died. Dar relived witnessing their deaths and found herself trembling. "It was horrible to see those killings. I think about them all the time. That's why you frightened me."

Kovok-mah gazed silently at Dar awhile. "That makes me sad," he said. Then he walked away.

Dar continued collecting firewood as she tried to sort out her feelings. Her encounter with Kovok-mah had only increased her disquiet. She found it hard to believe that the orcs would obey the tolum without question; yet she knew Kovok-mah did not lie. *He doesn't even understand the concept.* The idea of such obedience was disturbing. *If the tolum told Kovok-mah to kill me, would he do it?* She felt certain the tolum was capable of giving such an order. How Kovok-mah would respond was a trickier question. *Where do his loyalties lie?*

The simple answer was that the orcs' loyalties lay with their queen. Teeg had said as much. Yet, within the regiment, the situation was more complicated. *Here, men speak for the queen.* Dar wondered what distinctions the orcs made between their queen and the Queen's Man. Perhaps the two were interchangeable. *And what about the Queen's Man's officers? The orcs killed quickly enough for Tolum Karg.* Dar worried they might even obey a murdant. It was hard to figure out where things stood within such muddled allegiances. As Dar pondered them, she reached only one conclusion: There was no reason to believe that the orcs' loyalties included her.

By the time Dar returned to camp, the orcs had erected their shelters and the soldiers had pitched their tents. Only the women were busy. They worked around the cooking fires, which sorely needed wood. Dar tossed her load of branches beneath pots that Kari and Taren were stirring. "Are we only cooking porridge?" she asked.

"Aye," said Taren. "It was slim pickings last night. Soldiers had been there before."

"Do you suppose that's why the boy was so angry?" asked Dar.

"Who knows?" said Taren. "Poor fool."

Neena held out a pair of worn shoes. "Try these on, Dar. They might fit you."

Dar eyed the footwear. "Aren't those yours?"

Neena smiled. "Muut gave me a new pair."

Dar looked at Neena's feet. Her "new" shoes bore bloodstains. "But those are from . . ."

"Someone who no longer needs them," said Taren quickly.

So that's a man's generosity, thought Dar, *a dead woman's shoes*. She sat on the ground and tried on Neena's old pair. They were far too small.

Teeg was already in the tent when Kol entered and set down his saddlebags. The sound of bottles clinking caught Teeg's attention, and he sat up from his sleeping roll. "'Twas a dry march today," he said. "Makes a body thirsty."

"You're always thirsty," said Kol. "Rain or shine."

"Aye, that's true enough. So why don't ye share what's in yer bag?"

Kol opened his saddlebag. "I must save one bottle, but here's another."

Teeg grinned when he saw the bottle's shape. "Is that brandy?"

"Yes, honey brandy."

"I saw some fine cloth, too."

"A dress," said Kol.

"For yer woman?"

"It may prove useful."

Teeg used his dagger to pry the cork from the bottle. He took a long swig and sighed contentedly. "Why bother with a dress? Just tup her and be done with it."

"That would be your way," said Kol.

"Easiest is best," said Teeg. "That's my creed."

"So why hunt boars when you can get hogs from a pen?"

Teeg shot Kol a puzzled look. "What?"

"It's the chase that makes it interesting."

Teeg snorted. "Ye don't know what a woman's good for. It's not chasin'. Besides, why her? Ye can't like the look of her piss eye teeth." He took another swig.

"The black teeth are just one of her ploys," said Kol. "She's full of tricks. Did you know the piss eyes call her Weasel?"

Teeg laughed. "She's weasely, all right."

"Clever," said Kol. "And daring for a woman. Worthy quarry."

"Worthy? Are you daft, man? Just hold her down and poke her."

"She's the type that pokes you back . . . and with something sharper than a prick."

"Then why'd ye give her a dagger?"

"A boar needs tusks," said Kol with an enigmatic smile.

Teeg rolled his eyes. The two men regarded each other, each contemplating how different they were.

Kol took a swallow from the bottle. "I want to tame her, not just tup her," he said.

"And what will ye do with her once she's tamed?"

"Then you can have her," said Kol. "It's the hunt I enjoy."

Nineteen

By the third week of the march, the Urkheit Mountains filled the horizon. One peak rose behind another without any apparent end, marking the northern boundary of the kingdom. The ground over which Dar traveled was no longer flat, but rolled gently in anticipation of bounding upward. The land was less dry, and trees often grew between the fields.

The mountains appeared closer than they actually were. The Turgen Bridge, which lay south of their foothills, was still three days away. The far side of the bridge marked the end of the first leg of the march. The regiment would reassemble there, then merge with the rest of the king's army. When it resumed marching, it would be into hostile territory.

The nearness of the staging point brought a change among the soldiers that was gradual yet as marked as the change in the scenery. The men developed an edginess that mixed eagerness and apprehension. The approaching hostilities also affected the orcs. Though Dar still avoided them, it was impossible not to notice how quiet they had become.

Near day's end, the shieldron halted at a deserted farmstead. The soldiers rummaged through empty buildings that had been picked clean, either by fleeing peasants or by other soldiers. As Dar went to groom and feed Thunder, she anticipated meager rations that evening. At the barn, a soldier was grooming the officers' horses, but Murdant Kol's steed was absent.

"Where's Thunder?" Dar asked.

"The murdant went for a ride."

Dar left the barn to help prepare dinner. As she cooked porridge and waited for Kol's return, she wondered why he would go riding after spending all day in the saddle. Many of the murdant's actions puzzled her, but she understood him well enough to know that he did nothing by whim. The porridge was nearly ready by the time Dar heard hoofbeats and saw Kol riding toward the barn. She turned to Neena. "Will you watch over the pot? I've got to groom Thunder."

Neena took the stirring paddle from Dar. "That man sure fusses over his horse," she said. "I'd think he'd be more interested in you."

"I prefer it this way," said Dar as she headed for the barn.

Murdant Kol was still mounted when Dar arrived. He smiled. "You needn't feed Thunder tonight. I found a field of fresh spring grass. You can ride with me to it."

Dar was instantly wary. "I've never ridden a horse before."

"Then it's time you did. Climb on behind me."

Dar understood that, despite the murdant's smile, he was giving an order. Still, she hesitated to obey. Dar scrutinized Kol's face to determine his intentions, but it was bland and unreadable.

"Hurry up," Kol said. "Thunder won't graze in the dark."

Dar touched the hilt of the dagger that hung from a cord about her waist. She was unconscious of the gesture until she noticed Kol watching her hand. "Don't be nervous," he said.

Dar resolved to prove she was not. She hopped onto a box and raised her shift so she could throw a leg over Thunder's back and sit behind Murdant Kol. The saddle was too small for two, so her seat was precarious. Dar gripped the horse's flanks with her bare legs and feet and wrapped her arms around Kol's waist. Thunder's coarse coat felt rough against her skin and Kol's leather armor, sewn with metal plates, felt no better. Dar hoped it would be a short ride.

They rode out of camp at a pace that forced Dar to grip Kol tightly to keep from falling. The bouncing ride was uncomfortable, but it was also thrilling. Dar felt the horse's power and relished her connection to it. Yet she didn't let the experience distract her. Dar was careful to keep her bearings as they rode through the countryside. Thus, when they halted before an isolated cottage, she realized Kol had taken a roundabout route.

"Get off," said Kol. "Remove Thunder's bridle and let him graze. You can groom him when we get back to camp. I'm going to light a fire." Dar slid off the horse, then Kol dismounted and entered the small, thatch-roofed cottage.

While Dar unbridled Thunder, her mind raced. She suspected the moment she had long dreaded was at hand. *He calls me his woman. Tonight, he'll claim me.* The prospect roused a mixture of apprehension and anger. Yet Dar wasn't completely without hope. *Perhaps he's been truthful and only wants to protect me.* The notion ran counter to Dar's instincts, but it made entering the cottage seem less like capitulation. The only other option was fleeing. Dar touched the brand on her forehead. Its raised scar felt very prominent. *There's no refuge.*

Soon, Thunder grazed contentedly as the setting sun made the grass glow green-gold. Smoke drifted from the cottage chimney. The countryside—in contrast to Dar's inner turmoil—was calm and peaceful. Dar sighed, then steeled herself to face Murdant Kol.

The cottage smelled of herbs when Dar entered it. Some light came from an unglazed window, but the single room was mainly lit by a fireplace, where splintered furniture burned. Bundles of herbs hung from the roof beams and pegs that lined the walls. The only furnishings that remained were a straw mattress on the floor and a plank—probably from a tabletop—that was set before it. Murdant Kol sat on the mattress. Upon the plank were several hunks of cheese, a loaf of bread, sausages, dried fruit, and a dark green bottle. To Dar, it seemed a banquet.

Murdant Kol had removed his leather armor. It was the first time Dar had seen him without it. He looked less threatening in a cloth shirt. He smiled. "Why should Thunder feast while we get porridge?"

Dar's mouth watered at the sight of the food, but she remained put. Kol shook his head. "You look nervous."

"I'm not nervous," said Dar. "Just surprised. Why all this food?"

"Don't you think you deserve it? Come enjoy yourself. We'll have to return to camp soon."

Dar relaxed slightly when Kol spoke of returning to camp. She walked over to the mattress and sat down, trying to keep her distance from the murdant without being obvious. Kol handed her the bottle. "I fear I have no goblets."

"I'm not used to goblets," said Dar, lifting the bottle

for a sip. The liquid tasted of honey and warmed her throat and empty stomach. "What's this?"

"A treat," said Kol, "maybe the last for a long while. We'll be at the base camp soon. Thousands of orcs, men, and horses."

"*Thousands?*"

"Yes, it'll be chaos and short rations until the war begins."

"When will that be?"

"I'm not privy to the king's plans. Soon enough, I suppose. But not before you're sick of base camp."

Dar took another swallow from the bottle. "What's war like?"

"It's flesh meeting metal—a hard game. A man's game."

"An orc's, too?"

"Piss eyes spill blood better than most, but a game requires strategy, and they lack it. It's men that win wars."

"And the women?" said Dar. "What about them?"

"The smart ones get by. Some handsomely."

"War must be more than a game."

"All life's a game, and winning and losing are what matters." Kol gave Dar a meaningful look. "That, and whose side you're on."

Dar did not like where the conversation was headed. "Murdant Teeg said you knew the reason for this war, the one he called long-winded."

Kol smiled, but Dar couldn't tell if it was because of Teeg's remark or the transparency of her change of subject. "The tale's not too long," he said. "Old King Kregant loved peace overmuch, so when his wife's father died, he made no claim on the estate. Instead, he let the lands pass to King Feistav, who had no more right to them than he. Things changed when our present king took the throne. He renewed the claim."

"And started a war?"

"Strong men take strong measures."

That remark was on Dar's mind as she glanced about the herb-filled cottage. "This was a Wise Woman's home. Few would harm a healer. I'm surprised she fled."

Kol shrugged. "Her ill fortune isn't ours. You hungry?"

Dar grinned, already feeling the effects of Kol's brandy. "That's a silly question."

"Then it's silly not to eat. Dig in. You're not sitting at the Queen's Man's table. I'm only a lowly murdant."

"A lowly *high* murdant," said Dar. "They say even Tolum Karg's scared of you."

Murdant Kol looked pleased. "And why would he be afraid of me?"

"I don't know," said Dar. "They just say he is."

Kol reached out and stroked Dar's arm. "I hope *you're* not afraid of me."

Dar felt her hair rise. "No," she mumbled.

Kol broke off a chunk of cheese and handed it to Dar. She bit into it, savoring its flavor. The last time she had tasted cheese was at a cousin's wedding. The sausages, and even the bread, were novelties. Dar's hunger shifted her thoughts to the food, while the honeyed liquor relaxed her. As her belly filled and her head grew lighter, Dar eased her guard. She flopped back onto the cloth-covered straw. She was lying still, feeling pleasantly satiated, when Kol began touching one of her feet. She giggled. "What are you doing?"

"Seeing what size boots I should get you."

"Boots?"

"You highland girls are tough, but I doubt you walk barefoot in the snow."

Dar sat up. "I had boots at home. Shoes, too."

Kol pulled a garment from a bag and held it up. "Did you own a dress as fine as this?"

Dar gazed with wonder at the elegant blue-gray dress. She wiped her hand on her tattered shift before fingering its fabric. It was soft and finely woven. "I've had only homespun."

"It's yours."

Dar regarded Murdant Kol. The drink had loosened his self-control and his eyes betrayed a mixture of lust and triumph. "Try it on," he said.

A note of command in Kol's voice brought back Dar's apprehension. "I'd have to undress."

"So? I've seen women's bodies."

"You haven't seen mine."

"It's time I did."

Kol's smug tone rekindled Dar's resentment. She rose slowly, attempting to appear calm. "I don't want your dress."

Kol rose also. "Suit yourself. It won't change anything. You're still mine." His hand shot out and grabbed the neck of Dar's shift. With one downward pull, he tore apart its stitches and ripped it further. For an instant, Dar teetered between terror and rage. Then rage won.

Instead of covering her breasts, Dar reached for her dagger. Kol had apparently anticipated the move, for he seized her wrist as the weapon cleared its sheath. After a brief struggle, he twisted the dagger from Dar's hand and threw it into the fire. He still gripped Dar's wrist, and the two glared at each other. Kol answered Dar's fury with cool menace. "You'll regret that," he said.

The murdant grabbed the torn edges of Dar's shift to finish ripping it off. As he tugged at the fabric, she swung a knee into his groin. Kol gasped and let go. He stood still momentarily, and Dar landed a second and more forceful blow in the same place. This time, the murdant doubled over, and Dar dashed into the evening. She grabbed Thunder's bridle and tossed it onto the cottage's roof. Then she found a stone and threw it hard against Thunder's hindquarters. The horse reared up and galloped off. Dar sprinted in the other direction, stopping only when she reached the cover of a line of trees.

Twenty

♛

Dar hid in the undergrowth and watched the cottage. As her fury abated, she considered her next move. Her reaction to Kol's assault had been instinctive, but she knew only calculated actions would get her through the night. At the moment, she needed to size up her adversary.

Dar thought Murdant Kol would burst from the cottage enraged and shouting curses. Instead, he took his time coming out. When he did, he was silent, and Dar found that more chilling than shouting. Kol had donned his armor, and he carried a burning brand as a torch. Kol was too distant for Dar to see his expression, but he appeared to have mastered his emotions. He lit the thatch to set the roof ablaze, then methodically examined the ground by the fire's light. He cursed softly when he saw the bridle was gone. He gazed in the direction that Thunder had galloped, called his horse's name, and listened. After a spell of silence, he turned toward the trees.

"Dar!" he shouted. "Can you hear me?"

Dar didn't answer.

"Come out, and I'll forgive you. I like a spirited woman, but not a stubborn one." He waited before he spoke again. "There's no use fleeing. Peasants will kill you for the bounty." He paused. "They'll do it with stones and hoes." He paused again and waited for a reply. He received none. "This is your last chance. Think hard. How will you fare without my protection? The men haven't changed. They'll be worse for the waiting."

Recalling how a soldier had nearly cut off her nose, Dar was momentarily tempted to emerge from hiding. *Isn't the demon I know better than the one I don't?* She answered her question with another. *After Kol tups me, will he still protect me?* She realized that Kol had been playing with her and this evening marked the game's conclusion. *He abandoned Loral. Why would I fare better?* Dar surmised that any surrender would be the first in a chain of surrenders—a chain that only death would break. She decided to stay put.

Murdant Kol stood still awhile, illuminated by the burning cottage. Finally, he walked in the direction that Thunder had galloped. Dar was safe, but only briefly.

Dar moved among the trees, which marked the boundary between two fields with a line that snaked toward camp. Dar used their cover until she could see the farmstead in the distance. The officers and soldiers had taken over the buildings, but the women slept in their tent. The orcs' shelters stood a little way apart.

Dar scanned the open ground. There was no sign of Murdant Kol. *With luck, he's still looking for Thunder. I can go to the women's tent and change into my spare shift.* Yet Dar was paralyzed by a single question—*then what?* It had nagged her throughout her flight. She imagined various fearful scenarios. Murdant Kol could flog her for drawing a dagger. He might simply rape her. He could loose the men upon her. Only one outcome seemed impossible—that he would forgive her and let her be. Dar knew that whatever peace she had enjoyed was due to Murdant Kol. He had played the part of a powerful friend. *Now he's a powerful enemy.*

Every time Dar considered her quandary, it boiled down to facing Murdant Kol. She realized that he had many advantages—authority, strength, skill in arms, and men to do his bidding. All she had were her wits. Dar was certain that she would need more than wits to overcome Kol. As she pondered this, her gaze fixed on the orcs' encampment and a thought came to her. *To oppose a powerful enemy, you need a powerful friend.* There was no question that Kovok-mah was powerful. *But could he ever be my friend?* It seemed unlikely. Dar considered further and became convinced it was her only hope, however slim. Dar scanned the landscape one more time, then sprinted toward the orc encampment.

The ache in Kol's groin made it painful to walk, but he kept his gait natural through force of will. He thought Dar might be watching him, so it was important to betray no weakness. As he walked, he called out Thunder's name, keeping any urgency from his voice. Upon hearing a faint whinny from a dark hillside, he moved in its direction.

As the murdant searched for his horse, he pondered how he might turn the situation to his advantage. Kol knew Dar was daring, and he assumed she was too smart to run away. That meant she would probably return to camp. If he was right, she must be silenced, but in a way that gave no impression that she had thwarted him. Slowly, he pieced together a scheme. He would return to camp acting sated. Then, as an act of largesse, he would "share" Dar with the men. He could easily delay tomorrow's march to ensure that every man would have his turn. Dar's resistance would only enhance his reputation. Once the soldiers were finished, he would kill her. His men would have some fun, and they would never learn the true story. Kol smiled, despite his pain. By late tomorrow morning, his problem would be solved.

The orcs' sentry bounded over and seized Dar as soon as she entered the circle of sticks. He pressed her against his chest with one arm as he raised his sword toward her throat. Dar was squeezed so tightly she barely had the breath to shout, "Gat!" *Stop!*

Hearing his language made the orc hesitate. Dar shouted, "Mer sav Kovok-mah!" *I see Kovok-mah!* It was the closest she could come to making a request in Orcish. The sentry answered, but she couldn't understand him. Dar repeated, "Mer sav Kovok-mah."

The orc lowered his sword and gripped Dar's arm. "Sutat," he said.

Dar understood that word. It meant "come." The orc led her to one of the shelters and spoke to the orc inside. The reeds parted, and Dar saw a glint of green-gold in the dark interior. "Dargu? What are you doing here?"

"I need to speak with you."

Kovok-mah said something to the sentry, who left. Then he pushed some items aside, clearing a small space before him. "Sit," he said.

Clutching her torn shift against her chest, Dar knelt in the space. "Shashav, Kovok-mah." *Thanks, Kovok-mah.*

"I smell fear."

"Hai. A man almost raped me."

"What means 'raped'?" asked Kovok-mah.

"When min and muth do what changes muth into muthuri. What is word?"

"I do not understand."

"Min . . . muth . . . together," said Dar, using her hands to mimic lovemaking. "Make baby. What is word?"

"Thrim. We say 'Min thrimak muth.' "

"Washavoki tried to thrimak me against my will."

"Against your will? How is that possible?" asked Kovok-mah.

"Men are strong," said Dar. "They use force."

"But that would offend Muth la!"

"Men don't care about Muth la."

"Does this offend your Karm?"

"Hai."

"Yet, washavokis do this thing?"

"All the time," said Dar. Even in the darkness, she could see Kovok-mah's eyes had grown wide. It seemed bizarre that rape would shock him so.

"This happened to you?"

"Not tonight. I fought him. Now he is angry."

"Who is this washavoki?"

"Murdant Kol," said Dar. "He rides horse."

"Bah Simi?"

Dar mentally translated. *Eye Blue*. "Hai, he's the one."

"What will he do now?" asked Kovok-mah.

"He may try again. He may have others do it. He may hurt or kill me. I don't know."

"I have seen you with Bah Simi many times. You did not seem afraid."

"He said I was his woman. He protected me from other men, but only because he wanted me for himself. Tonight he . . ." Dar stopped as she heard hoofbeats. She peered into the darkness and saw the shadowy form of Murdant Kol on Thunder. Lowering her voice to a whisper, she said, "He's back."

Kovok-mah's eyes easily penetrated the darkness. He watched the murdant dismount, walk over to the cloth hut where the woe mans slept, and peer inside before leading his horse into the barn. He noted that Kol walked as though injured. The orc had difficulty reading the washavoki's expression, but his abrupt gestures betrayed anger. While Kovok-mah made the observations, Dar's scent grew stronger as the sour smell of fear mingled with pungent anger. When Kol disappeared into the barn, she whispered, "Can I stay here tonight?"

Kovok-mah was ambivalent. He didn't relish the idea of a washavoki inside his shelter. Her odor would linger long after her departure. Moreover, washavokis were strange and cruel. *Zna-yat is right*, he told himself. *I should avoid them.* Yet, though Kovok-mah wished to believe that Dar's fate wasn't his concern, he was unsure Muth la would agree. *If Muth la is honored when Dargu serves food, would Muth la be dishonored by Dargu's rape?* Kovok-mah regarded Dar as she silently waited for his answer. She seemed both fierce and afraid. *I called her mother*, he thought. Then he knew what his answer must be.

Twenty-one

At first, the touch was part of Dar's nightmare. Then Dar woke and realized the hand on her shoulder wasn't Kol's. She lay curled on the floor of Kovok-mah's shelter, so close to the sitting orc that his knees pressed against her back. Kovok-mah shook her harder. The nightmare faded, but not its sense of dread. "You must go," he said.

Dar peered outside and saw dawn was approaching. Her dread intensified. "Can't I stay?"

"Thwa. You leave now."

Dar wondered if Kovok-mah knew he was sealing her doom. *He probably does*, she thought. *He just doesn't care*. Dar considered—then quickly dismissed—begging for his protection. *I won't debase myself*. With that resolution, her last hope evaporated. She looked outside again. Everything was still.

"Vata," Dar said, hoping Kovok-mah understood the finality of her good-bye.

Clutching her torn shift to cover herself, Dar hurried to the women's tent. She hoped to change into her other shift and, perhaps, find a weapon before the men came. Taren sat up when she entered. "So, you're back," she said. She eyed Dar's torn garment. "Was it bad?"

"Worse than you can imagine," said Dar as she rapidly changed. "Where are the knives?"

"Why do you want a knife?"

"I just need one."

"They're on the wagon," said Taren.

Teeg's wagon, thought Dar. Her heart sank further. *I'll only have a stick of firewood or a ladle to defend myself*. Dar left the tent to avoid further questions. The kettle of cold porridge sat near the ashes of last night's fire. The serving ladle hung from its edge. Dar hefted it. The utensil felt light in her hand, but all the firewood had been burned. *I guess this is my weapon*. She dipped it in the cold mush to take her last meal.

Dar was still eating when Taren emerged from the tent. "Dar, what happened last night?"

Dar swallowed. "Murdant Kol finally made his move. He . . ." The sight of men leaving the barn made her stop. Usually, the soldiers straggled in to eat, bleary and grumpy. This morning, they swaggered from their sleeping quarters as a small mob and moved as purposefully. Dar noted none carried a wooden bowl. As she watched them advance, the urge to run became nearly irresistible. Dar stayed put only by summoning all her courage.

The soldiers halted a few steps from the kettle. By the time they did, Kari and Neena were also watching them, aware that something was about to happen. The men eyed Dar as a pack, united by belligerence and lust. Yet, as individuals, they hesitated to step forward. Dar could only guess what Murdant Kol had told them, but the result of his words was evident—she was for the taking. It was only a question of who would be the first.

After a tense moment, Muut decided it would be him. He advanced, grinning. "I've wanted a taste of this for a while," he said. He lunged at Dar and she swung the ladle, hitting his jaw. Dar heard a soldier laugh. Then Muut punched her in the chest. Dar's breath whooshed, and she was unable to take another. She doubled over, dropping the ladle.

Muut grabbed her arm and jerked. "To the barn, bitch."

Dar was able to gasp a bit of air as Muut began to drag her away. The other soldiers followed. Now that the first move had been made, each was eager for his turn.

Dar was halfway to the barn when Muut suddenly released her. Confused, Dar glanced about and saw that Kovok-mah stood where Muut had been. He was fully armed, and he held Muut by the neck, dangling him above the ground at arm's length. The orc ignored the man kicking and thrashing within his grasp and slowly regarded the other soldiers. "This is my woe man!" he bellowed.

Kovok-mah tightened his fingers around Muut's neck. There was a crunch of gristle. Then he casually tossed the man aside. The soldiers drew back, silent and cowed. The only sound came from Muut, who gurgled and gasped as if drowning. As everyone watched, his face turned bluish gray.

"Touch my woe man, and I kill you," said Kovok-mah. Then he turned and strode away.

The soldiers remained still, but Neena shrieked and ran toward Muut. She knelt beside him, caressed his face, and began to sob. Her actions broke the mob's inertia, and the soldiers gathered around their fallen comrade. By then, Muut lay still. A soldier examined him. "He's dead," he said, regarding Dar with revulsion. "Yer lover killed him."

"My *lover*?" said Dar.

"He called you his woman," said the soldier.

Neena glared at Dar, her grief mingled with repugnance. "How *could* you?" she said. "An *orc*! What kind of monster are you?"

Dar was too stunned to protest. She glanced at Taren and Kari and saw the same loathing in their faces.

"It's her black teeth," said a man. "Piss eyes fancy them."

"Well, they can have the unnatural bitch," said another.

The men embraced the idea that avoiding Dar showed contempt for her rather than fear of the orc, and their self-respect returned as fright became disdain. "Taren," said a soldier, "we won't have that one servin' us."

"Aye," chimed in several others.

Teeg appeared with a shovel, which he tossed at Dar's feet. "Ye can dig Muut's grave, bein' yer the one that got him killed." When Dar simply stared at the shovel, he added, "Hop to it, or ye'll feel the lash."

Dar took up the shovel and dug where the earth looked soft. As she dug, she felt both relieved and humiliated by Kovok-mah's intervention. By calling her "his woman," he had simultaneously saved and degraded her. Dar was appalled by how readily everyone believed the worst, no matter how far-fetched.

Kovok-mah stood at the edge of the sacred circle watching the washavokis. Their actions perplexed him. The washavokis were eating, ignoring the dead one. Kovok-mah wondered why there were no prayers or rites. Dargu stood alone, digging a hole in Muth la's breast. She didn't appear happy. Already, he wondered if he had acted wisely.

Zna-yat approached. "Mother's brother's son, you stink of washavoki."

"Hai. Strange things have happened."

"I know exactly what has happened," said Zna-yat. "You've become fool." When Kovok-mah tensed and exposed his fangs, Zna-yat's eyes narrowed. "Don't challenge me. I won't bend my neck this time."

Kovok-mah returned Zna-yat's stare. "Then you want to fight?"

"You are my kin and still strong in my chest. I'd rather speak wisdom instead."

"What is this wisdom?"

"Dargu has evil magic."

"I think not."

"Your chest has grown small," said Zna-yat. "This is Dargu's doing. It has learned our words so it can cast spells on you."

"You speak foolishness," said Kovok-mah.

"How else could it have slept in your shelter?"

"I allowed it for Muth la's sake."

Zna-yat gave a derisive hiss. "Muth la? How can sons speak for Muth la?"

"When we lack mothers to guide us, we must think for ourselves."

"Then you've thought poorly."

"I followed my chest," said Kovok-mah. "It told me I should protect Dargu from evil washavokis."

"Dargu is washavoki," said Zna-yat, "so it is evil, also. For your sake, I'll kill it."

"Don't!"

"Has your chest grown so small that you would spare washavokis?"

"I would spare this one."

"If you persist in this folly, others will not follow you. They'll meet and choose another. You'll lose your cape."

"If I lose it," said Kovok-mah, "killing Dargu will not get it back."

Zna-yat studied his cousin's face. At last he said, "I won't kill it . . . not yet."

As Teeg approached Murdant Kol, he could discern no emotion in his face. Kol merely stood in his rigid manner, watching Dar dig the grave from a distance. Teeg couldn't resist saying, "I'm glad to see she's not spoilin' her new dress." Kol's face darkened, alerting Teeg to watch his tongue.

"I burned that dress," said Kol.

"So, ye got yer fill without it," said Teeg, suspecting Kol had not.

Kol grunted.

"That piss eye was a surprise," said Teeg as casually as he could. "One of her tricks, I suppose."

"Yes," said Kol, his face growing even darker.

"I'm not fond of tricks, myself," said Teeg. "Weasels, either." He made a show of drawing his dagger. "It's best to get rid of vermin."

"Piss eyes don't bluff," said Murdant Kol. "He'll slay the man that touches her."

"He doesn't have to know who did it."

"Then he'd probably kill everyone to be sure. Piss eyes don't do things in half measures."

"There's only one of him," said Teeg.

"The men can't stand against a piss eye," said Kol. "That sorry lot only uses weapons for brawling or scaring peasants."

Teeg wondered how he'd fare against an orc and decided he would rather not find out. "So we leave her be?"

"There's no reason for that," said Kol.

"Still, we let her live?"

"For the time being," replied Kol. "Soon, we'll be at war, and anything can happen."

Teeg caught Kol's drift and showed his jagged teeth. "Aye, war's full of opportunity."

It was difficult to use a shovel barefoot, and Muut's grave was still shallow when the men had finished breakfast. Dar was still at work when Murdant Kol approached. As soon as she spotted him, she changed her grip on the shovel so she could swing it if necessary. The movement wasn't lost on Kol, who halted outside the shovel's reach. "That's deep enough," he said. "Dump him in and cover him."

"All right," said Dar, not taking her eyes from Kol.

"Afterward, give Thunder a good grooming before you saddle him. You neglected him last night."

"Last night . . ."

"Didn't change your duties," said Murdant Kol. "Neither did tupping that piss eye."

Dar's face reddened. "I never did that!"

"You're not fooling anyone," said Kol, pleased his words had the desired effect. "We all have eyes and ears. Now get to work."

Kol turned on his heel and strode to where the women were loading a wagon. Dar briefly watched him stop and talk with them. Then she dropped the shovel and walked over to Muut's corpse. It had lain untouched as the camp went about its business. *No one but Neena seems to care*, Dar thought. She glanced up and saw Neena was still talking to Murdant Kol. She dreaded to think what they were discussing.

When Dar dragged Muut to his grave, she spied his dagger. After depositing him in the hole and ensuring no one was watching, Dar used the dagger to cut its scabbard from Muut's belt. She quickly lifted her shift and tucked the weapon in the waist cord of her undergarment. Then she piled dirt on Muut's body.

The soldiers waited until Dar was grooming Thunder before they approached Muut's resting place. One emptied a bottle on it "to give him one last drink." The rest made remarks of feeble jocularity. Only Neena wept.

Twenty-two

♛

When the shieldron belatedly began its march, Dar tried to take her place among the women. Taren barred her way. "Go to your orc. We don't want your kind."

"What kind is that?" asked Dar.

"There's no word for it," said Taren. "None foul enough."

"Just what do you think happened last night?" asked Dar.

"We know what you did," said Taren, "and we're disgusted."

"Who told you? Murdant Kol?"

Taren nodded.

"And you believe *him*?"

"Look," said Taren, "you told me yourself you don't like men. And all of us heard what the orc said before it killed poor Muut."

"*Poor Muut*? How can you take his side? You know what he was going to do."

"He wasn't perfect, but he was kind to Neena. *And* he was human. More human, it seems, than you."

Dar nearly burst into tears, but she refused to give anyone the satisfaction, especially Neena, who was staring at her with undiluted enmity. Dar saw the futility of further argument; the women had sided with their oppressors. She felt as she had on her first day in the regiment—surrounded by others, yet utterly alone. As Dar turned her back on the women, she reminded herself that she had Kovok-mah. *Just like Cymbe had her bear.*

The tale of Cymbe and the Bear was familiar to every highland child. Dar's father had told it often. Cymbe was a little girl who, like Dar, lived in a small hut with her parents. She wasn't happy, for she had to work hard and every meal was porridge. Then, one day, a bear urged her to join him in the forest. "In the woods, you'll never toil," he said. "I know the trees in which bees hide their honey and the slopes where the berries ripen first. Every day, I'll catch fish or hares or a deer, and every night we'll feast."

Cymbe gladly ran off with the bear, and they lived an easy life together. The girl grew fat. Her hair lengthened and tangled until it covered her body, and she looked like a bear. After a while, Cymbe thought she was one. Yet, when summer ended, the bees went to sleep, the berries shriveled, and the fish and game fled. Then the bear spoke to Cymbe. "Hard times are ahead, so I'll sleep through the winter."

"What about me?" asked Cymbe. "I still must eat."

"I've fed you all summer," replied the bear, smacking his lips. "Now it's your turn to feed me."

Dar's father always laughed at the end of the story. The moral of the tale varied according to his need. Cymbe was invoked when Dar or her brothers grew tired of porridge. "Remember Cymbe" might answer a complaint about chores, warn of a stranger's approach, or rebuke discontent. Yet, even as a child, Dar devised her own moral—Cymbe's fatal error wasn't wishing for a better life, but misunderstanding bears. *Do I understand orcs any better?*

While Dar pondered that question, the shieldron

snaked out onto the road. The officers and Murdant Kol led the way on horseback, followed by the two wagons, the foot soldiers, the women, and finally the orcs. Dar saw no place for her in that procession, though she knew she must join it. She fell in behind the column of orcs, who hid her from the sight of the others.

The day was hot and Dar was thirsty when the march halted for a brief rest. The orcs carried their own water, but the soldiers and the women drank from a water barrel at the end of one of the wagons. Dar headed for it to quench her thirst. The soldiers always drank first. As Dar waited for her turn to use the common ladle, she became conscious that she was both the center of attention, yet pointedly ignored. Dar waited until everyone had drunk, then approached the barrel. A burly soldier brushed past her, knocking her aside to seize the ladle. "Don't want *her* lips where mine go."

"No telling where they've been," said another.

"Think about it," said Neena. "Can't you guess?"

Neena's question prompted speculation that grew ever filthier. Dar tried to ignore it as she cupped her hands and hurriedly drank. When she finished, she looked up and saw the soldiers had surrounded her. They seemed like dogs around a viper, filled with loathing and fear. Dar was uncertain which made them more dangerous. Rather than try to push her way through the men, she darted beneath the wagon and emerged out of their reach. As she retreated, she heard Neena laugh. "Did you see the whore blush? One of you men guessed right."

Dar headed for her refuge at the end of the column. As she passed the orcs, she sensed a change in them also. Dar had grown familiar enough with orc facial expressions that she could detect their resentment. It seemed directed toward her. *Why would they be angry with me?* wondered Dar, alarmed by the prospect. She glanced about for Kovok-mah. When she caught his eye, he looked away.

When the march resumed, Dar trudged behind the orcs, brooding that—like Cymbe—ignorance would be her undoing. Kovok-mah's actions had altered her life, and she needed to understand them. Dar picked up her pace until she strode beside Kovok-mah. "Pahav ta mer," she said. *Speak with me.*

Kovok-mah replied in Dar's language. "There is nothing to say."

Dar continued to walk beside Kovok-mah. Glancing about, she became aware that the other orcs were watching them. It occurred to her that Kovok-mah's deed might have caused him problems with the others, making his position a delicate one. If that was true, she would have to proceed with care. She needed to get Kovok-mah to speak with her, but he must not lose face by doing so.

In time, an idea came to Dar. She exposed her teeth and puffed up her chest in a comic imitation of an orc challenge. "Dargu is very fierce," said Dar in Orcish. Then she roared with a warbling, high-pitched cry that parodied the deep, thunderous sound made by an orc. Kovok-mah's initial surprise turned to amusement.

Dar roared again. "Talk to fierce Dargu."

Kovok-mah dissolved into laughter, slowing his pace as he did. Dar halted and bent her neck in the orcish sign of submission. Kovok-mah stopped walking also. The marching orcs flowed around the pair. Dar noted that a few were laughing and more were smiling.

Kovok-mah continued to stand still, as if he were laughing too hard to walk. He waited until there was a long gap between him and the other orcs before he resumed walking. By then, he regarded Dar with an expression that was more curious than amused. "What do you wish to say?" he asked.

Dar was suddenly at a loss for words. She felt as if she were balanced on a mountain peak where a step in any direction would send her sliding downward. Dar hesitated, knowing she must take that step and it was likely to determine the course of her life. She grew nervous and all she uttered was "Why?"

"Why what?" asked Kovok-mah.

"Why did you do it? Why did you call me your woman? What did it mean?"

"I protect you."

"Why? I'm washavoki."

"Ther nav muth." *You are mother.*

"Muth. Woman. What difference does that make? Why did you save me?"

Kovok-mah was slow to answer. When he did, he seemed to be groping for words. "Muth la is everywhere . . . yet . . . she is far away. Her voice is hard to hear. Even harder to understand. Muth la is first mother. She speaks through mothers. Sons have little wisdom, but we, too, try to hear Muth la's voice. I think . . . I think she says to me—protect this washavoki mother."

Dar said nothing. After a while, Kovok-mah asked, "Why do your eyes make your face wet?"

"All my life, I . . . I've been treated . . . treated like . . ." Dar wiped away her tears. "I'm only a woman. You talk like I'm worth saving."

"I do not understand you."

"Washavokis think women are worth little, that they are ruled by men."

"Then they lack wisdom," said Kovok-mah.

"They think you rule me now."

"Why would they think that?"

"Because you said I was your woman."

"I thought it meant I protect you," said Kovok-mah.

"It means more than that," said Dar.

Kovok-mah was puzzled to note that Dar's face had assumed a reddish hue. "What else does it mean?"

"Washavokis think that . . . that you and I . . ." She switched to Orcish to distance herself from the idea the words expressed. "Tha tep Mer da-thrimak." *You and I tupped.*

Kovok-mah's eyes grew wide. "Da-thrimak! They believe this?"

"They do, and they are angry with me."

"You must tell them it is not so."

"They will not believe me. Bah Simi has told them lies," said Dar, using the orcs' name for Murdant Kol.

"Why?"

"He wants to hurt me," said Dar. "You can hurt someone without touching them. I'm outcast now."

"What is outcast?"

"I have no place among my kind."

Kovok-mah didn't reply, and after a while, his silence disquieted Dar. She suspected that he was like someone who rescues a stray dog on impulse, then finds it a nuisance. *How worthy does he think I am?* Dar wondered. *I'm still a washavoki.*

At last, Kovok-mah made a sound that Dar thought was a sigh. "Where will you sleep?"

"I'll find someplace," said Dar.

"You could sleep in my shelter," said Kovok-mah.

"But my scent . . ."

"I will grow used to it."

Twenty-three

♛

For the rest of the day's march, Dar left her spot behind the orcs only when thirst drove her to the water barrel. Each time, she felt apart from those who drank there. Through practice, they perfected their techniques of exclusion. Dar gave up trying to use the ladle. Conversation was impossible. The air of scorn was palpable. Though no one threatened Dar, she felt menaced.

Every time Dar retreated, she found Kovok-mah waiting for her. She was unsure why, for he had grown taciturn and his thoughts seemed elsewhere. At first, Kovok-mah's quiet mood mirrored her own. The day's events had thrown her off balance, and she wanted to mull them over. Yet, by afternoon, Kovok-mah's silence began to make Dar uncomfortable. *I know nothing about him, and he might be my sole companion.*

"Where's your home?" asked Dar after she returned from another chilly visit to the water barrel.

Kovok-mah fixed his gaze on the mountains. "My mother's hall lies there."

"In the Urkheit Mountains?"

"That is their washavoki name. We call them Blath Urkmuthi."

Dar translated. "Cloak of mothers?"

"Hai. They sheltered mothers when we fled washavokis."

Dar had a hard time imagining orcs fleeing anyone. "Why would urkzimmuthi flee?"

"Have you not seen ants overpower larger creatures?" asked Kovok-mah. "There is strength in numbers."

"Do you mean washavokis took your land?"

"Hai. Long ago."

"I'm sorry," said Dar.

"Why? You did not take it."

"I'm sorry my kind did. Mer nav nervler." *I am sad.*

"Hai, Ma snaf." *Yes, I also.*

"Does your father's hall also lie in Blath Urkmuthi?" asked Dar, wishing to turn the conversation from human wrongs.

"Fathers have no halls," said Kovok-mah. "They move to hall of muthvashi."

"Muthvashi? What's that?"

"When muth and min live together and have children, what is that called?"

"Married?"

"I think so," said Kovok-mah. "Muth chooses her married."

"I think you mean her 'husband.'"

Kovok-mah looked confused. "These are words I have not learned."

"When man and woman—min tep muth—get married," said Dar, "muth is called 'wife' and min is called 'husband.'" Dar suddenly looked puzzled. "Do you mean muth *chooses* their husband?"

"Hai, but she must ask his muthuri first."

After a long and sometimes confusing conversation, Dar pieced together a picture of orc family life. In Kovok-mah's society, not only did the females choose their spouses, they had the higher standing. All the females in a hall were related—the daughters, granddaughters, and great-granddaughters of the clan's ruling mothers. A husband lived in his wife's hall and all his children belonged to her clan. His daughters would spend their entire lives in the same hall, their status increasing as they aged.

Females not only owned and ruled the clan halls; the surrounding land and the food it produced was theirs. They guided the males, who served as providers, protectors, and artisans. Dar tried to envision a life where men considered her wise and deferred to her authority, but it seemed too far-fetched. Yet Kovok-mah spoke as though this was the natural order of things, ordained at the world's creation.

Though such a life was beyond her imagining, it gave Dar an insight into why Kovok-mah had saved her. *Perhaps he felt obligated.* Dar suspected not many orcs would have done the same, for she saw few signs they believed human women deserved the same respect as their own females. *I doubt Kovok-mah fully believes it himself.* Dar recalled the slaying of the peasant women in the courtyard. *Those killings didn't seem to bother him. Why does he see me differently?*

After she and Kovok-mah ceased talking, Dar continued to ponder that question. She reasoned that it must have had something to do with their first meeting, for he spoke to her the next time they met. *He never spoke to women before*, thought Dar. *Memni said so.* Dar tried to remember their first encounter. *I cried. He made me bathe. I got mad at him.* She recalled that when she had glared at Kovok-mah, he had smiled and said Weasel was a good name for her. *I didn't under-*

stand what he said at the time. He must have been speaking to himself.

It occurred to Dar that by showing irritation, she hadn't behaved like a human. *The women here are fearful*, thought Dar. *A muth would be the opposite. Fearlessness must be the key.* However, Dar felt far from fearless. Orcs still frightened her. More than once, they had almost killed her. Even Kovok-mah made her nervous at times. Nevertheless, she reasoned that security lay in boldness and the more intrepid she acted, the safer she would be.

The shieldron camped early. Though Dar continued to receive the silent treatment, she had no illusions that it excused her from work. She was convinced that Murdant Kol would be watching her closely, hoping to find a reason to discipline her. Thus, the first thing she did when the march halted was go to tend Thunder. Both the horse and its master were nowhere to be found.

Dar went to the cooking area. "Get wood" was all Taren said.

When Dar searched for firewood, she discovered the land had been stripped as if plundered by the enemy. *To a peasant, every soldier is an enemy.* Mindful of that, she took Muut's dagger from under her shift and attached it to the cord about her waist. Thus armed, she collected what wood she could find. It took a while before Dar gathered an armload and returned to camp. When she dumped it down, Taren uttered, "More."

The sun was low when Dar returned with a second load and noted that Thunder was with the other horses. When she approached the fire, Dar spotted Teeg standing there. *Trouble*, she thought. Soldiers clustered nearby. Someone was crying. Dar didn't recognize her voice. When Dar drew closer, she spied a branding iron heating in the fire. Her heart sank. Dar glanced at the soldiers and saw they held a weeping, dark-haired girl. Thin and tiny, she was still a child.

Teeg seemed pleased by Dar's dismay. As he lifted the glowing brand from the fire, Dar realized he had been waiting for her arrival. She threw down the wood and fled to take care of Thunder. Before Dar reached the horse, she heard the girl scream.

Dar wasn't surprised to find Murdant Kol waiting. "Why did you take that child?"

Kol regarded her coolly. "She's here because of you. It's your fault."

"I don't know what you mean."

"You're so worthless, we had to find another woman."

"Woman? She's no woman."

"We'll use her like one," said Kol. "You brought this on her."

"You can't be serious!"

"I'm always serious," said Kol. "She'll curse you for the rest of her life."

"Why? Why are you doing this?"

"You seem upset," said Kol with mock solicitude. Then his expression hardened. "Didn't you know there'd be consequences?"

Dar bit her lip, recalling her first violation. "Look, I'll . . . I'll give you what you want. Just leave the girl alone."

"And what do you think I want?" asked Kol. "Just what are you offering?"

Dar averted her eyes. "I'll tup with you."

"You're soiled goods. I'm not interested."

"You'd rather abuse that girl? Why? To punish me?"

"You seem to think I care about your feelings," said Kol. "You'll learn how wrong you are when you see that girl tomorrow."

"This is crazy! Why should she suffer?"

Kol didn't bother to answer. He simply turned and walked away.

Dar reached for her dagger, but halted. *Even if I could kill him, it wouldn't help that girl.* She began grooming Thunder, thinking it was ironic that Kol trusted her with his horse when a quick cut with her dagger would cripple the steed. Yet Kol apparently understood that Dar couldn't take revenge upon an innocent animal, just as Dar knew that Kol would show no such scruples. The girl was doomed, and Dar felt responsible. As she worked, Dar wondered if there was some way to prevent what seemed inevitable.

After Thunder was groomed and fed, Dar headed for the cooking area with a heavy heart. The girl was sitting on the ground. She clasped her bony knees close to her chest as she whimpered softly. Ragged and barefoot, she reminded Dar of herself as a child. The king's mark was an ugly burn on her forehead and Dar didn't know if the girl cried from pain, terror, or both.

Ignoring the other women, Dar squatted beside the child and gently touched her shoulder. "Hello," she said. "My name's Dar. What's yours?"

"Twea" was the whispered reply.

"I know this is the worst day of your life."

Twea nodded.

"I can help you, but you must do exactly as I say."

"Leave the girl alone," said Taren.

Dar rose. "No."

Taren strode over. "I'm in charge here!"

"I know what the men have planned," said Dar. "I won't let it happen."

"You've caused enough trouble today," said Taren.

Dar placed a hand on her dagger's hilt. "Don't try to stop me. Twea must serve the orcs tonight."

"Why?" said Taren. "She's suffered enough already."

Dar whispered to Taren. "I'm certain she's a virgin, and I intend to keep her one."

Neena strode over. "Are you going to trust that perverted bitch?"

Taren glanced at Twea, who was watching them with wide-eyed terror, and lowered her voice. "What makes you think the men will abuse her?"

"Kol bragged about it. He'll do it just to torment me."

"Taren," said Neena, "don't listen to her lies."

Taren studied Dar's face, then glanced again at Twea. "How can you protect her?"

"I can't," said Dar, "but the orcs can."

"Don't you see what she's doing?" said Neena. "She wants to give the girl to them."

"Shut up, Neena," said Taren. She turned to whisper to Dar, "That girl's already terrified. How can she face orcs?"

"She has to," said Dar. "Otherwise she'll face something worse. I know what I'm talking about."

Taren eyed Dar suspiciously as she made up her mind. "All right," she said at last, "I'll agree for the girl's sake. Get her ready. I'll let you know when it's time to serve."

"Thanks," said Dar.

As Dar walked toward Twea, Neena grabbed her

arm. “You may fool Taren, but you’re not fooling me.” She recognized the dagger hanging at Dar’s waist and her eyes narrowed. “I know where you got that, you thieving slut!”

“From someone who no longer needed it,” said Dar, “the same way you got your shoes.”

Neena glared at Dar for a moment, then spit in her face.

Dar wiped off the spittle and went over to Twea. “Come with me,” she said to the trembling girl. “You can be safe, but only if you’re brave.”

Twenty-four

When Dar washed Twea in the women's tent, the girl was either too numb to protest or she lacked an aversion to bathing. Twea's passivity worried Dar, but she assumed it was the result of the day's traumas. To spare her from reliving those events, Dar refrained from questioning the girl about her capture. Instead, she concentrated on preparing her for what lay ahead.

"Twea," said Dar. "We'll be serving orcs tonight. Have you heard of them?"

"Aye," said Twea. "Auntie says they eat people."

"Do I look eaten?"

Twea shook her head.

"Orcs are not as they seem," said Dar. "When I was little, we had a dog that was part wolf. He scared people, but that dog slept with me every night. When he was with me, I was safe. Orcs are like that dog. They look scary, but they'll keep you safe."

Twea seemed dubious. "Orcs kill people."

"So do soldiers," said Dar. "Soldiers took you away and branded you, not orcs. Orcs protect me. They'll do the same for you. Do you believe me?"

Twea's expression remained doubtful, but she nodded.

"I'm going to tell them your name is Tahwee. That's their word for bird. They call me Dargu. It means 'weasel.' "

A hint of a smile came to Twea's lips. "Weasel?"

"Weasels are clever. They can be fierce, too."

"Is that why that lady doesn't like you?"

"Yes. She thinks I'm too clever."

Dar gave Twea a serving robe to wear. It nearly reached the girl's ankles. Then Dar washed and dressed. Afterward, she taught Twea the Orcish serving phrase. The girl was still repeating it when Taren poked her head into the tent. "The porridge is ready."

Dar and Twea carried the kettle to the orcs' encampment. Once they passed the circle of upright sticks, Dar halted. "The orcs call this circle 'Muth la's Embrace,' and you're safe within it," she said. "The Mother of All watches over this ground. Soldiers won't come here."

They set the kettle before the seated orcs. After Dar said "Saf nak ur Muthz la"—*Food is Muth la's gift*—and the orcs responded, Dar addressed them in their tongue. "This little mother named Tahwee. Cruel washavokis hurt her. I say urkzimmuthi honor Muth la. I say urkzimmuthi honor mothers. Tahwee fear not urkzimmuthi."

Dar touched Twea's shoulder, signaling her to say "Tava." Some of the orcs responded to her greeting, and Dar noted which ones. After the two finished serving, Dar led Twea to Kovok-mah's shelter. "Sit here," she said, "and have some porridge."

"Aren't we going to eat with people?" asked Twea.

"You're not. You're going to stay here."

"Why?" asked Twea. Despite everything Dar had said, she looked frightened.

"This is where my friend sleeps. This is where we'll sleep, too."

"I don't want to sleep here," said Twea, beginning to rise.

Dar grabbed Twea's arm. "Then you'll end up with the soldiers. They'll do bad things and won't let you sleep at all."

Twea sat down again, though she looked miserable.

The girl had finished eating by the time Kovok-mah arrived. "Weasel has caught bird," he said. His expression contradicted his playful words, and Dar knew he was unhappy.

She replied as best she could in Orcish. "You save little mother. Washavokis have big hurt for her. She sleep here. You say she is your woe man."

"Two washavokis in my shelter?" said Kovok-mah.

"No, two mothers."

Kovok-mah regarded Dar and his lips curled back in what she thought was a rueful smile. He squatted down before Twea. "Tava, Tahwee," he said. "I am Kovok-mah."

Twea gazed in awe at the huge face before her. "Tava, Kovok-mah."

"I have magic for your pain," he said, pointing to Twea's brand. He parted the walls of his shelter and took a dried leaf from a pouch. By its large size and fuzzy texture Dar recognized it as nayimgat. "Chew this, but do not eat it," said Kovok-mah. "It will make you sleep." He broke off a piece of the leaf and gave it to Twea. She put the leaf in her mouth and made a face.

"I know it's bitter," said Dar. "I've had some myself."

Twea chewed dutifully and soon had trouble sitting upright. When she slumped backward, Kovok-mah caught her. He cradled Twea in his arms and examined the crown-shaped burn on her forehead. His expression darkened. "I smell much fear, much pain."

"Men are cruel," said Dar.

"Hai." Kovok-mah carried Twea into his shelter. "I will use magic on her burn," he said, reaching into a bag.

"I must wash the kettle," Dar said. "I'll be back." She hurried off, lugging the kettle and its carrying pole.

Murdant Kol was standing just beyond the upright sticks. There was no way to avoid him, and Dar didn't try. "Where's the girl?" Kol asked, when Dar was clear of the circle. His voice was hard.

"She's with the orcs."

"Get her."

"Twea's under their protection. If you want her, fetch her yourself."

Kol drew his sword. "You'll do as I say."

Dar stood her ground. "Do you want to trade your life for mine? I'll make that bargain. When we meet upon the Dark Path, you must tell me how it feels to be torn apart."

Kol's sword wavered before he sheathed it. "This hasn't ended." Then he turned and strode away.

Dar didn't tremble until Kol was out of sight. She dragged the kettle to the cooking area and was scraping her dinner from its sides when Taren approached. "Where's the girl?"

"Twea's safe."

"So, she's with the orcs?"

"Yes, they'll protect her. They'd probably protect us all."

Taren shook her head. "I'd rather stay here."

"It's your choice."

An uncomfortable silence followed. Dar ate the orcs' leftover porridge while Taren watched. "I keep misunderstandin' you," Taren said at last. "I should have known you'd . . . you'd never . . ."

"Tup an orc?" Dar laughed bitterly. "How could you believe that?"

"This mornin' it seemed . . . Well, anyway, I've changed my mind."

Dar sighed. "You're probably the only one who will."

"Neena's mad 'cause Muut died wantin' you. She's happy to believe Murdant Kol. And Kari's her friend."

Dar shrugged and licked her fingers. As she began to clean the kettle, Taren retreated to the women's tent. Dar finished cleaning up and walked over to a wagon to get some washuthahi seeds before she returned to Kovok-mah's shelter. There were some soldiers playing knockem nearby, and Dar sensed their eyes upon her. The men's boisterous talk died away until the only sound was the bones being shaken and tossed. Dar took the seeds and hurried off.

The opening to Kovok-mah's shelter was closed and Dar had to part the reeds herself. She found the orc sitting cross-legged. A cloak covered his lap. Twea lay upon it, her brand wet and smelling of herbs. Kovok-mah raised a clawed finger. "Tahwee Ki zusak," he whispered. *Little Bird sleeps.*

Kovok-mah woke Dar before sunrise. Orcs slept sitting upright and made no provision to soften the floors of their shelters. Dar was stiff from sleeping in a cramped position on the hard ground. "You go," said Kovok-mah. "I will bring Little Bird."

Dar went down to the cooking site and lit a small fire to take away the morning's chill. She stole a quick breakfast before Taren and Kari emerged from the tent. The two women waited in silence to serve the men. As the soldiers began to arrive, Kovok-mah marched toward them dressed in full battle gear. Twea walked beside him, her small hand in his massive one.

Kovok-mah halted and drew his broadsword. The soldiers froze. "Know that I protect this little woe man," he said. "Hurt her and die."

When Kovok-mah released Twea's hand, she remained put. Taren took the ladle from the porridge kettle and held it out. "Come, honey," she said to Twea. "Serve the men."

Twea seemed more frightened of the soldiers than of the armored orc beside her, and she left his side reluctantly. "Who wants some breakfast?" she said in a tiny voice.

A soldier, who kept a wary eye on Kovok-mah, advanced and extended his wooden bowl. "I'll take some."

Twea served all the soldiers under the watchful gaze of Kovok-mah. He stood motionless and silent throughout the meal. In his ominous presence, the men ate quickly and left rapidly. Dar had just begun to help clean up when Murdant Kol approached. "Report to the tolum," he said to her. She scrutinized Kol's face for some hint of what the tolum wanted. A look of satisfaction made her wary, and Dar's concern grew when Kol followed her into the tolum quarters.

Karg was seated behind a rude table that held the remains of his morning meal. He regarded Dar testily. "I hear you're making trouble."

"Sir?" said Dar as meekly as possible.

"A man was killed on your account," said the tolum.

"An orc did that, sir. It wasn't my fault."

"That's a lie," said Kol.

"Sir, I'm only a woman. Orcs do as they please."

"Last night she incited disobedience," said Murdant Kol.

"Disobedience by whom?" asked the tolum.

"The new girl," said Kol. "I don't know her name."

"It's Twea, sir," said Dar.

The tolum eyed her sternly. "Is the murdant's charge true?"

"Sir, when I was Murdant Kol's woman, he used to brag that he was the real commander here." Dar saw Tolum Karg's face redden, but she had no clue where his anger was directed. "He said that if Twea didn't tup him, he'd make you punish me."

"*Make* me punish you?"

"Don't listen to the bitch," said Kol.

"I'll listen to whomever I please, *Murdant*," said Tolum Karg. He returned his gaze to Dar. "Go on."

"Sir, I know you dislike whores. Orcs feel the same way. They get annoyed when tupping makes women neglectful."

"Murdant, what disobedience did this girl incite? What duty did Twea fail to perform?"

Kol shot Dar a venomous look. "Sir, am I to have my orders questioned by the likes of her?"

"She's not the one who's doing the questioning," said the tolum. "What was your order?"

"I told her to fetch Twea, sir."

"Where was she?"

"With a piss eye, sir."

"And Twea's the same girl who served the men this morning?"

"Yes, sir."

The tolum appeared to enjoy Murdant Kol's newfound deference. He thought a moment, then said, "If a piss eye wanted Twea, that's its business. Did you really expect this girl to interfere?"

"That was my mistake, sir."

"Yes, it was. Now, have the men prepare to march. I want to be at base camp by the morrow."

"Yes, sir."

Kol turned to Dar, his face a mask of self-control. "Saddle my horse."

Twenty-five

Dar saddled Thunder, then held the reins for Murdant Kol. When he arrived with the tolum, Dar sensed tension between the men. She tried to be inconspicuous, aware the tolum was concerned with his authority and not her welfare. When she handed Kol the reins, she acted so subservient he failed to perceive her air of triumph.

When the shieldron moved out, Dar headed toward her place behind the orcs. She was pleased when Twea ran to her side. The girl had changed back into her tattered shift, which looked like it had been made from an adult's cast-off garment. The neck hole was far too wide and kept slipping over her shoulder. Besides being ill fitting, the shift was filthy, and Dar resolved to wash it at the first opportunity.

Before Twea said a word, Dar could tell her spirits had improved. She was animated and no longer seemed in pain. The swelling about her brand had lessened and lost its angry hue. More significantly, fear had disappeared from Twea's face. "Let's find Kovy!" she said.

The name made Dar smile. "Kovy? I'm not sure Kovok-mah would like being called that."

"Then you don't know him," said Twea.

"Perhaps not," said Dar. "If we walk behind the orcs, he'll probably join us."

When Dar and Twea reached the end of the column,

Kovok-mah was there, waiting for them. Twea darted to his side. "Kovy!"

Kovok-mah curled back his lips. "Little Bird. We walk together."

Twea seemed to understand that Kovok-mah was smiling, for she grinned back at him. Dar smiled at the mismatched pair and marveled at Twea's transformation. *She trusts him completely*. Dar had never imagined that Twea would reach that point so quickly. *Is it something he did or said, or is it instinct on her part?* Dar still had apprehensions about orcs, but as she watched Twea, her remaining doubts about Kovok-mah vanished.

Twea had also become talkative, and as she walked, she seemed intent on telling her whole life story. "I don't have a mother," she said. "Or a father. Just Auntie, and she's not a real aunt. Soldiers gave me to her. I don't remember, 'cause I was a baby."

Dar immediately thought of Frey.

"Auntie hid her real daughters. When the man on the horse came, she . . . she . . ." Twea grew upset. "She said I belonged to the soldiers and they were taking me back. Is that true?"

"You belong to the king," said Dar. "Just like I do."

"Urkwashavoki nuk tash," muttered Kovok-mah. *Washavokis are cruel.*

"What did you just say?" asked Twea.

"He said men are mean," said Dar, "and he's right."

"They will not be mean to Little Bird," said Kovok-mah.

"Auntie was mean. She beat me all the time. She called me worthless."

"She was wrong," said Kovok-mah. "You are mother."

"I'm *not*!"

"Orcs call all women mother," said Dar. "Even girls."

"That's silly."

Dar found herself repeating Kovok-mah's explanation. "If a bowl is empty, it's still a bowl."

Twea thought about this for a moment. "So you're a mother, too?"

"Hai," said Dar. "That's how the orcs say yes."

"Dargu lo-nat muthuri ala Tahwee Ki," said Kovok-mah.

Dar translated. "He said I'll be your mother."

"I don't want a mother," said Twea. "Mine threw me away. Just like garbage."

"Who told you that?"

"Auntie."

"She lied," said Dar, recalling Loral. "When the king's women have babies, the soldiers take them away. Your mother loved you."

Twea gazed up at Dar. "How do you know?"

"I've seen a mother's love. My friend, Loral, died so her baby girl might live."

"Is that true?" asked Twea, sounding more hopeful than skeptical.

"Yes," said Dar. "I swear by Karm's holy name."

Twea took Dar's hand and smiled.

"Since your mother isn't here," said Dar, "I'll take care of you for her."

"Will Kovy take care of me, too?"

"Hai," said Kovok-mah.

When Twea tired, Kovok-mah hefted her onto his shoulders. She straddled his neck, and he gripped her thin legs with his massive hands. Twea's perch was comfortable because Kovok-mah's cape cushioned the plates of his armored tunic. While Twea enjoyed her new vantage point, Dar took the opportunity to practice her Orcish. "Where did you know speech of washavokis?" she asked.

Kovok-mah corrected her. "Where did you *learn* speech of washavokis."

"Learn," said Dar. "Where did you learn it?"

"From my father."

"Where did he learn it?"

"His mother visited old washavoki king often. She learned his speech and taught all her children."

Dar was intrigued. "Why would she visit king?"

"She was queen. It was fitting."

Dar gazed at Kovok-mah with surprise. *He's a prince!* Not knowing the proper Orcish words, Dar switched to the human tongue. "I did not know you had royal blood."

Kovok-mah look puzzled. "What kind of blood is this?"

Dar replied in Orcish. "Your father's mother was queen. That makes you like her—leader."

"It does not. I herd goats. My father makes hard milk."

Kovok-mah's answer surprised Dar. *His father's only a cheesemaker? I guess orcs don't believe in royal blood.* Further talk confirmed Dar's assumption. Among the orcs, heredity didn't determine who ruled, and Kovok-mah's standing was not enhanced by his kinship to a queen. Dar learned that the cape he wore was less a sign of rank than recognition of his wisdom. It marked him as one to follow in the press of battle. The cape had been bestowed on him by the consensus of his comrades, who could remove it by the same process.

Dar continued practicing Orcish until Twea grew bored with riding and asked to be set down. Soon, the girl had Dar helping her gather flowers. Twea used them to decorate Kovok-mah's armor, employing its metal plates to grip the flowers' stems. Gradually, his rusty tunic took on the appearance of a spring meadow.

For the remainder of the day, Dar was often happy. Secure beside Kovok-mah, she opened her heart to Twea. Dar envisioned the girl's mother—branded and desolate—and felt she was passing on that woman's love. There was joy in being needed, and it filled an emptiness that had haunted Dar far too long. Yet, whenever she remembered the precariousness of their situation, happiness gave way to concern. They were marching to war, where lives and fates could be altered in an instant. Orcs weren't invulnerable; a single arrow or sword stroke could remove Twea's and her protection. If that happened, Dar was certain Murdant Kol's vengeance would come swiftly—first on Twea, then on herself.

Dar might have succumbed to despair if she weren't a highlander. Her hardscrabble life had taught her to cling to whatever happiness the present offered. She kept a wary eye toward the future, but she didn't let forebodings crush her spirit. She worried, but she also smiled. At times, when Twea was playful, Dar seemed as carefree as someone on an outing.

The road descended into the Turgen's broad floodplain. Though the river was still beyond sight, the black, fertile earth flanking the road was evidence of its nearness. The richness of the land contrasted with the state of its farms. Passing troops had left little in their wake. The homes along the way were empty and ruined, stripped bare by waves of soldiers. With no larders to commandeer, Murdant Teeg cut the grain rations that evening. For days, only porridge had been served. Henceforth, meals would be meager as well as monotonous.

After Teeg announced the news, Taren muttered to Neena, "The men will take it out on us."

"Then make the scabhead serve," said Neena. "Where is she, anyway?"

"Out with Dar, getting wood," replied Taren.

Neena's face darkened upon hearing Dar's name. "I heard you talking with that bitch last night. I thought we agreed to shun her."

"Maybe we were wrong about her," said Taren.

"We weren't. I know her kind. She dropped a murdant for an orc. She'd drop that orc for something better."

"I don't believe that," said Taren.

"Think twice about whose side you take," said Neena. "You're with us or against us. And remember—no orc's protecting *you*."

Taren didn't reply. Nevertheless, Neena was certain her threat had left its mark.

Twea and Dar served the orcs late because Twea had to serve the men first. As on the previous evening, Twea ate within Muth la's Embrace. Dar left her with Kovok-mah while she finished her chores. When she returned to Kovok-mah's shelter, Twea was curled up on his wide lap, sound asleep. Kovok-mah spoke softly in Orcish. "Dargu, we must speak about tomorrow. Time for killing draws close."

"Hai," said Dar, feeling a chill in the pit of her stomach.

"Soon, many urkzimmuthi will gather. They will

look at you and Little Bird and see washavokis, not mothers. There will be danger."

"Danger is everywhere," whispered Dar.

"You speak wisdom."

As Dar and Kovok-mah conferred in hushed voices, halting whenever Twea stirred, Dar realized that she would be starting over with new bands of orcs and no assurance of acceptance. She recalled how Zna-yat had almost killed her and how the sentry had nearly slit her throat. *Twea's and my fate are in the orcs' hands. It's too late to change that.* All Dar could do was wait and discover what that fate would be.

Twenty-six

The shieldron reached the Turgen River early the following day. Already broad, it was a formidable barrier. Its current, gray with sediment from the nearby mountains, was swift and so cold that it chilled the surrounding air. The river awed Dar. She was fascinated that frigid water could seem to boil as it rushed downstream.

The road followed the riverbank, and by afternoon a great stone bridge came into view, its arches linking rocky islands to span the river. The stonework had weathered until it was hard to tell where the islands ended and the masonry began. It was the most impressive structure Dar had ever seen. She stopped to gape at it, and Kovok-mah stopped also. "That is Flis Muthi," he said.

Dar translated. "Leap of Mother?"

"Hai. Great work of urkzimmuthi and cause of much sorrow."

"You built that bridge?" said Dar, trying to hide her surprise.

"Hai. Long ago. And long ago washavokis crossed it to take our homes."

As Kovok-mah spoke, a troop of horsemen rode across the span to the camp on the far shore. Not much later, Dar crossed the bridge herself. Up close, the structure revealed its antiquity. Centuries of rain and snow had rounded its angles and its paving stones were worn and rutted. In places, full-grown trees grew between them.

The base camp beyond the bridge was only partly filled, but it was already a busy, confusing place. Though Tolum Karg's shieldron was the first of the regiment's six to arrive, other orc regiments were already there. In addition to the orcs, there were units of human soldiers, both foot and cavalry, within the camp. With a single turn of her head, Dar viewed more people than she had encountered all her life. A din of voices, both human and inhuman, assaulted her ears. Mingled with them were the sounds of animals and the noise of an army preparing for war.

The shieldron waited at the edge of the camp while Tolum Karg reported to the camp commander. When the tolum returned, he led the shieldron to a patch of open ground. It lay next to a broad area encircled by upright branches that enclosed hundreds of conical shelters with ample space for many more. The orcs entered the circle while the soldiers and women remained outside and began to unload the wagons.

Dar had given up asking questions and relied on eavesdropping to find out what was going on. She learned from the soldiers' talking that the army would encamp until all its units had assembled. Some men thought that would take a few days, while others predicted weeks. The only consensus was that the invasion wouldn't commence until the king arrived.

Dar heard a lot of grumbling, for no one looked forward to camp life. "No helpin' ourselves to peasant larders," said Murdant Teeg. "Ye'll be livin' off His Majesty's generosity."

"With ol' Squeeze Purse feedin' us," said a soldier, "it'll be naught but porridge."

"You just wait," said another. "When camp's full o' bellies, a bowl o' mush will seem a feast."

"If yer lucky enough to get some," said Teeg. "Staying put makes for lean times. Wood's already scarce. All we got enough of is water." He glared at Dar. "Move yer arse, bitch. There's work aplenty."

Dar hurried off to help the women prepare for an indefinite stay. The soldiers, as usual, did as little as possible. Once they erected their tents, they left the women to set up camp. The women finished unloading the wagons, established the cooking area, and erected their own shelter before turning to other tasks. Neena and Kari went out to gather wood. Taren and Twea fetched water, then started dinner. Dar had been ordered to dig the latrines, which she finished just in time to serve the orcs.

Dar and Twea washed, donned serving robes, hefted the pole bearing the porridge kettle, and entered the circle that marked Muth la's Embrace. Dar was forced to wander about looking for Kovok-mah and his companions. Finding them among hundreds of strange orcs and their shelters took a while. By then, Twea was struggling to hold up her end of the pole.

Kovok-mah seemed tense when Dar served him, and he whispered that they must speak. After Dar and Twea doled out the porridge, they went over to Kovok-mah's shelter and waited for him. He arrived as the sun began to set.

Kovok-mah spoke in Orcish so Twea couldn't understand him. "You must not stay here tonight," he said. "It is not safe. Last night, guards kill washavoki."

"Just because some foolish soldier . . ."

"Not soldier," said Kovok-mah. "Woe man."

"Urkzimmuthi kill mother?" said Dar. "Why?"

"I am not sure," said Kovok-mah. "All I know is she

entered circle and guards killed her. They may do same to you and Little Bird. Both of you should leave now."

"Thwa," said Dar. "If we are not safe within Muth la's Embrace, we are not safe anywhere. We will wait for guards to come."

Kovok-mah didn't argue, though his expression betrayed his unhappiness. Dar was a mother, and he deferred to her judgment. Kovok-mah followed Dar's example and sat near his shelter where he could be seen easily. Twea, unaware of what was happening, snuggled close to him.

The women who served the other orcs departed. The sun sank below the horizon. It grew dark and a chill breeze came from the river. Without being too obvious, Dar watched the small bands of armed orcs that patrolled the circle's boundary. Eventually, one band headed in her direction. She remained perfectly still.

There were three orcs in the band, all with weapons ready. Two had broadswords. The third and largest one carried an ax. Its razor-sharp head was wider than Dar's neck.

"No washavokis here!" bellowed the ax bearer.

Kovok-mah started to rise, his hand reaching for his sword hilt.

"Zetat!" said Dar. *Sit!*

Kovok-mah obeyed, surprising the other orcs and causing them to turn their attention to Dar. She continued speaking in Orcish. "Two mothers sit here. This is good place for us."

"No washavokis," repeated the orc, although with less self-confidence.

"We serve food, and Muth la is honored," replied Dar in the orcs' language. "If you do not believe we are mothers, kill us. Kill all washavoki mothers. Then leave

Muth la's Embrace to eat with soldiers, for you will be like them."

The orc raised his ax, but Dar didn't flinch. "Kill little mother first," she said. "She does not understand your speech. She trusts urkzimmuthi. Surprise her with quick blow."

The orc hesitated before lowering his ax. He gazed at Kovok-mah. "What am I hearing?" he asked.

"Wisdom," replied Kovok-mah.

"Why are these two here?" asked another guard.

"They share my shelter," said Kovok-mah.

"You sleep with washavokis?" asked the ax wielder. "That is very strange."

"We are not like washavokis," said Dar.

Twea grabbed Kovok-mah's hand. "What's happening?" she asked.

Kovok-mah didn't answer. Instead, he addressed the guards in Orcish so Twea couldn't understand. "Little mother wishes to know her fate. Should I tell her she will die?"

"I cannot decide this," said the orc with the ax. He turned to his companions. "Come," he said.

When the guards left, Dar asked, "What will happen?"

"I think he will bring Wise Sons to speak with you."

"What should I do?" asked Dar.

"Show your wisdom."

A short while later, the guards returned leading a group of five orcs who wore short capes. Unlike men, the urkzimmuthi didn't ornament their weapons or armor as a sign of authority. Nevertheless, Dar sensed that these orcs were particularly distinguished, and the capes marked them as wise. The foremost had a mane that was shot with gray. He stepped forward and spoke. "I hear there is washavoki that speaks like mother."

"I am mother," said Dar, remaining seated, "so I speak like one."

"What is your name?"

"This camp is your home," replied Dar. "It is more proper for you to speak your name first."

The grizzle-headed orc looked surprised. "How can washavoki know this?"

"Think," said Dar, "and you will know answer."

The orc curled back his lips. "I am Nagtha-yat."

"I am Dargu."

"It is good name for you."

Dar curled her lips, displaying her blackened teeth. "So I have been told."

"Why do you wish to stay within Muth la's Embrace?" asked Nagtha-yat.

"Here, I feel close to Muth la," said Dar.

"Do you not miss your own kind?"

"Thwa," said Dar. "They have little sense."

Nagtha-yat grinned. "That is good answer." He turned his gaze on Kovok-mah, who responded with a seated bow. "Do you not mind their stink?"

"They are clean," Kovok-mah replied, "and smell not of fear."

Nagtha-yat bent over Dar and sniffed. "Yet why would you wish these two in your shelter?"

"To honor Muth la," said Kovok-mah.

"It is hard for sons to know Muth la's will," said Nagtha-yat.

"That is why they should listen to mothers," said Dar.

Nagtha-yat turned and spoke to the others who had accompanied him. "There is wisdom in what this mother says."

When Nagtha-yat said "mother," Dar knew no harm would come to Twea or her.

Twenty-seven

There were two communities in the base camp, human and orcish, and news of Dar spread quickly in each. The orcs came to treat Dar as a curiosity—a hybrid that was part mother and part washavoki. Some saw mostly the washavoki in her, while others accepted her as a mother. A few resented what they felt was her presumption. Among those, there were some whose resentment became hatred, but even they deferred to the Wise Sons who had permitted Dar and Twea to sleep within Muth la's Embrace.

Among the humans, Dar was notorious. Rumors besmirched her as unnatural—most likely a pervert and certainly a traitor to her kind. Though Dar was ostracized, she was too interesting to ignore entirely. The salacious stories and the fact that an orc had killed for her made Dar seem exotic. While other women tupped soldiers for extra rations, she was known as "the orc wench." The speculation as to what took place within Kovok-mah's shelter was as endless as it was fanciful. Dar was aware of the talk that swirled about her, but tried her best to ignore it.

Dar's reputation had some advantages. Everyone knew who she was. If the soldiers spoke ill of her, they also kept their hands to themselves. She intimidated some, and received grudging respect from others. Even Murdant Kol left her alone.

The other shieldrons in Dar's regiment entered camp over the next few days. Neena maligned Dar to the arriving women, and Murdant Kol made sure that anyone who was civil to Dar was treated harshly. Thus, Dar remained a pariah. Even Memni avoided her, and Dar never learned how her former friend had lost her front teeth.

After the regiment regrouped, routine set in. For the women, there was wood to be gathered, water to be carried, and porridge to be cooked, but little else to do. The men, who didn't drill like the cavalry and foot soldiers, mostly lay about. Many of the regiment's women spent the day with them, leaving those without lovers to do the bulk of the work.

The arrival of the Queen's Man in camp brought a change to Dar's routine. When he rode in with the last orc regiment, word went out that he would inspect his troops. The news worked a dramatic change on the murdants, who acquired a sudden zeal for discipline. For the first time since Dar joined the regiment, its men tried to put on a military appearance. Weapons were sharpened, and those men who had armor polished the rust from it. The women were ordered to clean up the regimental area and take down all the tents and erect them in a more orderly fashion. The orcs, however, were exempted from these preparations. In fact, they were oblivious of them.

At sunrise on the morning of the inspection, the officers made a rare appearance. They had all the soldiers line up in orderly ranks. The women lined up also. Then everyone waited for the Queen's Man to appear. He did so at mid morning, riding slowly on horseback, accompanied by Murdant Kol, who was also mounted. It was the first time Dar had ever seen the general. What struck her about him was how similar he was to his high murdant. The Queen's Man was heavier than Kol and darker, but both men had an air of seasoned authority. Dar saw it in their stern features and the way the soldiers responded. The general and the murdant were accustomed to obedience and expected nothing less. Dar was relieved when they passed by, and she was not alone in that feeling.

Murdant Kol's groom arrived with the Queen's Man, and afterward Dar was relieved of caring for Thunder. She missed the job. Kol was right—she had a feel for horses, which blossomed while she cared for his stallion. Dar discovered that she understood the animals. She liked them and felt at ease around them. Compared with humans, they seemed innocent and guileless. In that way, they reminded her of orcs, for while a horse might trample a person, it would go about it honestly.

Whenever possible, Dar lingered near the stables to be close to horses. She also had another reason—it was safer there, for cavalry and infantry camped nearby. When Dar encountered these units, she realized that the men who served with orcs were truly the army's dregs. The foot soldiers and cavalry troops were superior in every way. They maintained their weapons and armor. They drilled rather than lazed about. They were fitter, more disciplined, and often less crude.

One morning, as Dar carried water through the infantry's camp, she heard rapid hoofbeats and then a horse's frightened cry. She turned in its direction and spied the riderless animal rear up. The large black horse was within a cluster of panicked foot soldiers. When

Dar saw weapons being drawn, she dropped her bucket and rushed toward the animal. She found it surrounded by frightened men who were only making matters worse. Clearly, those who were waving pikes and swords had no idea how to calm a horse.

Dar stepped into the circle. "Get back," she yelled. "Put down your weapons." Then she faced the rearing horse, looking it in the eye and holding out her hands, palms upward. With the same soft, calm voice she used when Thunder was edgy, she spoke to the frightened animal. Soon, her soothing words had their effect. The horse stopped rearing. Without taking her eyes off it, Dar told the men to move farther away.

As the men stepped back, Dar slowly advanced, speaking softly, until she was close enough to gently touch the animal. The horse grew calmer as she stroked him. "It's frightening to be surrounded by fools," she said, "but you're all right."

Dar heard someone running and shouting "Skymere!" The horse turned its head in the direction of the voice. Dar followed the animal's gaze and saw a man dressed in a doublet of blue and scarlet. He was holding a bridle. "Is this your horse?" she asked.

"Aye," said the man. "You have an uncommon way with him, it seems. I thank you for your aid."

"I didn't want to see him hurt," said Dar. She stared at the man's long red hair with frank curiosity.

The man caught her look and smiled. "Have you na seen a Southerner before?"

Before Dar could answer, a second man, dressed like the first, ran up. "Sevren, is Skymere safe? That stupid oaf . . ."

"This lady has rescued him, Valamar," said Sevren. He bowed toward Dar. "Whom am I to thank?"

"I'm Dar."

"The orc wench," added a soldier with a laugh.

"Orc wench?" said Sevren.

"She sleeps with an orc!" shouted another soldier.

Sevren grinned. "Small wonder you're na afraid of horses."

Dar grinned back, revealing her black teeth. "Or men," she said. Without a further word, she left to retrieve her water bucket.

Sevren watched her go with an intrigued expression on his face. When Valamar noticed it, he laughed. "Best leave before you get in trouble."

"Trouble?" said Sevren.

"I've seen that look before. You lack sense when it comes to women."

"I'm just curious."

"The way you were curious about Cynda?" asked Valamar.

"You must admit, she had pluck," said Sevren.

"Enough to get her hanged."

"Cynda was never boring. I doubt Dar is either."

"Then you *are* interested," said Valamar.

"A mite."

"I'd think those teeth would kill any interest. They're disgusting."

"In Luvein, ladies blacken their teeth. It's a mark of refinement."

"Well, you're far from Luvein," said Valamar. "There's nothing refined about a branded woman. They're all whores."

"I do na think she is," said Sevren.

"How you can tell? And what about the orc? She's called the orc wench for a reason."

Sevren grinned. "That orc might present a problem."

"*Might?*"

"If the story were true."

"And you aim to find out," said Valamar.

"Aye, I do."

Dar put little significance upon her meeting with Sevren until she learned that his doublet marked him as a King's Guard. Ordinary soldiers didn't wear uniforms, but the king's special troop had a distinctive livery. The appearance of men in blue and scarlet always preceded the king's arrival. By eavesdropping, Dar learned that they had just entered camp. By afternoon, the royal compound had been erected on a choice spot close to the river. To Dar, the large scarlet-and-blue tents seemed like cloth manor houses, for she had never seen anything so beautiful or finely made. She was enchanted by them.

Since toting water from the river provided an opportunity to pass close to the royal compound, Dar took it upon herself to keep the water barrels full. She was slowly walking by the colorful tents, laden with two full buckets, when a horseman rode out. She remembered his red hair, but not his name. When he drew near, he slowed his horse to a slow walk. "Lady Dar," he said.

Dar turned her gaze away, and picked up her pace.

Sevren followed her. "Milady, why will you na speak?"

Without looking up, Dar replied, "I know when I'm being mocked."

"I did na mean to. I wanted to show my regard."

"Don't you know who I am?"

"Aye, they say you sleep with an orc."

"They speak true," said Dar, wishing the man would go away.

Sevren persisted in following her. "Since my arrival, I've heard many tales about you."

"Believe what you want."

"I'll believe anything you tell me."

"Then you'll believe nothing," said Dar. She quickly turned and darted though a gap between two wagons. There was a crowd of soldiers on the other side, and Dar made her way into the mass of men. Sevren, blocked by the wagons, could only watch her flee.

The water Dar carried ended up, warmed and scented with herbs, in the Queen's Man's bath. General Tarkum disliked bathing, but the chore was necessary when dealing with orcs. He was the only man, other than the king, who could enter the orcs' circle and expect to return alive; yet even he took care to scrub away his scent. Tarkum knew more about orcs than any man in the army. He knew they could smell fear. Tarkum doubted they could detect his contempt, though he took no chances. Besides, bathing was courteous, and the piss eyes liked a show of manners.

Tarkum had dressed in a clean linen tunic when Murdant Kol brought in his armor. Unlike other generals', the Queen's Man's equipment lacked ornamentation and resembled that of an orc in its utilitarian simplicity. The armor's steel plates, however, had been polished and oiled until they gleamed like silver. Kol had two women spend an entire day doing it, and Tarkum approved of his thoroughness. He often wished his tolums were as useful.

Kol laid the armor on the cot and stood by to help put it on. Having served with the Queen's Man since the latter was a sustolum, he was one of the few men unintimidated by his presence. There was mutual respect between the two hardened soldiers, and they dropped the formalities of rank when they were alone.

"Will you be dining with the piss eyes tonight or just paying your respects?" asked Kol.

"I'll be eating with them," replied Tarkum. "There's no avoiding it. It's the Night of the Eye."

"Then I'll have proper food and drink waiting for you," said Kol.

"That would be good," said Tarkum. "Especially the drink."

"Would this evening be a good time to bring up that matter I mentioned," asked Kol.

"That business of the girl?"

"Yes," said Murdant Kol. "The one called Dar."

Tarkum frowned. "I've been thinking about her. You said she's sleeping with a piss eye. You think she's tupping him?"

"I wouldn't put it past her."

The Queen's Man shook his head. "It's a touchy matter."

"I understand."

"The problem lies in the piss eyes' notions about women. They're quite bizarre," said Tarkum. "Thank Karm, our girls haven't noticed."

"Well, Dar's noticed," said Murdant Kol. "It's causing trouble."

"Just one dead soldier."

"I've sent many a man to the Dark Path," said Kol. "A murdant gains respect through fear. It wouldn't do to have the men fear a woman."

"So, what do you propose?"

"Ask the piss eyes to cast her out."

"That would be difficult," said Tarkum. "If they've let her stay, they probably consider her a mother."

Kol snorted. "Dar's no mother."

"It's what piss eyes call their women, though it'd be the first time they've called one of ours that."

"So what?"

"Piss eyes call their queen 'Muth Mauk.' It means 'Great Mother.' They obey me only because I speak for her," said Tarkum. "I can't ask them to question a mother's authority."

"*Authority?* Karm's ass! How can a branded bitch have authority?"

"Among piss eyes, all mothers have authority. Your branded bitch and their queen are different, but only by degree. It's daft, but that's what piss eyes believe."

"All the more reason to get rid of her," said Kol. "Let her be, and she'll end up running the regiment."

"You give her too much credit. She's just a simple hillbitch."

"What if she stirs up the orcs?" asked Kol. "What if more girls join her? One already has."

"Who?"

"A scabhead called Twea."

The Queen's Man frowned. "So, one bad fish is spoiling the broth. You're right. This can't abide."

"So, when do we squash her?"

"We'll have to rid ourselves of more than Dar. Find a rat in the wine cask and you dump the whole thing."

"Do you have a plan?"

"Those piss eyes that protect her will not return from battle. I'll see to that. Once they're gone, you'll have a free hand with the girl."

"I look forward to that day, sir," said Murdant Kol.

"Aye," replied the Queen's Man, giving his high murdant a knowing look. "I'm sure you do."

* * *

Dar and Twea sat outside Kovok-mah's shelter, enjoying the calmness of the evening. "Where's Kovy?" asked Twea. "It's way past dinner."

"He's praying," said Dar. "It's Nuf Bahi, the night when Muth la's eye is fully open."

"Her eye?"

"Look," said Dar, pointing to the full moon. "She's watching us."

"Is that why Kovy's praying?"

"Hai. It's a special night. The urkzimmuthi say Muth la sends visions to mothers on Nuf Bahi."

Twea looked about. "Where are they? I don't see anything."

Dar smiled. "Few receive them."

"Have you?"

"Never."

"Maybe I will." Twea stared intently.

"Don't use your eyes alone," said Dar. "What do you feel?"

"Cold," said Twea. "That's all."

Dar wrapped an arm about Twea. Though the air was still and warm, the girl was shivering.

"Do *you* see anything?" asked Twea.

Dar gazed about the moonlit enclosure. The deep voices of the praying orcs enhanced her feeling that she was within sacred space—both embraced and watched by Muth la. She glanced down at Twea, who still peered wide-eyed into the darkness. *She feels it, too.* The idea of visions no longer seemed far-fetched.

Dar spied movement. At first it seemed like fog rising from the river. Then it resolved into the figure of Twea walking toward her. She was naked, and an unfelt wind blew her hair. When the girl came nearer, Dar could see through her pale flesh.

Dar was both awestruck and shaken to the core. She felt that the solid, everyday world had cracked to spill a glimpse of something significant and perilous to ignore. *It's Twea's spirit! She's walking the Dark Path!* When Dar could no longer bear the sight, she squeezed her eyes shut. When she opened them again, the figure was gone. Dar became aware that Twea was shaking her arm. "Dar, why were you staring like that? What's the matter?"

"Nothing."

"You looked so sad," said Twea. "What did you see?"

"Nothing," said Dar, hugging Twea close. "It was nothing."

Twenty-eight

Dar's vision haunted her. Sometimes she thought it was a warning so she might prevent Twea's death. Other times she feared it foretold the inevitable. Either way, it made Dar anxious whenever she was separated from the girl. Murdant Kol noticed this, for he was always looking for ways to hurt Dar. While he dared not harm her directly, he saw Dar's attachment to Twea as a vulnerability he could exploit.

Each morning, women were sent out to follow a wagon and fill it with firewood. As the nearby countryside was stripped of fuel, the women's trek had grown longer until it took most of the day. Knowing this, Kol ordered Murdant Teeg to put Twea on firewood duty. As soon as Twea left, Dar began to fret.

By noon, Dar was convinced she would never see the girl again, but Twea surprised her by returning early. She was in a buoyant mood. "Dar! Guess what!" shouted Twea as she scampered to Dar's side. "I rode a horse!"

Dar's relief turned to alarm. "Whose horse?"

Twea's smile vanished, and she became defensive. "Someone nice. He says he knows you. His name's Sevren."

"I don't know any Sevren."

"He's a King's Guard. He has red hair."

"Him? What did he do to you?"

"He just gave me a ride. Why are you mad?"

"I'm not mad at you," said Dar. "But I don't trust soldiers."

"He's not a soldier," said Twea. "He's a guard."

"It's the same thing," said Dar.

"I assure you that's untrue," said a man's voice.

Dar whirled and saw Sevren walking toward her. "You!" she said, eyeing him suspiciously. "What are you doing here?"

"Seeing that Twea's safe," replied Sevren.

"She's under an orc's protection. She doesn't need yours."

"Then that orc should be more vigilant. Twea should na wander alone outside the camp."

"Alone!" said Dar.

"The wagon went too fast," said Twea. "I couldn't keep up."

"Twea," said Dar. "I need to speak to Sevren. Go ask Taren what job needs to be done." She waited until Twea had left before she turned to Sevren. "And what were *you* doing out there?"

Sevren saw the distrust on Dar's face and chose to be candid. "I was looking for her."

"Why?"

"I thought if I got to know her, I'd get to know you."

"You were mistaken."

"Well, I have a question of my own," said Sevren. "Why was a wee lass sent to get wood? Is your murdant daft?"

"You're the one who's daft if you don't understand."

"Then I'm daft."

"He put her in harm's way to punish me."

"Are you saying he'd permit her to be harmed?"

"Permit her!" said Dar with a bitter laugh. "He'd do it himself if he dared. Your army holds Twea worthless, though it'd pay five silvers for her head."

"It's na my army."

"You're pleased enough to be in it," retorted Dar, "with your fancy clothes and fine horse. They didn't have to brand *you* to make you stay!"

"Aye, I lack a brand," said Sevren. "Yet I'm na so pleased to be here. I dislike the Northern ways."

"Then get on your horse and ride away."

"I will, one day."

"Twea and I can never do that," said Dar. She turned to walk away, and felt a light touch on her arm. Dar whirled. "What?"

Sevren looked chastened, but still anxious to speak. "I did na fully understand," he said, "and that was a fault on my part. Yet now that you've instructed me, perhaps I can be of help."

"You can't. Now leave us be."

"It's clear you can take care of yourself. Can Twea do the same? I can give her safety."

"How?"

"The king arrives soon. They'll need extra hands at the royal compound. Your murdant can na touch her there."

"Do you mean Twea could work for the king?" asked Dar.

"It'd be kitchen duty, but safer than gathering wood."

"I . . . I'd appreciate that."

"Come with her and work together."

Dar hesitated.

"I'm sure it'd please Twea."

"All right," said Dar. "I will."

Sevren smiled. “Then look for me tomorrow morning.” Before Dar could say anything more, he left.

Dar watched Sevren go with mixed feelings. She felt hopeful, yet suspicious. Murdant Kol had been kind to her, and now he was her enemy. *Should I trust this man?* Experience told her that she should not.

After Dar served the orcs and cleaned up, she reentered Muth la’s Embrace and walked to Kovok-mah’s shelter. Twea was asleep in Kovok-mah’s lap. He sat so still that Dar thought he was asleep also. She pushed the reeds closed, wrapped herself in her cloak, and lay down within the space in front of his knees. She had just closed her eyes when Kovok-mah whispered, “Tava, Dargu.”

“Tava, Kovok-mah.” Dar continued speaking in Orcish. “I am glad you sleep not.”

“Why?”

“I wish to speak of visions,” said Dar.

“Sons know little of visions.”

“But I heard you . . .” Dar tried to think of the Orcish word for “pray,” but couldn’t. “. . . heard you speak to Muth la on Nuf Bahi.”

“Sons speak to Muth la, and Muth la listens,” said Kovok-mah. “But Muth la speaks to mothers.”

“I think Muth la may have shown me something that night,” said Dar. “I need to understand what I saw.”

Kovok-mah said nothing. After a while, Dar wondered if he had gone to sleep. “Kovok-mah?” she whispered.

“Hai?”

“Did you hear me?”

“Speak not of what you saw,” said Kovok-mah in an uneasy voice.

"Why?"

"Such things are not for sons to hear. They are deep matters, shown to few mothers."

"Perhaps it was not vision," said Dar, hoping it wasn't.

"Perhaps," replied Kovok-mah. "You will know soon enough."

Dar and Twea rose before dawn and left the Embrace of Muth la. A few sleepy women were at the cooking site, warming themselves by a small fire. Taren and Neffa were among them, along with Memni, who looked particularly miserable. Dar assumed most of the women were still sleeping with soldiers. The group about the fire fell silent as Dar approached. Twea received the same treatment, but it didn't prevent her from talking about riding a horse.

The sun rose and men began to arrive for their half ration of cold porridge. The other women appeared. Murdant Teeg arrived to assign work details. There was no sign of Sevren, and Dar feared he had raised her hopes falsely. Twea already had been assigned to gather wood when a stranger in blue and scarlet rode up. He was burly with a neatly trimmed blond beard. Halting his horse at the cooking site, he asked in a loud voice, "Who's murdant here?"

"I am," said Murdant Teeg.

"I need two women to work at the royal compound."

"Memni!" shouted Teeg. "Tasha!"

"*I'll* choose the women," said the man. He peered about and pointed at Twea. "I'll have that wee one there and . . ." He looked about some more. ". . . the one they call the orc wench."

"You'll have neither," said Murdant Kol, who had just appeared.

"And who are you?"

"High Murdant Kol."

The man appeared unimpressed. "These women will work for the king. If you do na like it, speak to him." He turned toward Twea and Dar. "Come, lassies, there's work to be done."

The man began to slowly ride away. Dar and Twea, after a moment of hesitation, tagged behind. Murdant Kol watched, silent and red-faced, as they departed. The man on horseback said nothing until they were halfway to the royal compound. Then he burst out laughing. "Your high murdant must be very fond of you. He looked heartbroken when you left him."

"Are we leaving for good?" asked Twea.

"Nay, only while we bide in camp," said the man.

"Sevren sent you, didn't he?" said Dar.

"Aye. I'm his murdant. Murdant Cron."

"Is he your superior?" asked Dar.

"Nay, I'm his," said Cron. "But we Southerners stick together."

"What will we be doing?" asked Dar.

"Na much until the king arrives. You'll help Davot. He's the cook."

When they entered the royal compound, Cron led Dar and Twea to a large tent. A wisp of smoke rose from a vent along its ridge, and soot darkened the red and blue fabric. When Dar entered the tent, she expected to find a fire pit. Instead, she saw a row of large metal boxes. "What are those?" she asked.

"Have ye never seen a woodstove?" asked a plump man wearing a greasy, food-stained doublet. He turned to Cron. "What kind of help have ye brought me?"

"Two fit for scrubbing and glad to do it."

"What're yer names?" asked the man, whom Dar assumed was Davot. After Dar and Twea answered, he looked at them with an amused expression. "Ye're *glad* to scrub?" he asked.

"It's better work than we usually do," said Dar.

Davot smiled. "Then pity there's so little of it. There'll be only the porridge pot to scrub until the king arrives."

"When will that be?" asked Dar.

"Whenever he pleases," said Davot. "Ye can be certain of that." He led Dar over to a kettle that held warm porridge. "Empty what's left into a bowl and clean the pot. Help yerself to porridge while ye're at it. There's no rationing here. When ye're done, ye can visit yer guardsman."

Dar stiffened. "*My* guardsman?"

The cook grinned. "Do ye really think I need two lasses to scrub a pot?"

"I'm staying with Twea," said Dar.

Sevren entered the cook tent long after the pot had been thoroughly scrubbed. He smiled when he saw Twea and Dar. "Twea," he said, "would you like to ride Skymere?"

Twea, who had been tidying the stack of firewood, jumped up excitedly. "I'd *love* to!"

Sevren turned to Dar. "You can come, too."

"Three can't ride a horse," said Dar.

"Twea will ride," said Sevren. "You and I can walk."

"Come with us, Dar," said Twea. "Please."

Dar gave Sevren a dubious look. "Why are you doing this?"

Sevren grinned. "I've always been partial to black teeth."

"An orc crushed the neck of the last man who touched me."

"I know."

"He'd do it again."

"Then my life is in your hands," said Sevren.

"It's in *your* hands," retorted Dar. "Watch where you put them."

Dar's warning had the effect of broadening Sevren's grin. "I knew we'd get along."

Dar shot him a quizzical and slightly irritated look.

The three left the tent. Skymere was outside. Sevren lifted Twea into the saddle, then handed Dar the reins. "You can lead him. He trusts you."

"Where are we going?"

"There's a path along the river," said Sevren. "It's a pleasant place. Quiet, too."

Soon they were walking by the Turgen. Dar and Sevren were silent. Skymere's hoofs upon the gravel, the rush of water, and Twea's gay chatter were the only sounds.

As Dar walked along, she studied the man beside her. He seemed only a few years older than her, but already marked by a military life. His lean frame had a hardened look—wiry, yet strong—and was animated by an alertness that made Dar think Sevren would be deadly with a knife or sword. His face had a battered look. A scar notched his cheek and the bridge of his nose. Whenever Sevren smiled, it gave his mouth a funny twist. But it was his eyes that Dar noticed most. They were as unusual as his red hair—pale brown, and when they caught the sun, Dar saw flecks of green and gold. Sevren smiled frequently at Twea's remarks, and those smiles lingered in his eyes. They lessened Dar's uneasiness.

Twea was talking about her home when Dar impulsively asked Sevren where he was from. He looked surprised that Dar had spoken. "Averen," he said.

"Where's that?" asked Dar.

"It lies far south of the Cloud Mountains. Past Luvein and Vinden, then to the west. Mountain country. As beautiful as Karm is good. There's no place finer."

"Then why'd you leave?"

"In the highlands, a boy can follow two trades—farming or fighting. Farming takes land. To fight, you only need a sword."

"So you were raised to be a soldier?" asked Dar.

"Nay, but landless sons must make their own way."

"And this is the way you chose."

Sevren detected scorn in her voice. "An empty purse chose it for me. I'm a farmer—just one who lacks a farm. But that will change. I've saved what I earned."

"Earned by looting farmers," said Dar.

"I protect the king," said Sevren. "That's different from soldiering."

"I've seen what's done in his name," said Dar. "Looting. You protect a looter."

Sevren's face turned grim. "Best keep such words behind your teeth. If they reach the wrong ears . . ."

"Have they?"

Sevren shook his head.

"Do you think I'm wrong?"

"I'm a King's Guard. I will na answer."

"Why not? Whisper so only I will hear."

"The king has a mage who's skilled in secret arts," said Sevren. "He can hear and see what others cannot. Even thoughts, they say."

"And you're afraid of him?"

"Cautious," answered Sevren. "If you're wise, you'll be cautious, too."

Dar grew silent. The path turned with the river, revealing a beach of gray sand. Sevren lifted Twea from the saddle. "We must let Skymere rest from his heavy burden," he said.

Twea dashed to the water's edge as soon as her feet touched the ground. Sevren smiled. "She's a sunny child, though she has little cause. In Averen, we'd say she's 'faerie-kissed.' "

"She's just ignorant of her future," said Dar.

"As are we all," said Sevren. When he glanced at Dar, he was surprised to see his remark had upset her.

Twenty-nine

While Twea played, Dar took advantage of her unexpected leisure to doze. Not only did she welcome a chance to rest, sleep allowed her to avoid Sevren. It was afternoon when he gently shook her awake. "I promised Davot I'd have you back in time to help with dinner," he said.

As they returned to the royal compound, Dar bombarded Sevren with questions about his life. He told her that he was the youngest in a family of nine and had left home in his teens to make his way in the world. Averen was part of a waning empire. Ambitious lords raised their own troops, and men-at-arms found ready employment. Sevren had made his way to the rich province of Luvein, where warring nobles were always looking for soldiers. There he honed his skills and learned to ride.

"What brought you here?" Dar asked.

"When I was young, I thought swordsmen could protect the weak." He smiled ruefully, as if astonished by his own naïveté. "I learned differently. The weak can na afford soldiers. The strong can and use them for their own benefit."

"Yet you still served them."

"For a while, I switched from lord to lord until I learned they were all the same. By then, I was used to soldiering. And you bond with your comrades. Many are good men who have only their lives to sell. One told me of a king who was a man of peace and justice."

"King Kregant?"

"Aye. The elder one. I rode north to join his guard and discovered he'd died."

"And the son was unlike his father?"

"Aye. But what was I to do? Ride back to Luvein? So I donned the blue and scarlet. I've worn it three years." Sevren's voice betrayed his weariness. "The king has claims in the neighboring kingdom, lands he says are his by right. We take towns and territory, but can hold neither. All we get is goods."

"Plunder, you mean."

"Choose your words with care. Kregant says those goods are his by right." As Sevren said this, his expression indicated that he agreed with Dar. What he said next confirmed it further. "This is my last campaign. Next spring, I'm done with this. I'll head south with the price of a farm in my purse."

As they neared the royal compound, Dar asked yet another question. "Why did you seek me out? Don't tell me it's my teeth."

"Your ways remind me of home," replied Sevren.

"A sweet-sounding lie."

"Nay, I swear 'tis true. Averen women are na meek."

"So, you think I have spirit?"

"Aye. 'Tis a grand thing."

"Grand? I'll show you how grand!" said Dar. "Touch my back."

Sevren hesitated.

"Come on. Touch it!"

Sevren ran his fingers down the back of Dar's shift.

"Feel those scars?" said Dar. "That how spirit's repaid here."

Dar fell silent and Sevren thought it best to say nothing. *This one fair day must make the rest seem all the worse.*

When they neared the royal compound, Dar silently handed Sevren the reins and ran the rest of the way back. Sevren didn't chase after her, but simply watched her go. When he looked up at Twea, she was regarding him with a serious expression. "Don't be mad at Dar," she said.

"How can I?" replied Sevren. "I have na cause."

Davot had a large staff of men, so Twea and Dar had little to do. Mostly, they stayed out of the way while dinner was prepared and served. They ate at the same time as the guardsmen and cleaned up afterward. When Dar and Twea were done, Murdant Cron escorted them back to their regiment. He departed after telling Teeg that he expected the two at the royal compound by sunrise. By then it was dusk.

Dar and Twea headed for the bathing tent, but Neffa barred their way.

"The orcs have already been served," said Neffa. "There's no reason to bathe."

"We must anyway," said Dar.

"The water's been dumped," said Neffa. "The serving robes are wet from washing."

Neena emerged from the bathing tent. "The bitch doesn't wear a robe, wet or dry, when she's with her piss eye," she said. "The brat doesn't either."

"That's not true!" shouted Twea.

"Ignore her," Dar said to Twea. She turned to face Neffa. "We have to wash."

"Then use the river."

Dar considered bathing in the Turgen but quickly rejected the idea. The river ran deep, and its cold, swift currents were treacherous. They might easily sweep Twea away.

"Men don't care how a woman smells," said Neena, "but you don't tup a man, do you?" She smiled maliciously.

This was Neena's idea, thought Dar. *She knows it'll cause mischief.* Dar worried how Kovok-mah would react when she and Twea came to his shelter unbathed and "snoffi va urkwashavoki"—reeking like washavokis. It appeared she had no choice but to find out. Dar took Twea's hand. "Come. It's time to rest."

Without looking back, Dar led Twea to Kovok-mah's shelter. He parted the reeds before they reached it, making Dar think he had been watching for them. She halted several paces away. Since she held Twea's hand, the girl was forced to halt also.

"Dargu. Little Bird," said Kovok-mah. "You did not serve tonight."

"We had to work elsewhere," said Dar, staying put.

"Come," said Kovok-mah. "Rest."

"Kovok-mah, merth dava-splufukuk thwa," said Dar. *Kovok-mah, we have not bathed.* "Merth snoffuk." *We reek.*

Kovok-mah held out his massive arms. "Come, Little Bird."

Dar released Twea's hand and she ran to him. The orc scooped her up and set her on his lap. Then he breathed in deeply. "You smell like Little Bird," he said. "This is good smell."

Twea giggled.

Kovok-mah looked at Dar. "I think you will smell like Dargu."

"Hai," said Dar.

"Come. That scent is also pleasing."

If Kovok-mah were a human, Dar would have assumed he was merely sparing her feelings. But Kovok-mah was incapable of lying, even with good intentions. *He actually likes the way I smell.* The idea both surprised and pleased her. She blushed. "Shashav." *Thank you.*

Dar and Twea reported to the royal compound at the first sign of dawn. After they left, a damp, sluggish breeze blew in from the river. It flowed around Kovok-mah's shelter, spreading Twea's and Dar's scent among the sleeping orcs, who awoke to discover the change in the air. The scent of washavokis in their midst, which had been a subtle note before, was difficult to ignore. Sitting in his shelter, Garga-tok fingered the ears sewn to the edge of his cape and decided the situation had grown intolerable. *I'll meet with others*, he thought. *It's time to act.*

After the morning meal was served, Dar heard the thunder of hooves as the guards rode from the base camp. "Off to meet the king," Davot said. "His Highness will be here on the morrow. Busy times ahead."

Davot and his staff were already preparing tomorrow's feast. Bread could be baked in advance, and dozens of bowls were filled with rising dough. Soon Dar and Twea were feeding fires in all the ovens, washing bowls and pots, hauling water, and replenishing the woodpile. The tent turned sweltering with the ovens' heat. Dar's sweat-soaked shift clung to her body, which was covered with soot from the stoves and dirt from handling firewood. By dinnertime, the baking was done and Dar approached Davot. "Can Twea go back to the regiment? She needs to serve the orcs tonight."

"She'll eat better here," said Davot.

"Yes, but if she serves the orcs, she'll get to bathe."

"Bathe? Why would she want to do that?"

"Orcs have sensitive noses."

Davot shrugged. "Aye, she can go."

After sending Twea off with a warning to scrub herself well, Dar worked until the ashes were cleared from the ovens and the last pot was washed. It was dusk when she finished and headed for the river. There was a section of riverbank where a grove of trees grew up to the water and offered enough privacy to bathe. She approached it only after glancing about to ensure no soldiers saw her. When Dar reached the trees, she made her way to the river.

The Turgen's swift current had gnawed at its channel to carve a steep bank. The roots of the trees closest to the river were exposed where the earth about them had been swept away. Dar cautiously climbed down the bank. She was unable to swim, and the water made her nervous. Entering the river slowly, she carefully felt its bed with her feet for firm places to stand. Just a few steps from the shore, the water reached her knees. The current pushed forcefully against her legs, gurgling loudly.

Dar removed her clothes and washed them in the swiftly flowing stream. Once her garments were as clean as she could get them, she wrung them out, hung them on an exposed root, and turned her attention to washing herself. She had no doubts that Kovok-mah liked her scent, but even her washavoki sense of smell discerned it had grown strong. She scrubbed away the day's sweat and grime, knowing that her essence would remain. When she was satisfied, she left the river and donned her damp clothes.

Dar didn't see Zna-yat until she climbed the bank. Standing silently among the trees, he startled her. Dar doubted this was a chance encounter, but acted as if it was. She curled back her lips and said, "Tava, Zna-yat."

The orc didn't reply.

Zna-yat spoke only Orcish, so Dar addressed him in that tongue. "Why are you outside Muth la's Embrace?"

"Washavokis do not own world. I go where I please."

"As you should," said Dar.

"My mother's brother's son lost his cape today."

"His cape?" said Dar, uncertain what Zna-yat meant.

"Hai. Sons say he has forsaken wisdom. They agreed he is poor leader. Another wears cape now."

"Why?"

"Leaders should not stink of washavoki."

Dar sensed where this conversation was headed. "I am mother," she stated.

"Thwa," said Zna-yat. "You mock mothers. You have disgraced Kovok-mah."

"I will ask him if he agrees," said Dar. She started to leave, but Zna-yat blocked her path.

"Thwa. Your words have evil magic."

Dar attempted to dart away, but Zna-yat seized her arm. "You have not washed well. I still smell you." He grabbed her other arm and dragged her to the crest of the bank.

"What are you doing?" asked Dar even as she guessed. An instant later, the orc flung her into the river.

Zna-yat saw Dar's arms and legs flail the air before she splashed into the gray water. Dar vanished beneath its surface. The orc watched to see if she would rise. Dar's head bobbed up far downstream from where she had landed, then submerged as quickly as it had risen. It was even more distant the next time Zna-yat spied it—a dark speck amid swirling gray. The head disappeared again, this time for good. Zna-yat waited, scanning the broad Turgen with his keen eyes. When he was satisfied that Dar had drowned, he climbed down the riverbank and washed her scent from his hands.

Thirty

With an icy shock, the world became an airless, gray blur. There was nothing solid to touch, only water. The cold seized Dar and rushed her along, tumbling her about as it did. It toyed with her—a gasp of air, a glimpse of sky, then grayness again. Dar struggled. Her arms and legs thrashed futilely. Cold invaded her body, turning it stiff and leaden. Her efforts became lethargic. Soon, her lungs ached for air, but there was only the Turgen to fill them.

I'll die, thought Dar. Strangely, the idea was devoid of terror. The river held her in a frigid embrace, carrying her to the Dark Path. Dar wondered when she would arrive. *Soon, I think. I only have to breathe*. The world began to fade even before she tried.

Something struck Dar and gripped her. In her confused state, she thought it was a hand. The hand fought against the river. Dar was no longer moving. Her body pressed against something hard and rough. Above her head, the gray was lighter. Dar tried to move toward the light and discovered she could push against the rough hand. Suddenly, she saw leaves. There was air. Dar gasped.

The hand was a tree that had fallen into the river. Its leaves screened the darkening sky and its roots still rested on the shore. Dar was entangled in its branches.

For a while, she felt she was dreaming, but when the tree didn't vanish, that feeling became astonishment. Eventually, Dar began to struggle toward the shore. The way was treacherous, even with her clinging to the tree, and it was night by the time her feet touched dry ground. When they did, she heard a soft groan as the tree began to shift and slide into the current. Dar stepped back and watched it drift away. Soon it was only a parting shadow swirling on the dark river.

Dar headed for Kovok-mah's shelter. When she entered Muth la's Embrace, a patrol of orcs approached her and halted. "Dargu?" said a guard in a voice that betrayed surprise. It made Dar suspect the orcs knew what Zna-yat had done.

"Hai."

"Were you not in river?" asked another guard, confirming Dar's suspicions.

"I was," Dar replied in Orcish, "but I have returned."

"How can that be?" asked the guard.

"Tree saved me."

The orcs' eyes grew wide, and one pressed his palm against his chest, splaying his fingers so they pointed upward. Dar had seen that gesture before, although she didn't know its significance. "Tree?" said the orc, in a hushed tone.

"Hai," said Dar. Then, with all the dignity she could muster, she walked to Kovok-mah's shelter. Behind her, she heard the orcs speaking in low, agitated tones.

Skymere moved down the dark road with a gait that betrayed his exhaustion. The long ride had pushed the stallion to the limits of his endurance, and Sevren was angry over it. Despite this, he rode silently and stoically. A King's Guard didn't complain. At least, a prudent one didn't.

Sevren's companions were equally quiet. None knew the reason for their journey, other than the king had willed it. They had received no explanation for the order, and experience told them to expect none. Sevren suspected it was merely an exercise of power for power's sake. The king liked pomp and probably wished to enter base camp accompanied by the full complement of his guards. Sevren wondered who would be impressed.

As the rising moon silvered the horizon, Sevren spied the fires of the king's camp. He hoped that meant he could tend his horse soon. Before long, he heard voices made boisterous by drink. *For some, war's a merry business.* Their gaiety made Sevren reflect how Dar would see only the grim side of battle. *Privation, not riches. Carnage, not glory.* Sevren hoped she would be spared the worst. *No one should see what I've seen.* Even as he had that thought, Sevren realized he had been luckier than many. *There are worse things than viewing horrors. Far worse.*

It wasn't the first time during the long ride that Sevren had thought of Dar. After spending time with her, what had begun as curiosity had blossomed into deeper feelings. Sevren had spent much of the day pondering why Dar, who wasn't eager for his company, attracted him. She had a special quality, and "spirit" inadequately described it. *She wears rags, but there's a grandness to her no lord or lady can match.* Sevren found it in Dar's rapport with Skymere, her protection of Twea, and her fearlessness among the orcs. He also saw it in the way she treated him. Unlike most women, Dar was unimpressed that he was a guardsman. To Sevren, that was a good sign. She showed contempt for that part of him he had come to disdain. In all his travels, he had never encountered a woman like her. Already, he was smitten.

When Sevren entered the camp, his thoughts of Dar were interrupted by the trumpet that signaled the arrival of the royal guard. The king, surrounded by advisers and courtiers, left a tent to receive their obeisance, and Sevren viewed the royal party as he rode past. Kregant II stood foremost, his corpulent figure clad in gold-embroidered scarlet. The king's florid face matched his attire, and unsteady legs marred his dignity. Though approaching middle age, he looked younger than his years. A wispy beard emphasized his callow appearance.

Sevren surveyed the men about the king. All were familiar, but one surprised him. Othar, the king's mage, appeared to have aged decades since the guardsman had seen him last. If Sevren didn't know better, he would have thought the sorcerer was an elderly man. Yet something other than years had sucked life from his features, leaving them hard and withered. It marked them in a way that caused Sevren to think no wholesome thing had ravaged Othar's face. Only his dark eyes remained unchanged. They were as baneful as ever. When they glanced at Sevren, his hair rose.

The king returned to his carouse, while his guardsmen dismounted and tended their horses. Sevren fed, watered, and rubbed down Skymere before he looked to his own needs. These were simple. He spread his sleeping roll on the ground and ate a hard biscuit washed down with water. After he supped, he took off his boots and, wrapped in his cloak, lay down to sleep. The night was clear. As Sevren gazed at the stars, he reflected how they were shining over Averen also. He imagined himself there, stargazing from his own farmstead. In his mind's eye it was nestled among mountains with a lake to mirror the night sky. It was an old dream, which hard years had rendered more alluring. Tonight, however, Sevren added something new: Dar gazed at the stars with him.

Twea was asleep when Dar entered Kovok-mah's shelter, but Kovok-mah was awake. He appeared anxious, yet his voice was restrained. "You are wet," he said in Orcish.

"Hai, I bathed and washed clothes," replied Dar. Though she had resolved never to lie to Kovok-mah, she didn't wish to tell him about Zna-yat. Thus, Dar was relieved when Kovok-mah refrained from questioning her further. She had a question for him, however. Dar mimicked the gesture that the guard had made. "What does this mean?" she asked.

"Tree," said Kovok-mah.

"Why would urkzimmuthi make this sign?"

"Tree is Muth la," said Kovok-mah.

"How?"

"Tree is in earth and sky."

"I understand," said Dar. "Tree is like Muth la."

"Thwa," said Kovok-mah. "Tree *is* Muth la."

An eerie sensation came over Dar, and she understood why the guards had appeared awed. Kovok-mah handed Dar her dry cloak. He had it handy, as if he expected her to need it. "You rest now," he whispered.

* * *

When Twea stirred the next morning, Dar remained on the ground, wrapped in her cloak. She had slept poorly, haunted by dreams of Zna-yat and drowning. She wondered if he would try to kill her again. Logic said he would. Facing that terrible prospect, Dar embraced the idea that the tree had been Muth la. If the Mother of All had saved her, perhaps she would protect her again. It was an irrational hope, but it gave Dar the courage to face the day.

Dar rose and left with Twea to work for Davot. It was before sunrise and only guards were about within the Embrace of Muth la. Dar was still inside the circle when she heard rapid footsteps behind her. She halted and turned to see Zna-yat running toward her. "Twea, hurry on to the cook tent," said Dar. "I have some business here."

"I want to stay with you," said the girl.

"Go!" barked Dar. "Now!"

Twea looked upset as she hurried off, but that was the last concern on Dar's mind. She took a deep breath to calm herself and waited for Zna-yat.

The orc slowed his pace and approached solemnly. He stopped a few steps away. Dar saw that he was fully armed. "You have returned," he said.

"Hai."

"I watched you die."

"Tree saved me."

"I heard this tale and went to river," said Zna-yat. "There is no tree."

"Yet I am here."

Zna-yat stared at Dar for a long while as he pondered her reply. "I do not understand how this can be," he said at last. Then he drew his sword.

Dar held her ground. *Better to face death and die quickly.*

Zna-yat, however, didn't strike. Instead, he asked, "Will you wear my blood?"

Dar had no idea what Zna-yat meant, but she didn't think it was the time to ask him. Instead, she relied on her intuition and agreed.

Zna-yat drew his blade across his forearm. Blood flowed from the wound. He dipped his finger in it and knelt before Dar to paint a red line from her forehead to her chin. "You wear my blood," he said. "It is done for now." The orc rose and walked away.

Dar watched him go, feeling relieved but puzzled. *Well, he didn't kill me*. It was possible that Zna-yat had just challenged her to a fight, but she didn't think so. *It seemed more like an apology or a truce*. Dar wanted to ask Kovok-mah, but there was no time. Also, she felt uneasy whenever Twea was out of her sight. Reluctantly, she hurried off.

When Dar arrived at the royal compound, the cooking tent was already bustling. Further provisions for the king's table had arrived, and barrels and crates were stacked everywhere. Davot had all his men hard at work, and he grabbed Dar's arm as soon as she stepped into the tent. If he noticed the mark on Dar's face as he ushered her outside, he was too preoccupied to comment. He led her to a cage filled with chickens. "Kill this lot and pluck 'em," he said. "The little lass can help with the plucking."

Davot rushed off as Dar opened the cage to seize a bird. She had seldom tasted chicken, but she knew how to wring one's neck and did it with a quick twist of her hands. The dead bird was still jerking about when Twea came out of the tent. "What's that painted on your face?" she asked.

"Orc blood."

"Why's it there?"

"I'm not really sure."

"Well, you should wash it off."

"I don't think I will until I ask Kovok-mah what it means."

"What if Sevren comes back?" asked Twea. "You don't want to look like that! What will he think?"

"I don't care what he thinks."

"Why not? Don't you like him?"

Dar shrugged. "I don't dislike him, not in particular. It's just . . . well . . . he's a man."

"A nice man," said Twea. "Why scare him off?"

"He's only nice because he wants something. Something from me, at least."

"What?" asked Twea.

"You're too young to understand."

"Oh," said Twea with a knowing look. "He wants to tup you. Why didn't you say so?"

Dar grabbed the dead chicken and thrust it at Twea. "Here, pluck this."

Twea wasn't so easily distracted. "So, when did he ask you?"

"He didn't," said Dar, beginning to feel cross. "But he's a man, and I understand men better than you."

"If you don't like Sevren, is it because he's a washavoki?"

Twea's question surprised Dar and made her wonder how much of the camp's gossip the girl had heard. More important, she wondered how much of it Twea believed. "I never said I don't like Sevren," said Dar. "I just don't trust him. Maybe I'll feel different if I get to know him better."

Dar's answer seemed to satisfy Twea, even though it evaded her question. Twea dropped the subject, but Dar continued to ponder the girl's inquiry as she slaughtered and plucked the chickens. It made Dar realize that she was beginning to see the humans about her from a new perspective. They were washavokis, and she was becoming something else.

Thirty-one

Dar and Twea plucked chickens until mid morning. Afterward, they peeled vegetables and washed pots while the tent filled with savory aromas. Dar had eaten little but bland porridge for weeks, and the smells became a form of torment. Fare for the royal feast gradually accumulated throughout the day. Besides bread, roast meat, grilled chickens, and stewed vegetables, there were dishes Dar had never seen, much less tasted; yet everything looked delicious.

Most of the day, Davot was frantic that the meal wouldn't be ready in time. Then there was a brief period when the preparations were complete and he was calm. Later he began to fret about the king's arrival. He had a sharp-eyed man watch the road to warn him as soon as the king's party came into view.

Night fell and torchbearers were called to light the banquet tent. Sauces were kept warm until they scorched. New sauces were made, thrown out, and made again. Flies buzzed over the groaning table. The cooling meats grew black with them. Twea fell asleep in a corner of the cooking tent. Finally, when the night was old, Davot came to Dar. "Wake the little lass and go. The king's not coming."

"What about the food?" asked Dar.

"Don't touch it. It's still the king's feast, though only maggots will partake."

"You mean it'll go to waste?"

"Aye, that's his way. Anyone who sups without his leave gets flogged. Tomorrow, we'll cook his feast anew."

Dar roused Twea and they returned to Kovok-mah's shelter, unwashed and exhausted. As before, he had been waiting for them. "Come rest, Little Bird."

As Twea climbed wearily onto his lap, Kovok-mah spoke to Dar in Orcish. "I smell Zna-yat's blood."

"I wear it," replied Dar in the same tongue.

"So I have heard."

"What does it mean?" asked Dar.

"You have agreed not to kill him."

Dar laughed, despite her exhaustion. "Kill *him*?"

"Hai," said Kovok-mah. "None can kill him for you, either."

"Did I do unwise thing?" asked Dar.

"To wear blood means there is honor between you. There will be no killing while scent lingers."

"Then what happens?"

"No one can say, not even Zna-yat. Blood time is thinking time. Zna-yat was unsure where wisdom lay. That is why he offered you blood."

Knowing Kovok-mah wouldn't presume to give a mother advice, Dar asked, "If you wore blood, what would you do?"

"I would not wash my face."

As resplendent as rich clothes, a fine horse, and a company of guardsmen can make a man, King Kregant II rode into the base camp the following afternoon. Dar heard the noise of his arrival, but she was too busy to pay much attention. The activity within the cooking tent was frenetic. Yesterday's untouched feast had been dumped in the river along with all the bread that had been baked in advance. As a result, there was more to prepare than the previous day, and less time to prepare it. Three other women were recruited to work alongside Twea and Dar, and they were kept busy the entire day.

As evening approached, servants dressed in blue liveries arrived to begin serving. The kitchen gradually emptied of food and the men who had cooked it, leaving the women to clean up. Dar knew none of the women, who were from another regiment, but her reputation ensured they shunned her.

"Heard they caught the one that runned away," said a woman as she scrubbed a pot.

"Aye, poor thing," said her companion. "She should've killed herself afore they grabbed her. It would've been an easier way to go."

The other woman shuddered. "Aye, easier by far."

"Who did the floggin'?" asked the third.

"I don't know his name," said the first. "They say he be high murdant."

Dar knew there was only one high murdant in all the regiments. "Who was the woman?" she asked.

None of the women would reply. Dar continued eavesdropping, but the talk turned to gossip about strangers.

After the pots were clean, empty platters began to arrive for washing. Dar and the others were still at work when a smirking man in blue entered the tent. "Come, bitches, you're to be presented at the banquet." The women were staring at him, uncertain if he was jesting, when Davot arrived and confirmed the order.

The man led Dar, Twea, and the three women into

the banquet tent. Large tables lined three sides of its interior, and all the diners faced the open space where the women stood. The king sat at the central table, surrounded by boisterous men. Dar recognized the Queen's Man among them, but no one else. Little remained of the feast except the bones and scraps spread over the tables and the food smeared on the diners' beards. Though the feasting was over, the drinking was not. Blue-clad servants scurried about, refilling drinking bowls and goblets. When Dar gazed at the drunken faces about her, she felt apprehensive.

Her escort shouted, "Hear this proclamation!" The tent grew only slightly quieter, and the man continued in a raised voice. "Our Most Gracious Sovereign has deemed it fit that these lowly wenches should share in his feast." One man cheered, which caused the others to laugh derisively. "Let it be known that His Majesty gives them leave to partake of whatever morsels strike their persons. Gentlemen, feed the bitches!"

This was the signal for the men to pelt the women with rinds, crusts, bones, and other slops. Their targets cowered under the barrage until the man who had brought them in shouted, "Shame! Shame!" The throwing abated. "These tidbits touched the lips of generals and royalty." He glared sternly at the women. "Are you too proud to eat them? Such ingratitude warrants flogging."

At the word "flogging," the other women grabbed scraps from the dirt and stuffed them in their mouths. Dar imitated them as the men began to laugh and throw more slops. Following Dar's example, Twea reached for a gnawed chicken back. As she bent over, the king hurled a large beef bone and struck her in the temple. The girl wobbled, then crumpled over, her head bloodied. The men erupted in a prolonged cheer, as if points had been scored in a contest. Dar said to Twea "Stay down!" and quickly stepped over her prostrate form. She remained there to shield Twea from further hits.

All the men were too drunk to note Dar's defiance, except one. He sat by the king's side, in the midst of the gathering yet apart from it. His sobriety set him off, as did his black apparel, but it was the man's eyes that seized Dar's attention. As soon as she met them, Dar knew she was standing before the king's mage. Tales that he could read thoughts didn't seem far-fetched. The dark eyes that stared at her were more disconcerting than tossed bones. They seemed to probe her beneath her skin, seeking secrets, and Dar was relieved when they turned elsewhere.

The men's sport ceased only when they ran out of things to throw. "Grab your supper, ladies," shouted the man in blue, "and be quick about it."

Dar seized some bread crusts and a bone with some meat on it, then helped Twea to her feet. She returned to the cooking tent to be met by Davot. He seemed appalled by what had happened, though he tried to hide his feelings. "Go rest," he said. "Any last washing can be done tomorrow."

As Dar grabbed a dishcloth to clean the blood from Twea's face, the girl began to whimper softly. "Hush," said Dar gently. "I have white bread for you and meat."

Twea was still sniveling when Dar led her away. At the edge of the royal compound, a man stepped from the shadows. "I heard there was 'sport' at the banquet. Are you all right?"

Dar recognized Sevren's voice. "I'm fine," she replied in a weary tone. "But the king struck Twea's head with a bone."

Instantly, Sevren was kneeling before Twea, examining the swelling on her temple. Dar could see that he was outraged, and his indignation made her think better of him. "It's not serious," she said. "The orcs have magic that can treat her."

"I thought she'd be safe with Davot," said Sevren. "I'm sorry."

"You did your best," said Dar. "No place is truly safe."

"Aye," said Sevren, his voice choked with rage. "Na in a kingdom ruled by a . . ."

Dar touched his arm to make him stop. "Remember the mage," she whispered.

Sevren swallowed his anger, then sighed. "I'll speak with Davot. He's a good man when they let him be. I'll see you in the morn." With those words, he slipped into the shadows.

Within Othar's tent was another one made of cloth so heavy and black that no light penetrated, even at noon. At night, the darkness inside that tent was more than an absence of light—it was palpable. It dimmed flames and chilled the atmosphere. Othar sat there, illuminated by a single oil lamp that scented the air with pungent smoke.

A voice said, "I have him, sire."

"Send him in," said the mage.

The flap of the inner tent moved and a hand pushed a small boy into the inky space. He was dressed in the tattered clothes of a peasant. Though he was sleepy from being awakened in the middle of the night, one glimpse at the mage startled him to alertness.

Othar attempted to smile, but his face wasn't up to the task, and his expression was more frightening than reassuring. "You're a very lucky boy," he said.

"Sire?" said the boy, who obviously didn't think so.

"I have some magic just for you."

"For me?"

"Would you like to know your future?"

"I guess so," said the boy.

The mage produced a large iron bowl from the shadows and set it before the boy's bare feet. "Kneel down. Gaze into the bowl and learn your fate."

The boy reluctantly complied. "I don't see nothing."

Othar knelt beside him. "You're not looking close enough."

The boy bent down. "There's only rust."

Othar seized the child by the hair and pushed him down so his face touched the iron. The boy struggled until the mage drew a knife across his throat. Blood filled the bowl, steaming in the frigid dark. Othar pushed the little corpse aside and put on a circular iron pendant. Then he took out the sack that had cost the king so much gold.

Othar dipped a brush into the blood and painted a large circle on the floor. He took great care that there were no gaps in the crimson line; his withered face reminded him of the price for a mistake. Once he was satisfied, he stepped inside the circle.

The man who had sold the spell was vague about the entity it summoned. Though it had no form or voice, its presence was unmistakable. As Othar chanted words in an ancient tongue, he began to sense it. The air grew colder and the flame paler. These physical signs were accompanied by an oppressive air of malice.

Othar opened the sack and spilled its contents outside the circle. The human bones that tumbled out were yellow with age and carved with runes. The sorcerer studied the patterns they formed. The sign for "threat" immediately caught his eye. Shadows from that sign touched the bones for "king" and "mage." Othar grew concerned.

It was nearly sunrise when the mage emerged from the black tent, his skin a deathly hue and his eyes rimmed red. The bones were subtle messengers and difficult to interpret, but they were clear about one thing—there was an enemy within the camp. Hours of study hadn't revealed that enemy's identity, but Othar had learned something almost as useful: If the orcs were to die, his enemy would vanish also.

Thirty-two

Dar was naked. She tumbled through darkness and fell upon the ground. As she lay there, unable to move, leaves covered her like a thin cloth. They hid her, yet she could gaze through them as if peering through a veil. Dar saw the shadowy form of the mage gazing downward. He held a dagger. Its bare blade gleamed, ready and lethal. He was seeking her.

A cold wind clawed at the leaves, threatening to tear them away and expose her. She looked about and spied the wind's source. As first she thought it was a black cloud. Then she realized it was something else—a presence that annihilated light and warmth while radiating malice. Dar sensed it was trying to reveal her, but a huge tree restrained it. *Muth la*, thought Dar. Then she woke.

It was nearly sunrise, and Dar lay clothed on the floor of Kovok-mah's shelter. She was shivering, and the mage haunted her thoughts. Dar wanted to dismiss her experience as a nightmare, but it felt like something else. *A vision? A warning?* Dar wasn't sure. Yet she felt it was important to avoid the sorcerer. She didn't understand why, but the strength of her feelings made her disinclined to doubt them. Intuition had kept her alive thus far, so she heeded it.

* * *

Sevren met Dar and Twea at the edge of the royal compound as they headed for the kitchen tent. "I've talked to Davot," he said in a low voice. "You and Twea will na work in the kitchen. You're to gather herbs. Look for them where we walked along the river bank, and I'll meet you there."

Sevren strolled away as if their encounter had been by chance. Dar and Twea reported to Davot, who produced two large baskets. He reached into one and pulled out some withered herbs. Dar recognized wild thyme, marjoram, cress, and the curling scapes of garlic. There were also some leaves that were new to her. "I need ye to gather these afresh," Davot said. "Fill the baskets . . ." He paused to wink. ". . . even if it takes ye all day."

Soon, Dar and Twea were walking along the riverbank. When they could no longer be spied from camp, Sevren appeared and addressed Twea. "Halt! Are those the royal herbs you bear?"

"Aye," said Twea with a grin.

"Then I must guard them," said Sevren. "For I'm a royal guardsman."

"And what of the bearers?" asked Dar, caught up in Sevren's playful mood.

Sevren knelt before Twea. "Milady, I'll defend you with my life. Your mother, also." He looked up at Dar. "For so the orcs name you."

"It seems you're also a royal spy," said Dar.

"I use only those arts that Karm gives every honest man. A pair of ears and a set of eyes."

"And an oily tongue," said Dar.

Sevren looked to Twea with a wounded expression. "Milady, I pray your mother is na your tutor in courtesy."

"Oh, don't mind her," said Twea. "Dar doesn't trust men."

"Then she is wise," said Sevren. He rose and peered into Dar's basket. "I know little of herbs. I fear I'll make a poor guide."

"Then you can carry the baskets," said Dar.

"If I did, I'd be an even poorer guard, for that would encumber my sword arm."

Dar's smile took on a hint of scorn. "Such a manly excuse for avoiding work."

"Each should do what each does best."

"So gathering herbs is women's work?" asked Dar.

"Is it na said that mothers own the food?"

Dar looked at Sevren strangely. "Kuum da-suthat tha suth urkzimmuthi?"

"What did you just say?" asked Sevren.

"I asked how you learned orcish wisdom."

"I've picked things up," said Sevren, "but I would na call it wisdom."

"What would you call it?" asked Dar.

"Fables."

"Like the fable women aren't worthless?"

"I never said they were."

"But you believe it," said Dar.

"Nay!" said Sevren. "That's why I like you."

Dar noticed that Twea was watching her intently. "Twea," she said, "this is grown-up talk. Go ahead, but stay in sight." After the girl reluctantly moved up the pathway, Dar turned to Sevren. "You *like* me?" she said, making it sound like an accusation.

"Aye, Karm help me. Even Twea can see it. Why can na you?"

"Your words come too easily."

"How can I prove I'm earnest?"

"You can start by being useful." Dar drew her dagger. "I want to learn how to use this. The last time I tried, it was taken from me."

"You want to learn to kill?"

"No. I want to learn how to protect myself and Twea, even if that means killing."

Sevren sighed. "I'd rather teach you a gentler skill."

"It's not a gentle world. This is what I need."

"Then I'll teach you," said Sevren.

Dar's instruction in the use of a blade began in the early afternoon, after the baskets were full and everyone had dined on the brown bread that Sevren had brought. First, Sevren examined Dar's weapon. Balancing it in his hand, he declared it well made but poorly maintained. "The blade is dull and rust-pocked." He took a stone and showed Dar how to use it to sharpen the blade. Once she restored the dagger's edge, he proceeded within her first lesson. "You'll na learn everything in an afternoon, or a moon's worth of afternoons. Skill comes from confidence, and confidence comes with practice."

"Maybe I can practice with the orcs," said Dar.

Sevren looked dubious. "Orcs rely on strength and doggedness in a fight, na subtlety. It's speed and cleverness you need with a dagger."

"You mean I'll have to practice with you?" asked Dar.

Sevren grinned. "Every spare moment." Dar's frown made him regret that he had looked so pleased, and he quickly turned to teaching actual moves. He commenced with defensive ones. He showed how a dagger could serve as a shield against a sword and how it could even catch a blade to disarm an opponent. Using a stick as a sword, Sevren attacked Dar so she could practice defending herself. As she improved, Sevren gradually increased the speed and ferocity of his attacks. Soon he wasn't holding back.

The ease with which Dar mastered the moves amazed Sevren. Though she lacked his strength, she made up for it in speed and an ability to anticipate his moves. Reading an opponent was a crucial skill, and Sevren knew men who had taken days to reach the proficiency Dar had already acquired. It was she who suggested that Sevren use his sword rather than a stick. Sevren was leery. "A sword might hurt you," he said.

"That's its purpose," replied Dar. "I must face the thing I fear."

"I do na believe you fear anything," said Sevren.

"That's because you don't know me."

Dar proved as proficient against steel as she did against wood, though Sevren couldn't bring himself to attack with full force. His arm was tired and Twea was bored when the lesson finally stopped. It was approaching dinnertime, and Dar thought it wise to head back. When they reached the spot where Sevren had met them, he bowed low to Twea. "Farewell, milady," he said. "I must part. Tell your fierce mother I will tutor her again tomorrow."

Twea began to giggle as she and Dar walked to the royal compound. "I told you he liked you," she said. "He didn't even mention the blood on your face."

Dar grew suddenly concerned. "Is it still there?"

"Aye."

"Good," said Dar.

"So, do you like Sevren now?" asked Twea. "Maybe, a little?"

"Are you his spy?" asked Dar.

"At least, tell me if you cut him on purpose."

"Of course not! That was an accident. And just a scratch, besides."

Twea looked unconvinced. "Well, he called you fierce."

"Dargu *nak* gaz," said Dar in a deep, dramatic voice. "Weasel *is* fierce."

Twea laughed.

Davot took the herbs from Twea and Dar. "Good job," he said, "but I'll be needin' more tomorrow." With that, and a wink, he sent them back to their regiment. Dar hoped they would arrive in time to serve the orcs their meal. The other women dreaded the job, and Dar was confident that no one would prevent her or Twea from performing it.

Twea was ignored when she entered the bathing tent, but Dar's entrance was met by sudden silence and cold stares. Her absence seemed to have only increased the hostility directed toward her. As Dar scrubbed in the tense stillness, taking care to leave Zna-yat's blood untouched, she scanned the faces about her, trying to determine who was missing. She didn't bother to ask who Murdant Kol had flogged to death, for she knew that would be futile. Instead, she sought to discover his victim's identity by a process of elimination. By the time she left the bathing tent, she had narrowed it down to two possibilities—Neena or Memni.

Dar went with Twea and the others to pick up the food. Taren was working at the cooking pit, and Dar managed to whisper, "Who was flogged? Neena?"

Taren gave a subtle sign that she heard Dar and then turned to speak to another woman. "I'm tired of cooking, but—oh well—we can't all be the high murdant's woman."

If Neena's Kol's woman, then . . . Dar had to know for sure. "Memni?" she whispered

Taren's look confirmed Dar's fears. *Poor Memni*, Dar thought, recalling her own lashes. Dar felt grief and anger at once, but she bottled up her feelings to maintain a stoic face. Still, she couldn't help but wonder what desperation drove her friend to run away. Dar knew that she was unlikely ever to learn the story, and that heightened the sting of Memni's death.

Dar felt less isolated when she served the orcs, for they often exchanged pleasantries. Some merely greeted her. Others made a point of calling her "mother." Thomak-tok always made her smile by extravagantly praising the excellence of the bland porridge. Zna-yat never spoke.

After serving, Dar changed back into her shift and helped with the washing before going to Kovok-mah's shelter. Twea was already there. Both she and Kovok-mah had been chewing washuthahi seeds. Dar could tell from the seeds' distinctive odor, which permeated the shelter, and by the distracted look in Twea's eyes. The girl exposed her black teeth in a manic smile and said, "Uthahi." *Pretty*.

"You shouldn't be chewing those now," said Dar, feeling cross. "They'll keep you up." She felt like scolding Kovok-mah, but didn't know the Orcish word for "spoiled." Instead she said to him in his own language, "You chewed many seeds."

"Hai."

"It is not raining," said Dar. "It is not cold. You have not marched. Why so many?"

"Sadness will come. I wish not to think of it."

Dar regarded Kovok-mah. His massive hand gently

stroked Twea's thin back as the girl fidgeted in his lap. His green-gold eyes, which had once seemed so alien, held the same depth of sorrow that she sometimes caught in Sevren's gaze. Both orc and man had witnessed war, and the seeing had left its mark. Dar's irritation melted. She, also, didn't wish to think of the future. "I would like some of those seeds," she said.

It rained hard the next day and the one that followed. Dar and Twea's herb gathering became only a pretext to spend the day with Sevren. He had found a sheltered spot where an overhang kept out most of the rain. Twea spent the hours watching Dar learn the basics of knife fighting. When she grew bored, Twea chewed a washuthahi seed. This new habit worried Dar, but she couldn't bring herself to nag the girl.

The constant rain washed away all signs of the blood on Dar's face, and she had no idea if its scent still lingered. Certainly, she couldn't detect it. The idea that the "blood time" was over and Zna-yat was free to attack again gave urgency to her lessons. Sevren taught her the classic attacks and defenses, the most lethal striking points, how to stab and how to slash, and moves to prevent being disarmed. Toward the end of the second day, he began another lesson.

Leaving Twea beneath the overhang, Sevren walked Dar over to a tree and borrowed her dagger. "There is one time when you have an advantage over a swordsman," he said. He threw the dagger into the tree's trunk. "You can kill at a distance." He pulled the weapon from the wood and gave it back to Dar. "But you gain that advantage at great risk. You only have one chance. Now, you try."

Dar's throw went wide and the dagger disappeared into the undergrowth. "Now you are defenseless," said Sevren. "If that tree has a sword, it will slay you."

"I think I can outrun it," said Dar.

Sevren didn't smile. "Throwing your dagger should be the last resort. 'Tis a desperate move." He joined Dar as she searched for her weapon. "This is one skill you can practice on your own. Do na let anyone see you throw until you're good. Then, show off. A reputation gives advantage."

Sevren found the dagger and held it out. "I think 'tis time for my fee."

"Your fee?" said Dar.

Sevren smiled. "Mine are costly lessons."

Dar eyed Sevren warily, then grabbed the dagger from his hand. "How costly?"

"A kiss will settle your account."

"I've none to give," said Dar, more abruptly than she intended.

Sevren tried to mask his embarrassment with a grin. "Perhaps, one day, you'll discover one and remember your debt."

Dar said nothing, but walked close to the tree and threw her dagger. It struck the wood, but didn't stick. She picked it up and tried again.

Dar kept silently practicing in the rain. Eventually, Sevren tired of watching her and joined Twea beneath the overhang.

The next morning was fair. Sevren met Dar and Twea before they reached the kitchen tent. "Twea," he said, "go see Davot. I need to speak to Dar."

Dar motioned to Twea that she should go, then looked at Sevren. "What's this about?"

"I can na go with you today," said Sevren. "I may na see you for a while. War has begun."

The news brought a chill to Dar's stomach. "So my lessons are ended?"

"I'll try to see you when I can," said Sevren. Then he added, "If that would please you." When Dar simply shrugged, he sighed. "You do na like me."

"It's not that. It's just . . . I've had bad times with men."

"You serve with scum, but I'm na like them."

"I know."

"If Karm favors us, we'll get through this and winter in Taiben. When the snows melt, I'll head for Averen. I'll take you with me, if you'll come. Your brand will na doom you there."

"I couldn't leave Twea."

"I'll take her, too."

Dar looked at Sevren suspiciously. "And in Averen, I'd be your woman?"

"You'd be whatever you choose."

"I don't know," said Dar.

"Do na tell me you want to stay!"

"I loved my father. I trusted him. Then, when I was sixteen, my mother died and he . . ." Dar looked away. ". . . he betrayed me. I've only known you a few days."

"You do na have to say aye or nay," said Sevren. "You can wait till spring."

"Then, why ask me now?"

"I know what lies ahead," said Sevren. "You'll want a reason to live."

Thirty-three

Dar found Twea standing outside the kitchen tent, which was being dismantled. "Davot said we're to go back to the regiment," said Twea.

Dar tried not to show the dread she felt. As she walked with Twea through camp to report to Neffa, she saw that a sudden change had taken place. There was much more activity than usual, and it was accompanied by an air of tension. Murdants cursed louder. Soldiers looked grimmer. Tents collapsed and disappeared. Wagons grew full.

Dar and Twea passed a wagon that was already hitched to oxen. It was mired in mud and two soldiers, directed by a murdant, were trying to push it free. "By Karm's dirty feet," cursed one soldier, "why move out after rains?"

"Because the mage says it's propitious," said his murdant.

"Pro-pissy-ass?" replied the soldier. "What's that?"

"It means the road's turned to shit," said the other soldier.

"If you don't like it," said the murdant, "go tell Blood Crow he's wrong."

The first soldier laughed. "Just give me your stuff before you go."

"Cursed sorcerers!" said the second soldier as he kept on pushing.

Dar hurried Twea along, afraid the murdant would make them help the soldiers.

Neffa was more harried than usual when Dar and Twea reported to her. "Help load," she barked. "Move it!"

"When are we going?" asked Dar.

"I'll give you orders," said Neffa, casting a wary eye toward Neena, "but I'll tell you nothing."

Dar also glanced at Neena. The other women were rushing to break camp and load the wagons; only Neena moved leisurely. Apparently, her new status as Murdant Kol's woman shielded her from Neffa's wrath.

Dar and Twea enjoyed no such protection, and they did whatever they were told. As Dar worked, it became clear that the order to move out was a surprise to everyone and the surrounding chaos was the result. Only the orcs seemed organized. They donned their armor, rolled up their shelters, fixed them to their backs, dismantled Muth la's Embrace, and formed orderly ranks long before the wagons were ready to roll.

The regiment hit the road before noon. With war commenced in earnest, the order of march was different. Orcs formed the spearhead of the invasion. Human officers no longer led the column, but rode alongside it on horseback. There were eleven orc regiments in all, well over two thousand orcs. They marched as shieldrons—squares six orcs wide and six orcs deep.

Behind this deadly force followed its baggage train—wagons with soldiers and women trailing after them. In contrast to the orcs, the baggage train moved as a disorganized mass, with wagons and personnel from different regiments mingled together. Confusion reigned.

The remainder of the army brought up the rear, and it was more disciplined. The foot soldiers moved almost as smartly as the orcs. Calvary squadrons scouted the countryside or patrolled the army's flanks. The king came last, with his guardsmen protecting him and carrying messages.

With the orcs marching in battle formation, Dar and Twea were forced to walk in the baggage train. It was High Murdant Kol's domain, since the officers rode alongside the orcs. To Dar's dismay, she discovered that—like the Queen's Man—his authority extended over all the regiments. Thus, she found no refuge among strangers. Their looks and muttered comments reflected their hostility. Evidently, Kol had fanned it while Dar served in the royal compound. As she slogged down the muddy road, Kovok-mah seemed as far away as Murdant Kol seemed close. Dar felt as if Kol had slipped a noose around her neck to tighten when the time was ripe.

Dar tried to distract herself from this ominous feeling by examining the countryside. Her viewpoint was different from what it had been on her previous marches. This time, she was part of a huge army and she saw things from the midst of a mob. The orcs blocked sight of the road ahead, and the trailing troops obscured what lay behind. Often, Dar couldn't even see the opposite side of the road. What little scenery she glimpsed bore the marks of earlier conflicts. The deserted fields were going wild, and nothing made by human hands was unmarred. All the buildings she passed were burned ruins. The only signs of their inhabitants were bones lying by the roadside, still dressed in weathering rags.

The landscape had been altered by death, and it had death's stillness. Yet the absence of the enemy heightened, rather than calmed, Dar's anxiety. The effect seemed universal. Everyone was edgy. Dar saw it in the soldiers' eyes and the frenetic riding of the scouts. Dar felt as she had when waiting for the lash to strike—the question was not if there'd be a blow, but when.

The tread of so many orcs churned the wet road until it was a morass. When the wagons bogged down, Dar, and even Twea, were pressed to help push them. Soon the march became mindless drudgery, which dulled Dar's apprehensions. By the time the army halted its march for the day, she was caked with mud and exhausted. Twea moved as if in a trance.

The women, tired as they were, had to set up camp and prepare porridge. When it was time to serve the orcs, bathing was cursory. The water in the small basin quickly turned muddy, but it wasn't changed. When the women returned from serving, few bothered to wash their robes before staggering off to sleep. Dar made the effort, then returned to the Embrace of Muth la and found Kovok-mah's shelter. Twea was sound asleep and Kovok-mah was also. Dar quickly joined them.

As Murdants Teeg and Kol walked through the darkening camp, it was quiet. Only sentries moved about. Teeg smiled appreciatively at the scene. "It's good to be campaignin' again."

"Yes," said Kol. "A man grows stale in camp."

"And poor," said Teeg. "I could do with some loot.

You're privy with the Queen's Man, when's the first chance for plunder?"

"We're headed for a small town," said Kol. "It's two days off."

"Walled?"

"Nothing the piss eyes can't handle. I don't think there'll be a siege."

"Quick is best," said Teeg. "It means full larders and plump women. When I tup, I like a bit of cushion."

Kol merely grunted.

"Ye don't seem fond of bony bitches yerself," said Teeg. "Ye seldom use yer woman."

"I use her all the time," said Kol. "She's the one that told me about Memni."

"That was a proud bit of work," said Teeg. "The bitches have hopped to it ever since."

"They need an example every once in a while, and I wanted the practice."

"For what? The weasel?"

Kol smiled. "Her day is coming."

"What about the piss eye?"

"Soon he'll be no problem," said Kol.

"How come?"

"This campaign will be different from the last. More than raiding."

"How'd ye know that?"

"The mage's auguries. Expect a battle. A big one."

"So? What does that have to do with the piss eye?"

"He and his friends will serve as bait," said Kol, "and you know what happens to bait."

"Why would the king forsake his piss eyes?" asked Teeg. "They're mighty handy."

"He can get more," said Kol. "After all, he holds their queen."

"I'm a simple man," said Teeg. "Such cleverness hurts my head."

The two men reached their tent and found Neena asleep upon Kol's bedroll. "Well, she's a cheeky slut," said Teeg, "comin' in without yer leave."

"She probably has some information," said Kol. "I told her to keep an eye on Dar."

Teeg eyed the sleeping woman. "Ye plan on pokin' her t'night?"

A sardonic smile came to Kol's lips. "Why do you ask?"

"Knowin' ye, she'll go to waste," said Teeg. "But since there's naught to drink, I could use a tup."

"I thought you disliked bony women."

"I'm a practical dog," said Teeg. "If I can't have meat, I'll make glad with a bone."

"I'm going to check the sentries," said Kol. "Don't take too long."

Teeg grinned and disappeared into the tent.

Kol began his rounds. They eventually took him to the outer edge of the orcs' encampment. The neat arrangement of their shelters contrasted with the muddled sprawl of its human counterpart. The orc sentries moved smartly within the confines of the upright branches. They watched Kol as he approached, their eyes glowing gold in the day's last light. Kol had served alongside orcs for years, but their gaze still gave him shivers. They didn't fear him, and that made him uneasy.

Dar's somewhere in there, thought Kol, *safe with her piss eye*. The idea provoked him. He clenched his fist and thought of whips.

* * *

The road was nearly dry the next day, and walking was easier. Everything else was harder. Rations were cut again, and hunger made everyone irritable. Two women from other regiments were flogged. Dar never found out why. Life was reduced to taking the next step and staying out of trouble. Dar marched when she was told, rested when she was allowed, and obeyed every order. She made sure that Twea did the same. In the harshness of the march, life at base camp seemed like a pleasant dream.

Dar endured the second day of marching, and then endured the third. It ended differently from the first two. The march stopped early in the afternoon, and the orcs didn't set up an encampment. They merely piled up their bundled shelters and regrouped to form a broad, deep mass of shieldrons. Human officers rode among them, shouting orders in broken Orcish. The orcs began to move slowly, while the baggage train stayed put.

Aware that something was happening, Dar became alert. She gazed about and saw the countryside was unspoiled. There were apple trees flanking the near side of the road, their fruit still green and tiny. The lanes between the trees had been newly scythed. The tool that had done it lay dropped at the edge of high grass. There was general confusion within the halted baggage train, and Dar decided to climb a tree to view what was taking place. She found an apple tree with a tall, stout trunk and climbed it easily.

The first thing Dar saw was a town of whitewashed stone buildings surrounded by a low wall. Work seemed underway to make the wall higher, but only a small stretch had been completed. The townsfolk's preparation for an attack had started too late. From her perch in the tree, Dar could hear bells ringing the alarm.

The town lay within a broad valley, close enough for Dar to see its panicked residents scurrying about. Lush fields surrounded it. A small river wrapped around part of its walls, but in the wrong place to be an obstacle to the orcs. From Dar's viewpoint, the king's forces appeared arranged like tokens in an old highland game called stone's battle. Orcs and men took the place of different-colored pebbles; yet Dar perceived the strategy of the forthcoming attack by their positions. The orcs stood massed on the high slope of the valley's side, preparing to advance when darkness gave their night-keen eyes the advantage. The king's cavalry occupied positions on the far side of the valley to cut off any escape. Foot soldiers were beginning to march around the orcs, to reinforce the horsemen and to loot the town after it was taken.

"Hey, bitch!" shouted a murdant. "Get down from there!"

Dar climbed down. The murdant struck her for shirking and ordered her to report to her unit. Dar wandered about the milling soldiers and women until she found Neffa. "Go to Teeg's wagon," said Neffa, "get those black seeds, and give them to the piss eyes."

Dar went to the wagon and filled a small sack with washuthahi seeds. Then she headed for the orc formation. The orc shieldrons didn't carry banners or other identifying devices, and their utilitarian armor varied little between individuals. Thus, Dar had difficulty finding the shieldrons from her regiment. Women from other regiments simply handed out seeds randomly, but Dar wouldn't do that. She searched until she found the orcs she knew. When she did, she said not only the serving phrase, but also added "Fasat Muth la luthat tha." *May Muth la protect you.*

When she spoke to Kovok-mah, he looked so sad that she impulsively stroked his cheek. Then she turned away quickly, so he wouldn't see her tears.

Thirty-four

There was no place for Twea or Dar to sleep. The orcs had left no encampment and the women wouldn't have them. Dar and Twea wandered about camp, dodging sentries until it was dusk. Then Dar returned to the apple tree she had climbed earlier. One of its branches was nearly horizontal and thick enough for Twea to lie upon. When no one was looking, they climbed into the tree, hoping its leaves and the growing darkness would hide them.

Twea fell asleep, but Dar could find no comfortable perch, and the looming attack weighed heavily on her mind. When it grew dark, she climbed until she could view the town. The waning crescent moon wouldn't rise until early morning, so it would be a dark night. As the last light faded, watch fires were lit along the town's walls. The orange flames reflected off the whitewashed buildings, making the town shimmer like a bright mirage in the night. Dar heard the soft sound of tramping feet. She could barely see the mass of orcs as they marched into the valley. In the darkness, they seemed like a shadow passing over the fields.

When the shadow reached the light from the watch fires, it resolved into an army. The orcs attacked where the wall was lowest and carried ladders to surmount it. They pressed against the meager fortifications, and from Dar's perch their movements resembled a wave striking an obstacle that could resist it only briefly before being overflowed. The fires went out where the orcs poured over the wall. The urkzimmuthi fought silently. All the sounds were human—only shouts at first, then cries more distressing to hear. Even at a distance, Dar was horrified as her imagination gave substance to what she could barely see. Still, she couldn't take her eyes away. The town grew slowly dark as its fires were extinguished until it was only a vague, gray shape in the black valley. Dar climbed downward, wedged her body between the tree's trunk and a limb, and tried to rest.

Sometime in the night, Dar sensed that the tree had changed. She opened her eyes and saw that it was leafless. Its branches held her high above a different valley, which was dark and filled with mist. Dar could see the lay of the land but little more, except for one thing: The valley seemed filled with stars. On second look, Dar realized that the "stars" were something else. They were gold, not white, and the mist couldn't obscure them. They gleamed undimmed, and Dar loved them.

The lights commenced to move through the valley. When they reached the midpoint, Dar saw an ominous darkness. Like two separate waves, it crashed against the lights from either side. When it touched them, they winked out. Each time a light disappeared, Dar felt a stab of sorrow. As more lights vanished, her grief grew until it became unbearable. "Why?" she cried out. "Why do you show me this?"

The tree became the old apple tree within the orchard, leafy with the growth of spring. Twea was calling in a frightened voice, "Dar, are you all right? Why are you crying?"

With difficulty, Dar suppressed her sobs but not the grief that caused them. "I just had a bad dream," she said. "Go back to sleep."

Twea said nothing more, and after a while Dar assumed she was asleep. Dar couldn't even shut her eyes. She waited for dawn to come, tearfully pondering what she had seen.

Kregant II also waited for dawn. He had spent the night in the company of his mage, drinking and pacing about his tent. Guardsmen reported frequently with news of the battle's progress. Their accounts were optimistic, but sketchy, for none of the king's human troops had entered the town. They wouldn't advance until sunrise. Thus, despite the encouraging reports, the king remained nervous.

"Othar," said the king. "The bones did say that we will win?"

"Yes, sire," replied the mage. Though he had lost count of how many times he had answered the same question, his voice didn't betray his weariness of it.

"And they say the town's a rich prize?"

"I saw gold, sire. The bones didn't say how much."

"By Karm's teeth, then what's their use?"

"They will repay their price," said the sorcerer. "Many times over."

"They'd better," said the king.

"Are you unhappy with my counsel?" asked Othar in a low, even voice.

"No," said Kregant quickly, his face growing pale. "I . . . I only meant the treasury is bare. I need victories."

Othar's withered lips formed what passed for a smile. "Wisdom is never cheap. You should be glad it only cost you gold."

"Maybe you should consult the bones again," said the king. "I wish to know more about the great battle they foretell."

"I'll need another child for that," said the mage. "Perhaps, after the town is taken . . ."

"There's a branded girl in camp. I'll have her fetched."

"Lads are best," said the mage, wishing to postpone another session in the black tent. "Besides, the bones have already revealed much."

"So about the battle, the great one, I mean. Are you certain of its outcome?"

Othar chose his words with care. "The bones say our ends will be achieved." He was thankful when the king was appeased by that answer and resumed drinking. The mage found Kregant's demand for certainty annoying. Necromancy was a subtle business, and the guidance it provided was seldom unambiguous. The entity behind the bones didn't reveal everything. Moreover, Othar was aware that it had a bias toward bloodshed. The bones' counsels often seemed excessive, but that never prevented him from promoting them.

The sorcerer was more disturbed by something that had occurred recently. He had become conscious that a second entity struggled with the first. This struggle was apparent in the omens he received when he cast the bones. Something was muddling them, rendering their predictions more vague than usual and their guidance harder to interpret. Yet Othar remained convinced that his auguries were sound. If the details were unclear, the broad outlines were not. There would be a great battle. Thousands would be slaughtered. The bones said he would benefit, and that was sufficient for him.

* * *

Kovok-mah was glad when the sun rose, for it meant the washavoki soldiers would arrive soon. Then he could leave and cleanse himself of the night's deadly employment. It hadn't been difficult work; the frightened washavokis upon the wall had been easy to kill and there were no orders to slay woe mans or small washavokis if they didn't carry arms. Kovok-mah didn't even kill the hairy-faced washavokis unless they tried to kill him. Others were less restrained—the fringe on Garga-tok's cape would have many new ears—but for his part, Kovok-mah was tired of death.

The soldiers' entrance into the town was noisy. There were shouting and women's screams accompanied by the crash and smash of looting. Kovok-mah was familiar with all those noises. Once the washavokis drank burning water, they would grow louder. Kovok-mah heard hoofbeats. A washavoki tolum rode down the cobbled street. He swayed slightly in the saddle, already betraying the effects of drink. The tolum stopped when he saw Kovok-mah, showed his dog's teeth, and addressed him in broken Orcish. "Queen's Man say 'good, good.' Sons keep promise. Happy queen. You go now."

Before Kovok-mah headed up the ridge, he walked into the river, still wearing death's hard clothes. He stopped only when the water reached his neck. Then he stood motionless, so the blood could wash from the iron that wrapped his body. He stood that way for a long time, for he wanted not only the blood to be gone, but also the scent of blood and the odor of fear and pain that accompanied it.

Glee spread through the camp with news of victory. Dar and Twea climbed down from the tree at dawn to the sounds of cheering. When they reported to Neffa, she put them to work digging a fire pit. The digging was necessary because there had been no cooking the previous night. Instead, the women had served "battle porridge"—uncooked grain soaked in water.

"Dig a long one," Neffa told Dar. "There'll be lots to cook today."

The other women showed up talking excitedly of delicacies that would come from the looted town and gifts the soldiers might bestow. The men disappeared, a sure sign that the orcs had vacated the town and it was ripe for plunder. Women drifted off to see what they could from the ridge. Every once in a while, one would run back with a bit of news: Livestock was being herded toward the camp. Buildings were ablaze. Bodies floated in the river.

Late in the morning, the first soldiers returned, most of them drunk. Rumors arrived with them: A duke had been captured. No, it was a prince—King Feistav's own son. There was a room filled with gold. The wine had been poisoned. The prince was, in fact, a princess, and soldiers had raped her. All the women would receive jewels.

Neffa sent Dar to gather firewood after the pit was dug. Twea came with her without Neffa's leave, but Dar didn't worry that it would cause trouble. There was a general air of jubilation, and even Neffa had been infected. When Dar and Twea gathered enough wood to appear to be working, Dar went to find the orcs. She discovered they had set up their encampment on the far side of the orchard, more distant from the humans than usual. The upright branches that marked Muth la's Embrace had been erected, along with shelters. These were arranged to form a wide circle, and in the center of the circle was a pile of wood. It was already large, and orcs were continuing to add to it. Close by, the bodies of their slain lay upon rolled-up shelters.

Dar and Twea entered the Embrace, still carrying the firewood they had gathered. In contrast to the increasingly loud and raucous sounds coming from the human camp, the circle was quiet. Dar sensed the solemnity of the occasion. She walked to the pile of wood and added the branches she had gathered. Twea did the same. Then they began to search for Kovok-mah. Most of the orcs Dar encountered were strange to her; yet all seemed to recognize her. Over and over again, she heard a phrase being murmured as she passed, "muth velavash," but she didn't know what it meant.

Dar finally spied Kovok-mah carrying a load of branches to the pile. She waited until he dropped them before she approached. To her relief, Kovok-mah appeared uninjured. When he saw her, he smiled sadly as he gestured toward the human camp. "Washavokis are happy," he said in Orcish.

"This mother is not happy."

"Because you are not cruel."

"Kovy!" said Twea. "I slept in a tree!"

Kovok-mah smiled, this time without sadness. "Tree is good place for bird."

"But not for Little Bird," said Twea. "It was hard and scratchy."

"For Little Bird, lap is better nest," said Kovok-mah.

"What will urkzimmuthi do now?" asked Dar.

"We will rest," said Kovok-mah.

"May we rest with you awhile?" asked Dar. "I did not sleep last night."

"Dar was crying," said Twea.

"What is crying?" asked Kovok-mah.

"Sound washavokis make when they are sad," said Dar.

"Hai," said Kovok-mah. "I have heard you make this sound. Were you sad for dead washavokis?"

"I had another vision," said Dar. "Though I didn't understand it, it made me cry."

Kovok-mah regarded Dar with an enigmatic expression, then raised his hand in front of his chest to make the sign of Muth la. Dar knew he wouldn't comment on her vision, so she changed the subject. "What does 'muth velavash' mean?"

"Mother who blesses," said Kovok-mah. "All who you blessed still live."

"When I said 'May Muth la protect you,' it was a wish, not a blessing."

"Those were words for blessing," said Kovok-mah. "Perhaps Muth la placed them in your chest."

Thirty-five

♛

Dar slept dreamlessly until she woke with a start. Kovok-mah slumbered, but Twea was gone. Dar quickly peered outside. The sun was low in the sky; she had overslept. Dar left the shelter and gazed about the Embrace. Twea was nowhere to be seen. Dar entered the shelter and shook Kovok-mah awake. "Where is Little Bird?"

Kovok-mah blinked sleepily. "Little Bird?"

"She's gone. Do you know where she went?"

"Thwa."

"Perhaps she's getting ready to serve."

"We will not eat this day, for slain join Muth la."

"Then I'd better find her," said Dar. She left the shelter and headed for the other camp. On the way, she grabbed a few sticks of firewood. The noise coming from the camp had grown to a dull roar, and Dar arrived upon a chaotic scene. Everyone was celebrating, and no one she encountered seemed sober. After days of short rations, food and drink were everywhere.

Dar made her way to the cooking pit. Her subterfuge with the firewood was unnecessary, for discipline seemed to have collapsed. No one was in charge. A small pig charred untended on a spit. A kettle smoked on the fire. The ground was littered with empty bottles, bread crusts, cheese rinds, and other half-eaten tidbits. Yesterday the litter would have been considered a feast.

Few women were about. Those Dar saw seemed as drunk as the soldiers. Some sported new clothes. One woman stumbled by in a lady's brocade dress, her lip swollen and bloody. Another staggered about naked.

Dar grabbed a bread crust from the dirt and ate it as she continued her search for Twea. Worried that the girl was in some soldier's tent, she looked among them first. The flaps on many were either missing or open, so Dar could see the activities inside. Most of the participants were too intoxicated to care who saw them. When a tent's flaps were closed, Dar parted them, peeked inside, and hurried on. As she moved from tent to tent, she grew more anxious. Drink had made the soldiers reckless as well as randy, and Dar feared that drunken men wouldn't be deterred by Kovok-mah's threat.

Dar heard Twea's laugh. She froze and listened. She heard the laugh again. This time, she traced to its source. It was a tent. Its flap was closed. Dar rushed over and threw it open.

Twea sat on a bedroll beside a soldier, a large fleshy man whose jerkin was open to reveal a chest covered with curls of thick black hair. Twea held a bottle, and her face had a silly, vacant expression. The hem of her shift was pulled high up her thighs and the soldier was walking his fingers up her skinny legs, pretending they were a tiny man. Twea laughed at the game, but Dar knew where the fingers were headed. "Leave that girl alone!" she shouted. "An orc protects her."

"Dar!" said Twea in a slurred voice. She started to get up, but the man pressed his hand against her thigh, forcing her to remain put.

The soldier regarded Dar. "I see no piss eye, and I

don't recall invitin' ye." He looked Dar over and smiled drunkenly. "But more's merrier. I'm man enough for the both of ye."

Dar smiled and entered the tent. "All right," she said, "but big girls first." She stepped over Twea's legs so she stood between her and the soldier. Then she knelt down, forcing the two apart. "Girls with tits are more fun. Don't you agree?"

The man flashed a stupid grin by way of reply. When he grabbed Dar's breasts, she said, "Twea, get out."

As Twea started to rise, the soldier yelled. "Hey! I didn't say . . ."

The point of Dar's dagger cut him short. Dar pressed it just hard enough against the base of his chin to dimple his flesh. Dar glanced toward Twea and saw that the girl was staring wide-eyed at the blade. "Move, Twea!" she shouted. "Close the flap and wait outside!"

After Twea stumbled out, Dar pushed slightly harder on the dagger, drawing some blood. "The orc's not here," she whispered, "so I'll tell you what he said. It was 'hurt her and die.' "

Terror turned the soldier sober. "I didn't hurt her," he said, his eyes pleading.

"I'm going to ensure you never do," replied Dar, readying to plunge the dagger in.

The soldier whimpered and closed his eyes, and that pathetic gesture made Dar pause. She couldn't bring herself to kill the man. She watched him tremble for a long moment, then withdrew the dagger. "The girl's unharmed, so I'll leave you be. Tomorrow, ask about. You'll find I wasn't bluffing about the orc."

Dar left the tent and looked sternly at Twea, who wavered on unsteady feet. Twea's wide-eyed stare remained. "You kill him?"

Dar sheathed her dagger. "No. What were you doing there?"

"He was nice," said Twea.

"You're drunk, and it's made you stupid," said Dar, grabbing Twea's arm. "Come with me."

Dar marched the staggering girl through the camp and orchard to Kovok-mah's shelter, then pushed her inside it. The orc was absent, and Dar assumed it had something to do with ceremonies for the slain. "You stay there," said Dar. "You got into enough trouble tonight."

"Will you tell Kovy?"

"He'll smell the drink on your breath, but I'll keep mum about the man. You'd better, too."

"Dar?"

"What?"

"I'm hungry."

Dar sighed. "Didn't you eat?"

"The man gave me some honeyed fruit. That's all."

"I'll get you some bread. It'll soak up the wine. But you stay here. Understand?"

Twea nodded, and Dar returned to camp to find some bread. The crusts and other scattered leavings had been further trampled, and she was hard-pressed to find anything suitable to eat. She was still searching when someone called her name. Dar turned and saw Sevren smiling at her. As far as she could tell, he was sober. "I've finally found you," he said.

"You have," replied Dar.

"What are you doing?"

"Trying to find something for Twea to eat. We seemed to have missed the fun."

"You sound like you do na approve."

"Do you?"

"Soldiering's a hard life. Men grab what pleasure they can."

"Doesn't this bother you?" asked Dar.

"Aye, but I can na change others' natures. Come, I'll take you to the royal compound. You need na pick your dinner off the ground."

"Davot said people are flogged for taking the king's food."

"Our king is generous tonight. There's bread aplenty."

"So, he's openhanded with others' things. At least, those things that spoil."

"I see you understand Our Majesty," said Sevren. "Come. The food will na taste the worse for coming from him."

Dar sighed. "A man once told me an empty belly's a great cure for a conscience."

"He must have been a soldier."

Dar and Sevren walked to the royal compound, which seemed just as opulent as it had at base camp. An unhitched wagon was outside, and it held a considerable amount of bread. "You should have seen it when it first arrived," said Sevren. "It was filled to overflowing with all manner of victuals." He climbed onto the wagon's bed and started sorting through the loaves. "It's been picked over," he said as he examined what was left. "Ah! They missed a prize." He handed Dar a large loaf of soft, white bread that had fruit cooked in it. Dar's mouth watered.

"I should take this back to Twea," she said.

Sevren looked disappointed. "Before you do, I have something for you. I'll get it." Then he hurried off.

Dar listened to the sounds of carouse as she waited

for Sevren's return. She recalled the cries she had heard the previous night and thought how the pleasure about her had been bought with others' pain and loss. She was still thinking this when Sevren arrived with a bundle of light brown cloth. He handed it to her. Dar unfolded it. It was a shift that looked nearly new. It was a simple garment, but its fabric was finely woven and well sewn. Sevren smiled broadly and stated the obvious. "It's for you."

Dar didn't return his smile, and her voice was cool when she replied. "Where did you get this? What woman died so I might have it?"

The smile vanished from Sevren's face. "Guardsmen do na loot. I got this from a wagon. It's part of my pay."

"A fine distinction," said Dar. "How can I wear this and not think of another's sorrow?"

"You do na know her fate, and na do I," said Sevren. "It may be a sad one. Yet, if you were to burn this dress, it would na mend her life."

Dar fingered the fabric. Nothing she had ever worn had been so soft. "I can't take this."

"Then your pride will leave you naked."

"It's not pride."

"Is it na pride to believe you can change the world? We are na kings and queens. We must live as best we can and do what good is in our power. Wear this dress, and by your deeds requite another's misfortune."

Dar silently gazed at the garment in her hand, loath to let it go and feeling guilty that she wanted it. Her "good" shift, twice torn and twice mended, was becoming a rag. Her other shift already was.

"All of us are naked when we journey westward," said Sevren, sensing Dar's turmoil. "When you stand before Karm, this dress will be forgotten."

"I fear I'll make that journey soon," said Dar.

" 'Tis my hope you'll journey south, instead, and have a long life as a free woman."

Dar hesitated awhile longer, then sighed and said, "I'll keep it."

"I'm glad," said Sevren.

"I must go. Twea's hungry."

"I'll walk with you," said Sevren. "The men are wild with drink."

Dar didn't protest, and Sevren accompanied her until they separated at the orcs' encampment. Dar entered Muth la's Embrace. The pyre at its center was ablaze. The slain orcs lay upon it. Dar had heard of men who burned their dead fully armed and decked out in war's finery. The orcs, however, left this world naked and resting on the same reed shelters that had comforted them in life. The living orcs encircled the pyre, sitting motionless. As flames reached higher into the sky, they began their lament.

The voices sang of neither valor nor glory. Instead, they addressed the slain with verses ending with the refrain:

"Your scent lingers,
And we think of you,
Though you have wandered
From sight and touch
Into Our Mother's arms."

Soon, the deep, mournful voices drowned out the sounds coming from the other camp.

Thirty-six

"Wake up, Twea," said Dar.

Twea moaned and rolled over in Kovok-mah's lap. "My head hurts."

"That's wine's way with silly girls. Now get up! We have to work."

If the exchange roused Kovok-mah, he gave no sign of it. His eyes remained closed as Twea joined Dar outside the shelter. The promise of dawn lit the sky. Twea moaned again.

"I hope your head aches all day," said Dar, "to remind you of how stupid you were. That man was *not* nice. You're lucky you didn't find out how unnice he really was."

Despite her throbbing head, Twea managed a smile. "Well, someone was nice to *you*. Where'd you get that dress?"

Dar's face reddened. "Sevren gave it to me. And not for the reason you think."

Twea put on an innocent face. "What reason is that?"

"He gave it to me because he likes me, the silly man."

"I'll say he's silly," said Twea.

Dar scowled. "Come on. Let's not rile Neffa. Her head probably hurts as bad as yours."

When Twea and Dar arrived at the fire pit, no one

was there. Dar found a ladle and poked it into a kettle of burned stew. Some of the stew was edible, though it had a scorched, bitter taste. Twea's stomach was too queasy for her to eat. Neffa dragged in at dawn and glared at Dar with bloodshot eyes. "Why aren't you making porridge? Do I have to tell you everything?"

Dar didn't point out that they hadn't cooked porridge in the morning since beginning the march. Instead, she merely asked how much to make. "A full ration," replied Neffa. "The men will be in foul temper. Hot food may help."

Dar went to the supply wagon and measured out a full ration of grain, then returned to the cooking pit, where Twea was starting a fire. Twea grinned and nudged Dar. "Neffa's wearing new shoes," she whispered.

Dar looked and saw that Neffa's ratty sandals had been replaced by new footwear. "Some soldier must have got very drunk last night," she replied.

Twea giggled.

Other women arrived slowly, most of them hungover. Their misery didn't prevent them from comparing the gifts each had received from soldiers. Some wore new clothing—dresses, cloaks, or shoes. Others had trinkets.

"Have you seen Neena?" asked one woman.

"Aye," said another. "Murdant Kol gave her a fine new dress . . ."

"I heard two," said a third woman.

". . . and a pair of boots *and* jewels."

"They're only glass beads," said the third.

"Well she puts on airs like they're rubies."

"I wish I were the high murdant's woman," said the first with a sigh.

With that wistful comment, all three women glanced at Dar. They noticed her new dress and began to whisper among themselves. It pleased Dar that they were unable to satisfy their curiosity.

The soldiers staggered in even later than the women, and the murdants appeared last of all. When they did, discipline returned with a vengeance. In the course of the morning, several floggings were meted out. Before noon, everyone was hard at work. The soldiers were sent into the town to systematically pillage supplies. The women spent the day cooking and preserving food. When Dar and Twea took the orcs their meal, it included meat and roots for the first time in weeks. Dar was surprised to find that the only trace of the funeral pyre was a darkened patch of ground; all the ashes had disappeared. As she served the orcs their food, the soldiers torched the town.

The following morning, the army resumed its march with clear heads and full bellies. Dar, Twea, and five other women were assigned to drive a mixed herd of cows and sheep on the march. Each day, the herd grew smaller as it was devoured. The army took new ground as it advanced; yet that was all it took. The farms the soldiers overran were empty and whatever food or supplies they contained had been carried off or destroyed. The next town they reached was equally barren. By then, the sheep and cows were gone, as was most of the other food. The larders that were expected to replenish the army's rations were bare. The soldiers burned them, but their ashes didn't fill their growling stomachs.

The army had been on the march for days when it torched the empty town. By then, even Dar understood their situation. From the conversations she overheard and her own observations, she surmised the defenders' strategy. An invading army lived off plunder, and King Feistav had destroyed his own subjects' goods lest they fall into King Kregant's hands. The invaders were marching into a wasteland, and the farther they marched, the more desperate became their circumstances. Dar wasn't privy to the meetings in the king's tent, but she saw the scouts ride out into the countryside and she went on the forced marches when they brought news of an unspoiled prize.

Every forced march ended in disappointment. Three more times they reached empty, smoldering towns. Rations were halved, then halved again. Each day's march was an exhausting and fruitless ordeal. Kovok-mah became withdrawn. Dar was uncertain of the cause, though she suspected it was the weariness that afflicted everyone. Only Twea could raise his spirits, and only occasionally. Twea grew ever thinner. The soles of her feet cracked from days of walking and Dar often carried her, feeling both relieved and distressed that she was so light a burden.

The king's party always stayed safely at the rear. King Kregant kept his guardsmen close to his person, sending them out only to bear messages to his commanders. Dar saw Sevren occasionally upon such errands. He always waved, but never stopped. Dar suspected that he wasn't allowed.

One night after another trying day, Dar was roused from sleep by an orc sentry. "Muth velavash," he called from outside Kovok-mah's shelter.

"Hai?"

"There is washavoki that calls for Dargu. It will not go away."

"Who is this washavoki?" asked Dar.

"I do not know. It wears red and blue."

Sevren, thought Dar. "I will see this washavoki." She

left the shelter and followed the sentry. Though a gibbous moon shone brightly, Dar could see no sign of Sevren. The sentry led Dar toward a thicket of weeds that lay just outside Muth la's Embrace. When Dar approached the thicket, Sevren rose from it and softly called her name.

"Sevren, what are you doing here?"

"Keep your voice down," he answered. He waved for her to join him before sinking into his hiding place. Dar found Sevren and squatted next to him. "What's this about?" she asked.

He handed her a loaf of bread. It felt hard and stale, but it was intact. "For you and Twea," he said. "The king's finest."

"How'd you get this?"

"Be careful," said Sevren. "You'll be flogged if you're caught with it."

Dar guessed the answer to her question. "You stole this from the king!"

"You deserve it more than he does."

"But you could be flogged for taking it!"

"'Twould be my least penalty for tonight's offenses," said Sevren. "All were worth the risk. I had to see you."

"Why?"

"I know you and Twea are hungry. I was worried."

"We're all hungry."

"Other things worry me, too. Something's amiss."

"What?" asked Dar.

"We're being led into a trap. It's obvious. Each town is dangled as bait, then destroyed just before we reach it. Tomorrow, we'll do another forced march into the Vale of Pines. 'Tis the perfect spot for an ambush."

"Have you told the king?"

"He has generals to do that, and they're more clever than a guardsman. They know what's going on. They're doing this with open eyes."

"Why?"

"I've na idea, except the mage is involved. The Queen's Man has a part, too. They've been thick together."

"Why are you telling me this?"

"For two reasons. Warn your protectors . . ."

"You mean the orcs?"

"Yes, the orcs. They'll lead any attack. Warn them they're going into a trap. And you should know that if the orcs are slain, the soldiers will abandon you. They care only for their own skins. Move clear of the baggage train when the attack begins. I swear by Karm I'll find you."

"You frighten me," said Dar.

"There's na helping that. I want you safe. Twea, too."

"You've risked your life to tell me this, haven't you?"

"I've risked my life many times, but seldom for so good a reason." Sevren peered over the weeds and looked about. "The way's clear," he said. "I should go."

"Wait! I have something for you."

"What?"

"Something you may want," Dar said. "I just discovered it." Then she kissed him.

Dar returned to Kovok-mah's shelter and shook him awake.

"Atham?" he asked in a sleepy voice. *What?*

Dar replied in Orcish in case Twea overheard. "I've learned of great danger."

"What is it?"

"Tomorrow, if you fight, there'll be . . ." Dar couldn't think of the Orcish word for "trap." Neither could she think of words for "trick," "deceit," or "double-cross." A moment's reflection made her realize that the orcs lacked terms for every form of deception she could imagine, and she lacked the words to describe the threat. ". . . there'll be much danger."

"There's always danger," said Kovok-mah.

"But urkzimmuthi will die and washavoki soldiers won't."

"This often happens."

"Thwa, thwa, thwa," said Dar. "Tomorrow will be different."

"Each battle is different."

"Washavokis will hide like cat to jump on mouse," said Dar, trying to describe an ambush.

"That has happened before. I've seen it in other battles."

"But washavokis have spoken words without meaning. Urkzimmuthi will die for no reason," said Dar.

"Words spoken by washavokis often make little sense. Yet I know they want us to kill. Our queen has promised we would. If we die, that is reason."

In the darkness within the shelter, Dar couldn't see Kovok-mah's face, only the faint green glint of his eyes. They pierced the gloom better than hers. "Dargu, don't be sad," he said in a gentle voice.

"Why don't you understand? You must understand! Who leads urkzimmuthi fighters?"

"Queen's Man and his tolums."

"Thwa," said Dar. "Which son leads fighters?"

"There is no such son."

"Some sons have capes," said Dar. "Are they not leaders?"

"They're not like washavoki tolums that tell us what to do," said Kovok-mah. "Cape is sign of wisdom. Sons choose to listen."

"You're wise. Sons will listen to you."

"What should I say? Fighting is dangerous? Washavokis are cruel? This is common wisdom."

"Tomorrow will be different," said Dar. "Many sons will die."

"You've seen little fighting. Many often die."

As Dar pondered how she might make Kovok-mah understand how the orcs would be betrayed, she recalled how Murdant Teeg had compared them to hunting dogs. "They're strong and tough," he had said, "but they lack guile. It's guile that wins battles." *How can creatures unable to lie comprehend treachery?* She envisioned Kovok-mah and the others marching to their annihilation, and she couldn't see how to prevent them.

Thirty-seven

The next day's forced march seemed to Dar like listening to a long, sad tale that she already knew. She must endure the telling, though she couldn't change the ending. As the day progressed, her dread grew. Dar's one consolation was that Twea was oblivious of the danger ahead. She had been delighted by Sevren's bread. She, Dar, and Kovok-mah had eaten some in the morning, and the girl behaved as if it were a feast. The unexpected nourishment had perked up Twea's spirits and, for a while, livened her steps. Yet Twea's energy was quickly spent. By afternoon, Dar carried her. She seemed a light burden compared to her worries.

The army marched over grasslands, not bothering to pause at the empty farms along the way. The soldiers were spurred on by news of a great prize—not a town, but the goods from the emptied towns. Scouts had reported that a small force of the enemy escorted many heavily laden wagons. These slowed their escort's flight, which was headed for the Vale of Pines.

As the march continued westward, the rolling land began to rise. Soon, dark green hills came into view. The Vale of Pines wound through them. For a while, the army headed in its direction. Then, before the enemy was sighted, King Kregant's forces halted. The orcs and their baggage train remained in place while the foot soldiers and cavalry regrouped into two forces. These took separate routes to the hills around the valley. The king and his guards followed one of them.

As the human forces moved out, the Queen's Man rode alongside the orc column and halted midpoint. All the orcs turned to face him. General Tarkum rose up in his saddle and shouted in Orcish, "Hear words your Great Mother spoke to me!"

The orcs grew still and silent. Dar listened with them.

"Great Mother wants sons to aid Great Washavoki. There are evil ones ahead. They must die. That is her wisdom. Soldiers go to hills to protect you. Your path is different. Tolums will show way. Obey them. Soon, Great Mother will hear of your deeds and be pleased."

The Queen's Man finished his speech by making the sign of the tree. To Dar, it was the crowning duplicity. Though she was enraged, the orcs remained placid and watched without a murmur as the general rode off to join his retreating sovereign.

The orcs resumed advancing only after the human troops neared their destinations, which were the far sides of the hills that flanked the vale. By then, even Dar could see the plan. The laden wagons were King Feistav's bait to lure King Kregant's starving army into the valley. Feistav's forces were hidden on the tree-covered hilltops. When the invaders took the bait, Feistav's men would attack them on two sides from high ground. King Kregant's strategy took the same ploy to the next level. The orcs were his bait to lure his opponents from their ambush. After King Feistav's troops left the hills, Kregant's men would occupy them. From there, they would watch the orcs kill as many of their attackers as they could. When the orcs were vanquished, Kregant's men would charge and finish the work the orcs had begun. Feistav would lose, the orcs would lose, but Kregant would win.

Dar wondered why the orcs couldn't envision this when she saw it so clearly. *They've been in battles before*, she thought. *Surely they've seen ambushes*. Then she finally grasped the depth of the orcs' loyalty. *They're honoring their queen's promise, knowing it will cost their lives*. Dar saw that the orcs' error was in thinking the Queen's Man was as honorable as their queen. Dar marveled how a ruler could inspire such devotion and how men could so treacherously abuse it.

Yet for all her thinking, Dar saw no way to change anything. *Sevren was right. Only kings and queens can change the world. All I can do is keep Twea and myself alive*. That, alone, would be difficult enough.

The sun was low by the time the orc column marched into the Vale of Pines, and the valley's grassy floor was shadowed. A meandering stream ran through it, broad but shallow from lack of rain. The hills on either side were steep, but not too steep for a charging horse or a running man to descend. Their upper slopes were covered with pines and other evergreens. In the failing light, they looked nearly black. Dar scanned them fearfully, looking for hostile faces. She saw none.

Lacking cavalry, some mounted officers rode ahead to serve as scouts. Soon after they returned, the orcs and all who followed them halted. From her position in the midst of the baggage train, Dar could see little, and no one about her seemed to know what was going on, beyond that the march had stopped. Soldiers and women milled about the wagons, uncertain what to do or what would happen next. Dar wondered if this was the time that she and Twea should get clear of the baggage train.

The tension in the air convinced her that it was. She grabbed Twea's hand and said, "Come with me."

Twea followed Dar without question, and the two made their way to the edge of the mob. Dar glanced about, looking for the best avenue of escape. Farther up the valley, the orcs were unstrapping their rolled-up shelters and setting them in a pile. It was a sign that they were preparing for battle. Dar surveyed the surrounding hills. The valley had become narrower, but there was still a wide expanse of open ground to cross before she and Twea reached the slopes, which they would have to climb to hide among the trees. Dar wondered if Twea was up to the effort. Flight was desertion. If they were caught, it meant execution.

As Dar weighed their chances, she saw Murdant Kol riding toward them, leading a group of soldiers. He was still distant, but Dar could see he was shouting orders and scanning the faces in the milling crowd. Dar guessed he was searching for someone, most likely her. She pulled Twea back. "Where are we going now?" asked Twea.

"I have to hide you," replied Dar.

Dar pushed their way through the confused women and soldiers until she spied an untended wagon. She made her way over to it, and when it seemed no one was paying attention, she tossed Twea on its bed. "Hide under the cover and stay there," said Dar. "I'll be back when it gets dark." She saw the frightened look on Twea's face. "It'll be all right. Rest while I'm gone."

Dar ran off, keeping her head low. Instead of fleeing Murdant Kol, she decided to move in his direction. If she could slip by him, it would buy her time while he scrutinized the rest of the baggage train. Also, she would be headed toward the orcs.

Dar's plan worked, and she reached the head of the baggage train without getting caught. From where she stood, she could view the orcs assuming battle positions. The shieldrons—each thirty-six orcs strong—moved into place like bricks in a wall. Soon they formed a thick line of fighters that stretched from the hills on one side of the valley to those on the other. Kovok-mah had told Dar that his shieldron would be on the right flank. *Close to the hillside!* A chill ran through her as she realized he would be one of the first hit in an ambush.

Dar had a sudden urge to see Kovok-mah one more time. *I could hand out the washuthahi seeds. That way, I won't attract attention.* She turned back to find Neffa and volunteer for the job. Locating Neffa in all the confusion took a long time, especially since Dar had to watch out for Kol and his men. When she found her, Neffa seemed more distracted than usual. "I'll take out the washuthahi seeds," said Dar.

"The what?" asked Neffa.

"The black seeds orcs get before battle," said Dar.

"Oh," said Neffa. "Too late. It's already been done."

Stymied, Dar returned to the head of the baggage column. The orcs were in position, waiting for darkness to attack. The sun had set, but there was still light in the sky. Dar thought that she should return to the wagon soon and attempt her escape with Twea.

As Dar pondered their chances, an unrelated thought popped into her head—*All the orcs I blessed survived the battle*. Up to that moment, the idea that any words she uttered had special power seemed absurd. Casualties had been light when the town had been taken, and it didn't seem extraordinary that the orcs she had blessed were unscathed. Yet, desperate and with no other means to affect the upcoming battle, Dar suddenly became a believer in the potency of blessings. Her urge to see Kovok-mah became irresistible. Dar didn't question the impulse; she obeyed it and ran toward the orcs.

No one chased after Dar as she sprinted through the high grass. When she reached the orcs, she anxiously searched the ranks for Kovok-mah. When Dar finally spied him, she rushed over to where he stood. "Dargu?" he said, clearly surprised to see her.

"Fasat Muth la luthat tha," Dar said. *May Muth la protect you.*

Dar felt she didn't have time to explain. *If these words have any power, I must bless as many as I can.* She moved over to the orc on Kovok-mah's side. "Fasat Muth la luthat tha." Then she blessed the next orc, and the next.

"Hey bitch!" shouted a mounted officer. "What are you doing here?" The man didn't wait for Dar's reply but spurred his horse as he drew his sword. Dar started to run, but the officer caught up with her in a few paces and swung his sword. The flat of his blade slapped hard against Dar's buttocks. She gave a yelp and the man laughed. Dar darted between the ranks to evade another blow, and the officer gave chase.

Dar ran as fast as she could, slipping between the motionless orcs to use them as obstacles for the horseman. She was well aware that a slight twist of the wrist would transform a stinging blow into a lethal one. Dar passed beyond the last of the orcs and halted at the base of a hill. Her pursuer had ridden into the open space between the orcs and the baggage train. Dar was unsure if he had abandoned the chase or was waiting for her. She decided not to find out the hard way. Instead, she dropped to her hands and knees and began crawling through the high grass on the slope.

Dar slowly climbed the hill, staying low to the ground to keep from being seen. Partway up the hill, the ground became level for a stretch. A huge spruce rose from this natural terrace. The tree was dead and much of its bark had fallen away. The gray, bare wood gave the tree a skeletal look, the numerous branches its ribs. Dar crawled over to the tree and hid behind it. There, she tried to figure out how to get back to Twea. Dar thought if she climbed the tree, she could spot the safest route.

The spruce's branches were close together and horizontal, making it easy to climb. Soon Dar was high above the ground with a commanding view of the valley. The campfires of the enemy were visible in the distance. She saw that the Queen's Man's officers had gathered behind the massed orcs. She spied a group of soldiers leaving the baggage train. They were headed in her direction. Though that discovery was disturbing, it wasn't as unsettling as another one—the landscape was familiar. She had seen it before in her vision of the golden lights.

Dar recalled watching the lights wink out, and the memory brought ominous forebodings. She started to climb down, but saw soldiers ascending the hill. Dar froze and waited. There were over two dozen men in all, mostly murdants. A few brought women with them; Neena was the only one she recognized. To Dar's dismay, everyone halted beneath the tree. "This is the spot," someone said.

Anxious minutes passed, then Dar saw more soldiers headed in her direction. There was a horseman in front. It was getting too dark for her to make him out, but when he shouted, she recognized Kol's voice. "Did you get her?"

"Nay, High Murdant."

Kol spurred his horse up the hill. "By Karm's holy ass! Then why are you here?"

"We searched high and low," said a soldier.

"Then search again!" shouted Kol. "Find the brat and you'll find Dar. Tear apart the wagons if you must, but get Dar! Don't return empty-handed!"

As Kol dismounted, soldiers scrambled down the hill, passing others ascending it. Dar heard Teeg's voice call out: "Did they catch the weasel?"

"No," said Kol, startling Dar with the venom he poured into that single word.

"There's still time," said Teeg, breathing heavily from climbing. He surveyed the landscape as he rested. "This is a good spot," he said. "High enough to see and not too close. Are those their campfires?"

"Yes," said Kol. "You'd think at least they'd pretend to flee."

"Don't make no difference to piss eyes," said Teeg. He gazed at the bright moon high in the sky. "That will bother them, though. They'd have a better chance in the dark."

"Light or dark, they've no chance at all," said Kol. "The scouts reckon there are six thousand in the hills."

"It'll be bloody work," said Teeg. "How fine to watch it from here."

Kol tied Thunder's reins to one of the tree's lower branches, then joined Teeg to view the night unfold. By then, Dar realized that those around the tree were the favored few who had been warned of the upcoming danger. They wouldn't be going anywhere soon. She considered climbing down the tree, jumping on Thunder, and galloping off to get Twea. Having no experience riding, Dar realized that the idea was more a measure of her desperation than a practical plan. She rejected it. The terrible truth was that she was stuck, unable to reach Twea. Throwing her life away wouldn't help the girl. All Dar could do was wait and hope events would turn in her favor.

The night grew as dark as it was going to get. A damp chill came to the still air and mist rose from the stream in the valley. The orcs were easily seen in the bright moonlight, as was the baggage train, a hundred paces behind them. Dar could even discern that it was mostly women who remained with the halted wagons. Men on horses shouted orders, and the orcs began to silently advance. Careful to be quiet, Dar climbed higher for a better view.

Thirty-eight

From her perch high in the tree, Dar watched strategy dissolve into chaos. The battle began in an orderly enough manner. The orcs advanced to where the campfires burned. As they did, the mist rose until it appeared as if they were wading through water. Upon some signal Dar couldn't hear, they charged. The campfires were quickly extinguished. This, it turned out, was also a signal. Shouts reverberated from the wooded hilltops and men boiled out from them like angry ants from agitated nests. Their bodies blackened the slopes as they charged down them, the moonlight sparkling off the bare steel of their blades.

The battle was joined and the night quickly filled with the sounds of slaughter. Dar couldn't distinguish between man and orc in the writhing mass. The horrific deeds performed there were too far away to see; yet Dar felt them in her heart. Only fear of discovery kept her from sobbing. The fighting went on and on. Dar lost all sense of time, and for a long while she had little idea how the battle went. Eventually, the dark mass of fighters began to move toward the baggage train, slowly at first, then ever more rapidly. *Are the orcs retreating?* Dar wondered. *Have they been overwhelmed?*

The sounds of combat grew louder. At first, Dar thought it was because the fighting in the valley was closer. Then she realized that most of the sounds were coming from a new direction. The soldiers about the tree sensed it, too. They turned their attention from the valley to the slopes above them. Murdant Kol sent a man to investigate. He climbed the rest of the way up the hill and disappeared into the trees. He reappeared a few minutes later, running and shouting. "Retreat! Retreat! Kregant's been surprised!"

The soldier sped down the hill and probably would have continued running if Murdant Kol hadn't blocked his way. The man was still more afraid of Kol than the enemy, and he babbled a quick account of what he had seen. High in the tree, Dar could hear little of it, but the panic in the soldier's voice was unmistakable. Other soldiers began to emerge from the trees. They, also, were from Kregant's army. One of them was a tolum from a foot regiment. "Fall back!" he yelled. "Regroup at the valley entrance."

Murdant Kol mounted Thunder and drew his sword. "Follow me!" he shouted.

Kol led the soldiers down the slope, and the frightened women joined them. When they reached the valley floor, they were engulfed by mist and became vague, fading shapes. Soon they disappeared altogether. The valley was filled with the noise of combat, but the mist obscured it. Trees hid the fighting on the hilltops. Dar was surrounded by death, but it was invisible, which made it all the more terrifying.

At long last, the sounds of fighting became distant, leaving only disembodied voices in its wake. Moans, screams, and sobs filled the night, their din softening as the sufferers died, one by one. After the valley grew quiet, Dar climbed down from the tree. The night was old and the moon was near the horizon when she descended the slope into the mist and walked toward the baggage train, fearful of what she would find.

The damp air smelled of blood and Dar walked only a short way before she encountered the first corpse. A man stared at the sky, his gore-covered face frozen in a grimace. Dar quickly looked away, but soon it was impossible to walk without stepping over the dead. They were everywhere, both men and orcs. Dar looked at each orc's face, afraid he might be Kovok-mah.

Thus Dar made her gruesome way to the baggage train. There she found her first dead woman, still clutching her weapon—a serving spoon. The scene about her looked like the aftermath of a storm. Wreckage extended in all directions until it was hidden by the mist. Slain oxen lay among piled corpses and ruined wagons. Most of the wagons were overturned, their contents smashed and scattered.

Dar continued to stumble though the mist and discovered a miracle. The wagon where she had hidden Twea was intact. It stood out in the devastation like a piece of unbroken pottery in a ransacked house. Dar rushed toward it, her heart pounding with anticipation.

The wagon appeared just as Dar had left it. As she approached, she spied a figure standing by its rear. The figure was a woman. The mist obscured her features, so Dar was quite near before she recognized her. It was Taren. Arrows protruded from her chest, pinning her to the wooden wagon. Taren still gripped a bloody knife, and three dead soldiers lay at her feet. Dar gazed at her with sorrowful gratitude. "You gave your life for Twea." Only the jutting arrows prevented her from embracing the dead woman.

Dar stepped over the soldiers' corpses to peer into the wagon. Through a force of will, she turned her thoughts from everything but hope. Dar looked about. A small bare foot protruded from the cover. "Twea, it's time to go."

Stillness.

Dar didn't move, so she might prolong the possibility that the girl was only sleeping. "Twea, get up. You can rest later."

Reluctantly, Dar shook the foot. She already knew it would be cold; yet that didn't lessen the shock. Dar lifted the cover. Twea returned Dar's gaze with a look of terrified surprise. Her eyes were wide. Her parted lips seemed gasping. Blood darkened the front of her shift.

Ever since her vision of Twea's spirit on the Dark Path, Dar had foreboded the girl's death. Yet foreknowledge didn't lessen her pain. Grief hit her like a sudden blow. Dar felt her chest would burst. She arched back to scream her agony, and the scream became a long wail that echoed through the valley. When Dar had spent her breath, but not her sorrow, she lifted Twea from the wagon and carried her into the night with no idea where she was headed. Dar stopped walking only when the body of a slain orc blocked her path. It was Thomak-tok, who used to make Dar laugh with his quips about the porridge. *Washavokis killed him, just as they killed Twea.*

With cruel symmetry, men had killed both the one Dar protected and the ones who protected Dar. She was left stranded among the dead, unsure which army was the greater threat. As Dar thought how men had so thoroughly shattered her life, grief gave way to rage. She felt cornered, and like a cornered animal, she could only lash out. In her pain, Dar craved a chance to strike back. Only vengeance offered solace—vengeance for

Twea's death, for her abuse, and for all men's injustices. *Men are filth. Dog's teeth. Washavokis.*

Dar gently set Twea down. Then she pried Thomak-tok's broadsword from his fingers. Standing protectively over Twea's body, Dar screamed defiance into the night. "Kusk washavoki!" *Washavoki filth!* "Come and die! Die! Die! Kusk washavoki!"

The broadsword was heavy, and Dar needed both hands to swing it. Most likely she would manage only a single blow. Dar didn't care. The sword's weight and size matched her fury. There was no reason to live and there were many reasons to die. *They have to come! Stragglers. Looters. Anyone.* Dar's only desire was that her challenge would be met. It didn't matter if King Feistav's or King Kregant's men came forth, she would gladly slaughter either.

Dar's arms felt leaden and her voice was raw when she finally heard the sounds of movement in the mist. She blinked the tears from her eyes, raised the sword to strike, and hoarsely shouted, "Thayav kusk washa-voki!" *Die washavoki filth!*

Five shadowy forms appeared.

Dar prepared for death. "Mer nav su, kusk washa-voki!" *I am here, washavoki filth!*

A voice called out. "Dargu? Lat ther?" *Dargu? You live?*

For a moment Dar thought the dead had spoken. Then she saw it wasn't so. Her rage lessened. The sword wavered in her hands, then lowered. "Hai," she said in a low voice. "Mer lav." *I live.*

Kovok-mah hurried toward her, his lips curled back in a broad smile. "Dargu nak gaz." *Dargu is fierce.* He froze when he saw Twea's body.

Dar said in Orcish, "Washavokis killed Little Bird."

Kovok-mah responded by making a low, keening sound deep in his throat. Dar had never heard it before, but its anguish was unmistakable. The other orcs joined his side. All were from Kovok-mah's shieldron. Dar knew three by name, but not well. They were Duth-tok, Lama-tok, and Varz-hak. The fourth was Zna-yat.

Dar spoke to them in Orcish. "I hate washavokis for this."

Duth-tok and Lama-tok gestured their agreement.

Kovok-mah stopped making the noise and said, "We'll honor Little Bird before we join soldiers."

Dar looked at Kovok-mah as if she couldn't believe what she had heard.

"Come, Dargu," said Kovok-mah with a gentle voice. "Little Bird should go to Muth la properly."

"How can you honor Little Bird," said Dar, "then join washavoki soldiers?"

"We must join them," said Kovok-mah.

"Thwa," said Dar. "It makes no sense!"

"Queen made promise."

"I don't care," replied Dar. "You cannot go."

"It doesn't matter what you care," said Zna-yat. "I see no cape upon your shoulders."

"Sons give capes, but Muth la gives wisdom," said Dar. "She gave me visions to show washavoki king should not be obeyed."

"You, too, are washavoki," said Zna-yat.

"Yet I speak for Muth la," replied Dar. "Queen is far away, but Muth la is everywhere. She wants no more sons to die for washavokis."

"Are we to die for you?" asked Zna-yat. "It would be same thing."

"I only know that Muth la speaks to me," said Dar.

"Am I not called Muth velavash? Those words came from Muth la."

The orcs exchanged glances. Then Duth-tok spoke up. "Dargu blessed me, and I live."

"I was blessed," said Varz-hak.

"I, too," said Lama-tok.

"I was not," said Zna-yat. "Yet, I'm here."

"Hai," said Dar. "You're here. What will you do now?"

Zna-yat hesitated for a moment. "I won't listen to you."

"Do you love washavoki king so much that you would die for him?" asked Dar. "Muth la wants you to live. Why do you question that?"

"I'm not listening," said Zna-yat.

"Then look around and see, instead," said Dar. "Do king's soldiers lie among dead? Did any soldiers aid you? Queen cannot see how king treats urkzimmuthi, but you can."

Zna-yat didn't reply.

"Who wants to live?" asked Dar.

"I do," said Varz-hak. "With foes so near, it's safest to go with soldiers."

"Go home, instead," said Dar.

"How?" asked Lama-tok. "Washavokis surround us."

"Take paths washavokis don't expect," said Dar. "I can help you find them."

"What you say, Kovok-mah?" asked Varz-hak. "You're wise in battles."

Zna-yat turned to Kovok-mah. "I live because of you," he said, "not because of Dargu's words. Speak, mother's brother's son, and I'll heed your wisdom."

"I, too, will heed Kovok-mah," said Lama-tok.

Dar gazed at Kovok-mah also and said in the human tongue, "I wish to be with you, but I cannot return to soldiers."

All eyes fixed on Kovok-mah. He stood silently for a long while, struggling to resolve his mind.

At last he spoke. "I'm not wise," he said. "Dargu saw things I couldn't understand. She warned me of battle, but I didn't listen. Now few live. I'm unsure how we can get home, but this time I'll listen to Dargu." He bowed his head in Dar's direction.

Duth-tok, Lama-tok, and Varz-hak looked relieved as they bowed their heads toward Dar. Zna-yat's face grew stony, and though he bowed, he bowed to Kovok-mah, not Dar.

"Mother," said Kovok-mah, "what should we do?"

Hearing those words kindled a feeling within Dar that fought both rage and despair. It was a sense of worth. Dar took only a moment before answering Kovok-mah's question. "Foolish washavokis say urkzimmuthi are dogs," said Dar. "We'll become wolves."

Dar's eyes gleamed in the moonlight, fierce and triumphant. She had found a way to hurt the king and his army. She would help the orcs desert and, by deserting, live. *Somehow, we'll make it*, she told herself. *The orcs have the toughness and the strength, and I'll provide the guile.*

Thirty-nine

The dead made Skymere skittish, so Sevren dismounted rather than ride among corpses. He led his horse to a tree and tied him to it before entering the battleground on foot. Valamar did the same. "Sevren, this is foolhardy," he said, "and pointless, too."

"I made the oath, na you," replied Sevren. "You did na have to come."

"Feistav's men may be about. Someone has to watch your back."

"A skill, apparently, you think I've lost."

"Well, you've lost your wits, I know that. The girl's dead, and if Kregant learns we've come here, our backs will pay for it."

"That coward's too busy fleeing to count his guard," said Sevren.

"The king has cooler heads to do it for him."

"Kregant's lost too many men to lose two more through flogging. I'll keep my oath and take my chances. If Dar or Twea live, they'll na be left behind."

Valamar held his tongue and followed his friend. The fighting was only two days past, but the air in the valley was already putrid. The dismal scene before him didn't inspire hope, and Valamar, a seasoned warrior, knew what Sevren would almost certainly find. That Sevren, an equally experienced soldier, would think differently caused him concern. *Women make men reckless,* thought Valamar, *even dead women.*

The grim walk up the valley told a tale in piecemeal fashion, and the two men had to travel the battleground twice before they learned the gist of it. The orcs had carried the brunt of the fighting, and almost all of them had lost their lives. Most died in the ambush, but one shieldron counterattacked and apparently fought its way into the hills. Sevren thought they must have rejoined the surviving orcs when they retreated down the valley. The retreat was orderly, for all of the dead orcs appeared to have died while fighting, not fleeing, the enemy.

Only a few of Kregant's human soldiers were found among the slaughtered women at the baggage train. Sevren searched there for a long time, but found no trace of Twea or Dar. Most of Kregant's men had died in the hills or at the valley's entrance, where they made a stand against the troops that had surprised them. The orcs that survived the ambush helped Kregant's men fight that battle to a bloody draw. When dawn came, both armies were too exhausted and mangled to fight further. Kregant had lost half of his foot soldiers, a quarter of his cavalry, and almost all of his orcs. Judging from the battlefield, Kregant's foes also had paid a heavy price, for the orcs had fought valiantly for the king who had betrayed them.

With the fighting over, King Kregant's army was in retreat, and Valamar was anxious to rejoin them. With that in mind, he and Sevren separated to speed their search. As Valamar climbed a hillside, he had conflicting hopes. Part of him wished to find Dar's and Twea's bodies so they could leave. Yet another part worried what Sevren would do when he discovered Dar was dead. If Sevren chose to avenge Dar's death, even Kregant had cause to fear. Valamar wondered what course he should take if Sevren turned against the king. Would he honor his oath as a guardsman or side with his friend?

Valamar was still pondering this question when he discovered Twea's body beneath a tall dead spruce. He called to Sevren, who rushed over to find his friend standing outside a circle marked by twigs pushed into the ground. The girl lay in its center with a bunch of wilted flowers upon her thin chest. "Someone placed her here," said Valamar, "and marked the spot."

"Aye," said Sevren, wiping his eyes. "Someone who cared for her."

"Dar?"

"That circle's an orcish sign," said Sevren, "and they like to place their dead beneath trees."

"Orcs leave their dead unclothed and unadorned," said Valamar. "This girl's dressed, and there are flowers."

Sevren's face lit up. "Dar lives! She's with the orcs!"

"We looked among the orcs before we left," said Valamar. "She wasn't with them."

"What if the orcs that fought into the hills did na join the retreat? Mayhap they joined with Dar instead. Twea's resting place shows both human and orcish ways."

"If that's true, where are they now?"

"Far from here, most like," said Sevren, the gladness leaving his face as he realized he would never see Dar again.

"May Karm watch over her," said Valamar. "Should we bury Twea?"

"Nay," said Sevren. "She was left this way by those who cared for her most."

"An orc caring for a human child? I find that hard to believe."

"So do I," replied Sevren, "but Dar had a strange way with them."

"She had a strange way with a certain guardsman, too," said Valamar. "But since she's gone, we should head back."

Sevren sighed as he scanned the deserted countryside. "Aye, we might as well. She'll na be found."

"For her sake," said Valamar, "I hope she's not."

END OF BOOK ONE

The story continues in Book Two, *Clan Daughter*.

A Glossary of Orcish Terms

Adjectives: In Orcish, adjectives follow the noun they modify. Nouns and verbs often become adjectives by the addition of an "i" at the end. Example: snoof (to reek) becomes snoofi (stinky).

ala preposition—For.

armor: Warfare was unknown to the orcs before they encountered humans, and their armor is based on human designs. It is strictly functional, being devoid of ornamentation, and more massive than its human counterpart. Orcs call armor loukap, which translates as "hard clothes." The basic item consists of a long, sleeveless tunic made from heavy cloth reinforced with leather and covered with overlapping steel plates. The plates are small and rounded at the lower end to permit ease of movement. The effect is that of fish scales. This tunic is worn most of the time in the orc regiments. Its protection is supplemented by additional armor strapped to the arms and legs. These pieces tend to be worn only while marching or in combat. A rounded helmet completes an orc's armor. Simple in design, it encloses much of the head. There are small holes opposite the ears, and the area about the face is open to permit good vision and communication. Some helmets have nose guards.

Orcs regard their armor as a tool necessary for

distasteful work. They take no pride in its appearance, allowing it to rust.

Articles: Orcs do not use articles. The equivalents of "a" and "the" do not exist. When a sense of specificity is required—*the* girl as opposed to *a* girl—the noun is followed by *la*. The expression for the Divine Mother always includes la—*Muth la, Muthz la*, and *Muthi la*.

asa interrogative pronoun—Who.

atham interrogative pronoun—What.

avok noun—Dog.

bah noun—Eye.

bathing As opposed to humans, orcs bathe frequently. If given the opportunity, they will do so daily. This fondness for cleanliness is probably related to their keen sense of smell.

blath noun—Cloak.

Blath Urkmuthi proper noun—Orcish name for Urkheit Mountains. *(cloak [of] mothers)*

cape, as a sign of leadership. See "Military ranks and units—orc leaders."

d verb root and noun—To touch, touch.

dargu noun—Weasel.

Dark Path proper noun—The human term for the afterlife. Also known as the "Sunless Way," it was conceived as a plane of existence that paralleled the living world. Spirits of the dead would travel the path on a westward journey to the goddess Karm, leaving their memories behind in the process.

death song The human term for the *thathyatai*, a song

sung by orc males prior to going to war. Though mournful, it is not principally about death. Its purpose is to cleanse the spirit and beseech Muth la's comfort. The origins of the song are lost, though it undoubtedly dates from the beginning of the human invasions.

deception Orcs do not have words for any form of deception, such as "trickery," "lying," "betrayal," etc. Sometimes, lying is called "speaking words without meaning," but the understanding of this expression comes closer to "speaking nonsense" than to "lying."

di adjective—Two, second.

falf noun—Water.

falfi adjective—Wet.

fas verb root—May.

Fath noun—Spirit or soul.

flis verb root and noun—To leap or jump, a leap.

Flis Muthi proper noun—Orcish name for the bridge over the Turgen River. *(leap [of] mother)*

funeral practices Orcs send the bodies of their dead to Muth la in the same state in which they entered the world—naked. Corpses are cremated or left upon the ground (*Te far Muthz la*—On Muth la's breast). In the latter case, the body is placed within Muth la's Embrace (see separate entry), preferably under a tree.

fwil verb root—To please.

fwili adjective—Pleasing.

g verb root—To stop.

gat verb root—To bring.

gatash adjective—Worthy.

gav verb root—To seem, to have the appearance of.
gaz adjective—Fierce.
geem verb root—To wait.
git verb root and noun—To find, a discovery.
grun verb root and noun—To fight, a fight or battle.
grut adjective—Good, pleasing.
gusha adjective—Silly.

ha noun—Sky.
hafalf noun—Rain. *(sky water)*
hai adverb—Yes.
high murdant See "Military ranks and units."
high tolum See "Military ranks and units."
hiss verb root and noun—To laugh, laughter.
human noun—Human word for *washavoki*.

kala demonstrative pronoun—This or that.
kalaz demonstrative pronoun—These or those.
kam adverb—Why.
Karm proper noun—Goddess worshipped by humans. Called the "Goddess of the Balance," Karm was supposed to weigh one's deeds after death.
kaz verb root and noun—To hate, enmity.
ke relative pronoun—Who.
ki adjective—Little.
kram verb root and noun—To fear, fright.
kusk noun—Filth.

l verb root—To live.
luth verb root and noun—To protect, protection.

man noun (human word)—There is no specific term in Orcish for human males, although they are sometimes called "hairy-faced washavokis."

Military ranks and units: Orcs did not develop a highly organized military, and all the following terms are of human origin. In the orc regiments, all the officers are human.

general—The highest-ranking officer. The general for the orc regiments was called the **"Queen's Man"** because the orcs believed he derived his authority from their queen.

high murdant—The highest-ranking noncommissioned officer. A high murdant reports directly to a general.

high tolum—Usually commands a regiment.

human ranks: Ranks in ancient armies were less specific than in contemporary ones, and the modern equivalents are only approximate.

murdant—A noncommissioned officer, the equivalent of a sergeant.

orc leaders: Orcs had no officers or murdants, but did recognize leaders among their own kind. Such leaders lacked the authority of human officers and led by their example and through the use of persuasion. They wore capes as a sign of wisdom. These capes were bestowed by the consensus of their comrades and could be taken away in the same manner. The authority of Wise Sons derived from the Clan Mothers who appointed them to act in their absence. They guided the orc males in nonmilitary matters. Outside the orc regiments, they had no more authority than ordinary orc males.

sustolum—The lowest-ranking officer, the equivalent of a lieutenant.

tolum—The equivalent of a captain. Usually commands a shieldron (see below).

Military units: An orc regiment was composed of orc fighters commanded by human officers. Human soldiers served support roles, and women served both the orcs and men. A *shieldron* was the basic orc fighting unit. It consisted of thirty-six orcs. The term was also applied to a shieldron of orcs and the humans that commanded and supported them. An orc *regiment* had six shieldrons of orc fighters, accompanied by a human contingent of officers, support troops, and serving women.

min noun—A male orc, regardless of age. Usually translated as "son."

minvashi noun—Husband. *(blessed son)*

moon noun—Human word for *bahthithi*, which translates as "silver eye." The eye referred to is Muth la's.

mother noun—The human translation for the Orcish word *muth*, although the two terms are not completely equivalent.

murdant See "Military ranks and units."

muth noun—Often translated as "mother," it is the word for any orc female, regardless of age or whether she has borne children. Orcs occasionally use this word to describe human females. Mothers wield the real authority within orc society because Muth la's guidance always comes through them.

muth verb root—To give birth, to nurture.

Muth la proper noun—Orcish word for the Divine Mother who created the world and all living things. Muth la sends guidance to mothers through visions.

Muth la's Embrace proper noun—Human translation for *Zum Muthz la*. This sacred circle symbolizes the Divine Mother's presence. It may be temporary or permanent. Orcs always sleep and eat within its confines. Walls, upright sticks, stones, or even a line drawn in the dirt can mark the circle. Orc dwellings always incorporate Muth la's Embrace, and tend to be circular for this reason. The Embrace is hallowed ground; the dead are placed within it and worship takes place there. It is said that mothers are most likely to receive visions within Muth la's Embrace.

Muth Mauk proper noun—Orc queen. *(great mother)*

muthuri noun—A mother in the reproductive sense. *(giving mother)*

muthvashi noun—Wife. *(blessed mother)*

names Orcish names consist of two parts—a given name followed by the individual's clan. Thus Kovokmah is a member of the Mah clan. Children belong to their mother's clan, and a son's clan does not change when he marries. In the intimate form of address, only the given name is used.

nayimgat noun—A healing herb with large, fuzzy leaves that is also a sedative.

Negation: Thwa (not) follows the verb negated. Example: He doesn't bathe.—Fu splufukak thwa.—He bathes not.

nervler adjective—Sad.

Nouns: Orcish nouns are often formed by the descriptive combination of other words. Example: "Rain, *hafalf*, combines "sky," *ha*, with "water," *falf*. Verb roots often function as nouns. Example: *Ma urav ur.*—I give gift. Single-consonant verb roots, such as *s*—to see, have an "ai" added to the root to form a noun. Examples: *nai*—being, *sai*—seeing, and *tai*—killing.

nuf noun—Night.
Nuf Bahi proper noun—Night of the full moon. *(Night [of] Eye)*

orc noun—Human word for *zimmuthi.*
orcish adjective—Human word for *urkzimmuthi.*
Orcish, as the term for the Orcish language, noun—Human word for *pahmuthi.*
orcs noun—Human word for *urkzimmuthi.*

pah verb root and noun—To speak, speech.
pahmuthi noun—Orcish language. *(speech [of] mother)*

Personal pronouns: Orcs always distinguish between masculine and feminine among their own kind. Humans, animals, and things are genderless, the equivalent of "it." There is no distinction between objective and nominative cases.

	masculine	*feminine*	*genderless*
1st person singular	**ma**	**mer**	[none]
2nd person singular	**tha**	**ther**	**ga**
3rd person singular	**fu**	**fer**	**gu**
1st person plural	**math**	**merth**	[none]
2nd person plural	**thath**	**therth**	**gath**
3rd person plural	**futh***	**ferth***	**guth**

*Mixed-gender plurals are always feminine.

Plurals are indicated by placing the prefix *urk*, which translates as "many," before a noun. The human word for "orc" derives from the shortening of the orcs' name for themselves, *urkzimmuthi.*

Possession is indicated by the addition of a "z" at the end of a noun.

Possessive pronouns:

my	**merz** (fem)	**maz** (mas)	
your (singular)	**therz** (fem)	**thaz** (mas)	
your (plural)	**urktherz***(fem)	**urkthaz*** (mas)	
his	**mat**	their (mas)	**futha***
her	**mert**	their (fem)	**fertha***
its	**gut**	genderless plural	**gutha**

*Mixed-gender plurals are always feminine.

Queen's Man See "Military ranks and units."

regiment See "Military ranks and units."

s verb root and noun—To see, (noun form—*sai*) sight, vision.

saf noun—Food.

shash verb root and noun—To thank, thanks. *Shashav* translates as "thank you."

shieldron See "Military ranks and units."

simi adjective—Blue.

sleep Orcs sleep sitting upright in a cross-legged position, with only a mat as a cushion. Only babies and the extremely ill rest lying down.

smell Orcs have an especially keen sense of smell, and their language contains many terms for scents that humans cannot distinguish. They are also capable of smelling some of the emotional and physical states of others. They can detect anger, fear, love, pain, and some forms of sickness. This ability has affected their culture in fundamental ways and may partly explain why orcs do not easily grasp deception.

snaf adverb—Also.
snoof verb root and noun—To stink, stench.
splufuk verb root and noun—To bathe, bath.
sun noun—Human word for *bahriti*, which translates as "golden eye." The eye referred to is Muth la's.
sustolum See "Military ranks and units."
sut verb root—To come.
suth verb root and noun—To learn, wisdom or learning.
suthi adjective—Wise.

t verb root—To kill.
ta preposition—With.
tahwee noun—Bird.
tash adjective—Cruel.
tava interjection—Hello, greetings.
tep conjunction—And.
tham interrogative pronoun—Which.
thay verb root and noun—To die, corpse.
thayati adjective—Dead.
theef verb root and noun—To name or call, name.
there adjective and noun—Human word for *fa*.
these (those) demonstrative pronoun—Human words for *kalaz*.
thrim verb root—To have sexual intercourse.
thus verb root—Heal.
thwa adverb—No, not.
tolum See "Military ranks and units."
tul adjective—Real, having a verifiable existence. This word approaches the meaning of the human expression "true," although the orcs have no term for its opposite.
turpa adjective—Proper, correct, appropriate.

ur verb root and noun—To give, gift.

urk Prefix that makes nouns plural. Often translated as "many."

urkzimmuthi noun—The orc race, also the plural of orc. *(children [of] mother)*

urkzimmuthi adjective—Orcish.

uthahi adjective—Pretty.

v verb root—To have.

va preposition—Like.

vash verb root and noun—1. To bless, blessing. 2. To marry, marriage.

vata interjection—Good-bye.

velazul noun—Lover. Unlike the human term, it is used only in the chaste sense. *(give love)*

Verbs and verb roots: Orcish verbs consist of two or three parts. A verb root plus an ending that inflects person and number are used to convey the present tense. Other tenses are conveyed by adding a prefix to the present tense

Some Orcish verb roots consist of a single consonant. Examples: **n** (*to be*), **l** (*to live*), **t** (to *kill*), and **s** (*to see*).

Conjugation. Verbs are always conjugated regularly:

1st person singular	**av**	1st person plural	**uv**
2nd person singular	**at**	2nd person plural	**ut**
3rd person singular	**ak**	3rd person plural	**uk**

Tenses:

Past tense is indicated by adding the prefix **da** to the present-tense form.

Past perfect tense is indicated by adding the prefix **dava** to the present-tense form.

Future tense is indicated by adding the prefix **lo** to the present-tense form.

Example: sut + ak = [He] comes. da + sut + ak = [He] came.

verl verb root and noun—To forgive, forgiveness.

wash noun—Tooth.

washavoki noun and adjective—Human, either male or female. The word translates as "teeth of dog" and refers to the whiteness of human teeth.

washuthahi noun—A black, pea-shaped seed that is mildly narcotic and stains the teeth black when chewed. *(teeth-pretty)*

weapons Orcs did not make weapons before the human invasions, and their arms are adapted from human designs. Swords, axes, and maces are primarily used for combat, but orcs also carry daggers and sometimes hatchets. All their weapons are strictly utilitarian in design. They reflect the orcs' strength, being larger and more massive than those humans carry. Spears and pikes are not unknown to orcs, but are rarely used. Although orcs use bows and arrows for hunting, they do not employ them in combat.

wife noun—Human word for *muthvashi.*

wind noun—Human word for *foof Muthz la*, which translates as "Muth la's breath."

woman noun—An orc female is called a *muth*, but the term is not commonly applied to human females. There is no specific term for them in Orcish, although "woe man," a corrupted pronunciation of "woman," is occasionally employed.

yat verb root—To go.
yes adverb—Hai.

zar adverb—Very.
zet verb root—To sit.
zim noun—Child.
zimmuthi noun—An orc.
zùl verb root and noun—To love, love.
zus verb root and noun—To sleep, sleep.

Read on for an excerpt from

Clan Daughter

the second book in the

QUEEN OF THE ORCS trilogy

On sale August 28, 2007

One

♛

Three nights of hard travel had cooled Dar's rage. Considered dispassionately, her prospects looked grim. *One woman and five orcs*, she thought, *deep in enemy territory. I promised to get them home, and I don't know the way*. Nevertheless, Dar didn't regret convincing the orcs to desert. The human king had betrayed them all. The orc regiments had been slaughtered and the women who served them had perished also. Not even Twea had been spared. Whenever Dar recalled the look on the slain girl's face, her grief returned.

It was late afternoon and Dar was awake, though the orcs still dozed. Sitting upright within a small circle, they resembled idols and seemed as placid. Dar envied the ease with which they slept, while she—despite her exhaustion—napped only fitfully. Dar studied their faces, which no longer seemed bestial or alien. Kovok-mah had saved her life and sheltered her when she was an outcast. Duth-tok, Lama-tok, and Varz-hak were virtual strangers. Kovok-mah's cousin, Zna-yat, had tried to kill her twice.

Gazing at the massive orcs, Dar was still amazed that she was their leader. Yet she had chosen the escape route. It had been her decision to travel at night, "when washavokis cannot see." All female orcs, who were always called "mother," had authority among the urkzimmuthi. As long as Dar's companions regarded her as a mother, she possessed it also. That was why she led, even if she stumbled in the dark.

Dar and the orcs were still in the hills, though far from the site of the ambush and battle. The steep, wooded slopes made walking difficult, but the rugged terrain provided safety. So far, they had encountered no one, for the hills were barren except for tangled trees whose low branches hindered every step. The journey had already taken a toll on Dar. Her legs, arms, and face were crisscrossed with scratches, her bare feet were sore, and her empty belly ached. Dar's fatigue made the journey seem more daunting, especially considering how ill prepared she was. Their destination, the Urkheit Mountains, lay to the north, but that was all she knew. The orcs were just as ignorant of the way.

Dar's sole consolation was that her branded forehead brought no bounty in King Feistav's realm. *That won't help me if I'm caught with orcs.* Avoiding capture would be difficult. They were surrounded by enemies, so their hope lay in stealth; yet orcs had no aptitude for subterfuge. They were perplexed even by simple stratagems, and Dar had difficulty persuading them to avoid the roadway. If Kovok-mah hadn't followed her, the others might never have. Yet, while Kovok-mah supported her decisions, Dar doubted he truly understood them.

Unable to sleep, Dar decided to scout the route ahead. She ascended the slope until she emerged from the trees to stand on a cliff at the hill's summit. The hilltop proved to be the last high ground, giving Dar an unobstructed view of the rolling plain ahead. Haze obscured the more distant features, and Dar saw no trace of the Urkheit Mountains.

The land appeared well populated—a quilt of fields, orchards, and woodlots, all demarcated by dark green hedgerows. A nearby rise was crowned by a wall that encircled a small village. Dar also spotted dwellings shattered among the fields and orchards and grew apprehensive as she imagined all the hostile eyes the countryside contained. She was trying to plot a safe route through it when Kovok-mah emerged from the trees. "Why did you leave?" he asked in Orcish.

"To study way," replied Dar in the same tongue. Speaking it had become second nature. She gazed at Kovok-mah and read his expression. "Hai, there'll be many washavokis."

"Then there'll be much fighting."

"Thwa," said Dar. "There are too many to fight. We must pass unnoticed."

"So we travel by night?"

"More than that," said Dar. "You must not look like urkzimmuthi."

Kovok-mah curled his lips into a grin. "Have you magic? How will you change us?"

"You'll change yourselves," said Dar. "Leave your iron clothes behind, speak softly or not at all, and wear cloaks I took from dead washavoki soldiers."

Kovok-mah looked puzzled. "We'll still be urkzimmuthi."

"In darkness, washavokis may not think so," said Dar. She could tell Kovok-mah was struggling to grasp her idea. "Washavokis don't expect to find urkzimmuthi in their land. They may not understand what they see."

Kovok-mah pondered Dar's words awhile before he spoke. "After battle, I said I'd heed your wisdom. I haven't changed my mind."

"Will others heed it also?"

"They'll follow my example."

"Cloaks smell of washavokis," said Dar. "I fear Zna-yat will object."

"Hai, I think he will."

"Still, he must wear one."

"He swore to follow me, so I can make him do it, if that's your desire."

"It is," said Dar, fearing that if her ploy failed and the orcs were attacked, they would sorely miss their armor. She slumped down on a rock, realizing her plan gambled with their lives.

Kovok-mah sensed Dar's turmoil and laid his hand on her shoulder, surprising her with the delicacy of his touch. "I'm pleased you guide us."

Dar sighed. "I'm not used to leading."

"It's natural for mothers to guide sons."

Perhaps among orcs, thought Dar. "Still, it's new to me. I worry about making mistakes."

"When you feel uncertain, remember Muth la guides you."

"Does she?" asked Dar. "I foresaw big battle and Little Bird's death, but I couldn't prevent either. What good are such visions?"

"I'm not fit to answer."

"Muth la is new to me, but not to you," said Dar. "What can you tell me of her ways?"

"She may be preparing you."

"For what?"

"I don't know," said Kovok-mah. "But I think you will when time comes."

"I hope you're right."

"When I have doubts, I follow my chest," said Kovok-mah. "That's why I'll wear washavoki cloak."

"Because of Muth la?"

"Thwa. Because of you. I feel safe with you."

Dar stared up at Kovok-mah, who looked so formidable, and wondered at his words. Insincerity was alien to his thinking. As incredible as it sounded, he was speaking the truth: She made him feel secure. The idea that a woman could do that ran counter to everything Dar had ever been taught. It made her smile, partly because it was so ludicrous and partly because it was so pleasing.

While Dar and the orcs hid and rested, the remnant of King Kregant's army rested also. After several skirmishes, King Feistav had abandoned pursuit. Many of Kregant's men believed they were heading home, but experienced soldiers, such as Sevren and Valamar, suspected not. Rumors were about that the mage would use his arts to reverse the king's fortunes, and those rumors seemed confirmed when some guardsmen were ordered to transform a peasant's abandoned hut into a site suitable for necromancy.

The mage's black tent had been lost in the retreat, and the hut was to be its temporary replacement. The guardsmen labored the entire day under the sorcerer's watchful eye to seal every crack where light might enter. After sunset, they completed the work by blackening the hut's walls and ceiling with a mixture of ash and blood. As the men painted, the mage burned incense that fouled the air. All who breathed it had disturbing dreams that night, especially the two men who fetched the final item the mage required.

Othar waited until the night's darkest hour to return

to the hut. Inside, a single oil lamp illuminated the bound child, who shivered in the unnatural cold. The mage closed the door and covered it with a thick curtain before getting to work. Taking a dagger and his iron bowl, he sacrificed the boy and used his blood to paint a protective circle. Once inside the circle, Othar opened a black sack embroidered with spells stitched in black thread.

The bones inside the sack had grown heavier, as if they weren't bones at all, but objects crafted from iron or lead. The sorcerer had first noticed the change after the slaughter at the Vale of Pines. Othar didn't understand its cause, but he hoped it foretold a change in his fortunes. He needed a change, for he sensed that the king's anger might overcome his fear. If it did, Othar's life was forfeit for his disastrous counsels.

Despite this, Othar remained devoted to the bones that had placed him in jeopardy. They had become more than tools. The bones had such a hold on him that he was as much their servant as they were his. Without them he was only a sham, for auguring with the bones was the only real magic Othar could perform. Before they came into his possession, Othar's sorcery relied on deception and a knowledge of herbs and poisons. His daunting presence had been all show, for his skills had scarcely exceeded those of a knowledgeable Wise Woman. The bones had changed that. When their unearthly coldness stung Othar's hands, he felt powerful—a true sorcerer at last.

Othar tossed the bones on the earthen floor and studied their portents. Never had the signs been so clear or promising. It occurred to him that the entity behind the bones was pleased by the battle's bloody outcome, and it was rewarding him much the way a sated master throws his slave some meat.

That night, Othar learned much that pleased him. He discovered where rich plunder could be had—enough to appease his greedy king. He saw that the mysterious threat was far away and retreating farther still. Additional study yielded even greater satisfaction. Othar's unknown enemy was moving into peril. The mage read the signs for "betrayal," "bloodshed," and "soon."